# INTERNAL COMBUSTION

A siren wailed through the messdeck. The coffin lids slowly lowered. Hark found that his fists were clenching and unclenching. Inside the coffin, all he could hear was his own breathing. Cold sweat beaded his back. Hark waited, resigned to the coming agony of the jump.

Suddenly a vibration ran through the coffin as if the ship had shifted or stretched. For no logical reason, Hark had somehow imagined that the pain would start slowly and gradually increase in intensity. As the first shock seared through him, he knew that he had been completely wrong.

There was molten fire in his bones. At the same time he was being twisted out of shape. Every deformed nerve was being tortured; the teeth were being dragged from his gaping mouth. His own screams beat inside his head until his skull started to fragment. His surroundings had gone; he was alone...

# THEIR MASTER'S WAR

## Mick Farren

A Del Rey Book

BALLANTINE BOOKS • NEW YORK

A Del Rey Book
Published by Ballantine Books

Copyright © 1987 by Mick Farren

Librry of Congress Catalog Card Number: 87-91662

ISBN 0-345-34554-1

Manufactured in the United States of America

First Edition: January 1988

Cover Art by David Schleinkofer

# ONE

THERE had been a madness, and the river crossing had become a place of horror and death. The teroes had sensed the blood of men and mounts, and they were circling in the hot iron-gray sky, gliding on leathery wings and uttering hoarse, raucous cries. The bolder ones had already started to land, flapping and stretching, their long beaked heads turning this way and that, always poised for instant flight but, at the same time, always moving toward the fallen prey with their scrabbling sideways gait. A mount thrashed and contorted in its final agony, snapping at the hideous gaping wound in its stomach. The huge Brana-ma hunting dogs had caused this particular animal's downfall. The flying reptiles retreated to a safe distance and crouched, waiting for its dying struggles to end. The mount clawed at the loose sand, trying to rise, but the effort was too much for it. It shuddered and died. The teroes started to close in again.

For a while, the waters of the scant, high summer river had run red, but now, once again, they sparkled clear. The awful stain of mortal combat had been borne downstream, and it had already become history. Harkaan splashed through the shallows, staring with dull

1

horrified eyes at the wreckage that was left by the fighting. There was blood running down the side of his face from where a spinning platee had sliced his forehead. An angry, throbbing pain still pulsed through his shoulder and extended all the way up to the nerve clusters in the back of his neck. The Brana-ma warrior, the one with the black and yellow diamond-patterned snake painted on his left cheek, had been looking to finish him with a single blow from his war club. It had been intended to crush his skull, but at the last minute, Harkaan had desperately pivoted from the hip and the club had smashed down on his shoulder. In shock from the pain and driven by the strange new instincts of madness, he had gutted the man with his glassknife. The warrior's blood still stained his breechclout, his leggings, and his beaded chest piece.

Some of the bodies sprawled as though sleeping. Others were twisted into grotesque and unnatural parodies of what they'd been when alive. Harkaan avoided looking at the expressions on their faces. A mount lay half in and half out of the water. Its neck was stretched out, and its powerful back legs angled into the air. Spears stuck up like sinister leafless reeds, their points buried in the river mud or the dry, bare ground. The harsh hot Lawka-a wind that made men so quick to anger was still blowing, making streamers of the ribbons that decorated the weapons.

It was hard to remember how or why the conflict had started. When the twenty young men of the Ashak-ai had left the village, they had been nothing more than a simple hunting party, wearing the bands of ocher paint that designated them as such. Even then, though, there had been an awareness that something was wrong. The dry season had gone on far too long. Wells had run dry, and streams had dwindled until they were little more than trails of drying mud. The hot winds blew relentlessly. The nights brought no relief. A terrible lethargy had set in, punctuated only by bursts of sudden, out-of-control anger. Game had become so scarce on the high plains that a hunting party could go out for days and return with nothing more than a single sobore. The reserves of meal and dried meat were dangerously depleted, and even water had to be rationed. The old people of the village had become so sere and brittle that they seemed in danger of blowing away. The children were wide-eyed with hunger, and very soon the bellies of the youngest would start to swell and and starvation death would be among them. The omens and portents offered no hope or consolation. Brood mounts dropped their eggs long before the appointed time, and two human babies were stillborn. The elders and the shaman spent long hours in the Lodge of the Spirits, offering prayers to the ancestors and even making supplication to Ka-La-Lan, the Mother of the Hunt, a deity who was never trivially bothered. No help came. If anything, the heat grew worse and the Lawka-a blew as hard as ever.

For the first four days out, the hunting party found nothing; it was as if all life had fled from the plains. The grass itself was dying. As the hunters ranged farther and farther afield, they were increasingly aware that they were starting to infringe the treaties by moving into the traditional hunting grounds of other peoples. It was a serious offense, but they had little choice. They could not return to the village empty-handed.

When they saw the cloud of dust for the first time, a great surge of hope welled up in the heart of each of them. The meetha herds had returned. The cloud was relatively small, and there was no way that any of them could pretend that it was one of the huge armies of the waddling, duck-billed fehlapods whose vast migrations took them across the high plains soon after the start of the rainy season, but it might be an isolated group, thrown off track by the unnaturally long drought. Whatever it was, it was certainly better than nothing. They could return to the village with both honor and the desperately needed fresh meat. It took another half day for the disappointment to fall on them. At first they resisted the unpleasant truth. It had to be a meetha herd. Finally they could deceive themselves no longer. The dust cloud was moving too quickly and with too much purpose. It couldn't be meetha causing it. If anything, it was a hunting party similar to themselves, most likely from the Brana-ma, also pushing to the limits of their accepted territory. Despite the gut-wrenching realization that there was still no game and probably none in the direction from which the other party was coming, a certain excitement spread through the Ashak-ai hunters. If they kept on going, there would undoubtedly be a confrontation with the young men of the other tribe.

This kind of confrontation wasn't uncommon, and it was conducted according to a time-honored protocol. The formal insults were exchanged, and then the warriors would engage in the largely simulated ritual violence of toucou, in which combatants would attempt to strike each other lightly with the blunt end of their stabbing spears. The worst that could happen was that a few tempers would be lost, heads might be cracked, or an arm or a leg might be broken.

The two parties had met at the Great Maru River, which had dwindled to a number of shallow rivulets that meandered between banks of damp sand. The riders of the Ashak-ai had halted at the top of a line of low bluffs that followed the outswing of the river's curve. Below them, across the riverbed, the Brana-ma also stopped. As the two hunting parties cautiously approached each other, a certain unease spread through the Ashak-ai. The Brana-ma—by then it was easy to recognize the tribal markings on their mounts—had a pack of large, semi-wild hunting dogs with them. And the Brana-ma themselves wore the swirling black and yellow devil paint of a raiding party.

At first, the meeting had followed normal protocol. The insults were exchanged. Ga-Niru, the eldest of the Ashak-ai hunters and the leader of the party, stood up in his stirrups and yelled across the river.

"The young men of the Brana-ma must copulate with their mothers and sisters! No normal woman would lie with them!"

The Brana-ma leader was a disturbing sight. His whole body was painted a uniform yellow—the paint of one who is no longer sane. But his reply was comfortingly normal.

"And the young men of the Ashak-ai copulate with their dogs because their mothers and sisters are too filthy and hideous for even them to lie with."

Taunt and countertaunt had escalated until the leader of each party let out a bloodcurdling scream. They charged at each other.

Ga-Niru never had a chance. His stabbing spear was reversed in the position of toucou. The Brana-ma leader swung his war club in a lethal arc that ended by crushing the Ashak-ai's skull. The explosion of violence had been immediate. The two parties had hit head-on in the middle of the river in a flurry of clubs and spears. All ideas of toucou were forgotten in the howl of rage. They killed and went on killing. At the end, the surviving Brana-ma had turned and run, but they had taken the remaining mounts with them. The Ashak-ai probably could have claimed some kind of moral victory, but by that time there were only three Ashak-ai on their feet.

As the Brana-ma fled the field, the yellow-painted leader reared his mount and screamed back at them. "You think that this is Brana-ma madness, Ashak-ai? This is the madness of the wind." He'd thrown back his head. "Sniff the air, Ashak-ai! Don't you smell the madness on the wind?"

The words still rang in their ears. No one spoke. No one had the words. Harkaan, Valda, and N'Garth had taken the lives of men, and their shame was immeasurable. They could hardly face each other. They had no idea how the madness had come upon them or why the Brana-ma had triggered such a deadly combat. In the grip of shock and pain, they were beyond even grief. Their only course was to retreat into what they knew was their obvious duty. First they checked that their comrades were really dead. There was no good news in this operation. Two of the fatally injured mounts, though, still panted and thrashed in pain. The young men had to finish these creatures, to whom they were almost as close as they were to their own families, by hacking through their thick scales with glassknives until they hit a crucial vein. The work was agonizing and dirty. If more of the hunting party had survived, they would have felt bound to remain until all the bodies were buried, even those of the enemy. As this was plainly impossible, they simply dragged their own dead into a single pile and lit thornbush fires at regular intervals around it. The fires would keep the teroes at bay for a while.

With their obligations to the dead at least minimally discharged, they seated themselves in a small, close circle. One by one, they removed the feathers from their topknots and took off their chest pieces. They were no longer worthy of these hunters' tokens. N'Garth had brought the spirit bag from Ga-Niru's fallen mount. He took out the painting sticks. With slow, methodical strokes, they painted their bodies. The design was stark and unmistakable: one-half black, one-half white. It was the symbol of the ultimate outcast. It identified them as killers of men. Harkaan and Valda sat very still while the paint dried on their skin. N'Garth had removed the prayer levers from the spirit bag. As he worked them through the complex sequence, rocking backward and forward where he sat, he recited the pattern of the dirge. The acrid smoke from the fires drifted around them. Finally they stood and, still without a word exchanged, started the long walk back to the village and whatever fate would await them there.

It took them twelve long days of thirst, hunger, guilt, and horror to walk back to the village. By the sixth day, even their grim determination had started to fail. They couldn't shake off the feeling that something was very wrong on the high plains. They were stumbling through the worst drystorm that any of them could remember. They had never seen the land and the sky in such furious conflict. The winds screeched and tormented, tearing and twisting the dust into shapes of tortured demons. Were they the dead demanding burial, even after the prayers and the lighting of the fires? Colored lightning split the sky, and in the brief periods when the wind let up, it was possible to see even more monstrous storms on the horizon. Was the world being consumed by violence? Through the dust, the moons appeared blood-red. More and more, it looked as if the insane Brana-ma leader had been right. There was a madness on the wind.

The storm still raged when they reached the village. It swirled dust between the lodges and tore at the coverings. The three expected that their approach would go virtually unnoticed, that they could creep in, and only after water and rest would they reveal their condition to the elders. They had assumed that most of the tribe, with the exception of maybe one or two unhappy, blanket-swathed lookouts, would be huddled inside the lodges, sheltering from the dust storm and nursing their hunger. Instead of lookouts, the three found that the black talis poles had been set out around the perimeter of the village. Their braids and tokens and bleached animal skulls streamed and spiraled in the wind. The black poles were the tribe's most potent symbols of power, and in more normal times they would signify that a major magic was being conjured by the shaman and the elders. But how could magic be conjured in the teeth of such a storm? The only other reason for raising the talis poles was that the village feared a most awful supernatural threat.

Within the village, a shock awaited them. More than half the tribe was standing in the open, buffeted by the wind and scoured by the dust, exactly in the center of the inner ring of lodges, clustered around the pylon. It was the most sacred and magical spot in the whole village. The elders and the shaman were in the middle of the group. The wind snatched at the elders' robes and the matted locks of the shaman. The young men who had not gone with the hunting party flanked them, standing stoically as though trying to pretend that the storm didn't exist. Less was expected of the maidens who huddled beside them and the children who clung to their mothers' skirts and howled, too young to have learned the code of suppressing. The whole tribe seemed to be defying the storm, waiting for the return of the hunters.

The chief of the elders, Exat-Nalan-Ra, regarded the three arrivals with eyes that were impossible to read.

"You have killed men."

Exat-Nalan-Ra's face was wrinkled and brown, a miniature representation of a battered arid landscape. The feathers that held his topknot in place were nothing more than worn bare quills. The gray hair itself was so thin that it almost seemed as if the violent wind would pluck it out by the roots. Exat-Nalan-Ra's body, wrapped in a dirty white robe, was equally ancient and frail, and he leaned heavily on his ceremonial staff, but the fathomless depths of his icy blue eyes hinted at the power that made him the unquestioned leader of the Ashak-ai.

Harkaan nodded. "We have killed men."

"Such a thing has not occurred in generations."

It was as if Exat-Nalan-Ra already knew about the battle at the river.

"It was not of our own choosing."

"That does not change the color of the blood on your hands."

Harkaan looked down at the ground, avoiding those cold blue eyes.

Exat-Nalan-Ra's right hand, the one that held on to the staff, trembled slightly. "You have no answer for that?"

Harkaan raised his head and reluctantly met the penetrating gaze. "I have no answer."

Exat-Nalan-Ra's attention moved on to N'Garth and Valda. "You have no answers either?"

They looked equally uncomfortable.

"We have no answers."

"Unless it was the madness of the Brana-ma."

"It's a terrible madness that costs a simple hunting party all but three of its number," the elder said.

"Their leader already wore the paint of the insane."

"So you blame it all on his madness?"

"He howled like an animal."

"And you felt no part of this madness? You only defended yourselves against it?"

All three hesitated. The eyes of the tribe were on them, and they felt naked. Harkaan finally found his voice.

"I felt it."

Harkaan felt himself in the grip of a dull, exhausted recklessness. The wind still tore at them, burning their skin and turning their eyes red and raw. With every gust, Exat-Nalan-Ra visibly swayed. Harkaan was slipping past the point where he cared what the tribe's elders intended to do with him.

Exat-Nalan-Ra looked at the other two. "You also tasted madness?"

Their faces were as blank as was expected.

"I was mad."

"And I."

Exat-Nalan-Ra turned to Quetzyloc, the master shaman. There was a whispered conversation. The other shaman and most of the other elders joined them in a huddled discussion. Harkaan glanced quickly at the other two. Even the death paint couldn't disguise their apprehension. The sky picked that moment to crack open in multicolored bolts of lightning. Exat-Nalan-Ra beckoned with his staff.

"You will all come."

The villagers stepped back, leaving a path that led straight to the Lodge of the Spirits, the holy sanctum that occupied pride of place in the inner ring of lodges, on a direct line between the pylon and the spot on the horizon where the red sun rose. Harkaan had only once been inside the Lodge of the Spirits, and then only for a brief moment at the culmination of his manhood trials. Now the three walked slowly forward. It was an occurrence without precedent. Nobody ever entered the Lodge of the Spirits without an elaborate and lengthy ritual of purification. They had neither eaten nor drunk nor even brushed the dust from their leggings. There was a single-mindedness about the crowd's urgency. No one had screamed out in grief for the ones who had not returned. Death and the wind overshadowed everything. The wind itself seemed to acknowledge this, dropping in a brief moment of respite. Exat-Nalan-Ra swung back the entry flap to the lodge. There was a strange new deference about the old man that had Harkaan completely at a loss. A minute earlier he had been imagining what kind of punishment the elder might have in store for them, and now they seemed to be receiving an odd respect.

The Lodge of the Spirits was little different from any of the other lodges, a low dome of shaped and stitched hides molded to a framework of split and curved canes. The real difference was in what lurked, invisible, in the smoky scented air, what entities watched from among the blackened relics, totems, and charms that hung from the roof or found solace in the patterns of beadwork that lined the walls. Marjooquin, the senior woman, tended the fire-that-must-never-die. She was quite as old and frail as Exat-Nalan-Ra, and equally determined. Her only concession to her great age was that she had Conchela the maiden to assist her. As the three young men ducked into the lodge, she fed a handful of aromatic wood spills to the fire and nodded them toward three beaded cushions that had been set side by side as if in anticipation of their coming.

Only two of the assembly followed them inside. Exat-Nalan-Ra and Quetzyloc the master formally seated themselves at opposite sides of the circular lodge, facing each other, directly along the axis of the invisible line that ran from the pylon to the rising red sun. For a long time, they faced each other in silence.

Marjooquin sprinkled a handful of white powder over the fire, and it immediately burned a rich, deep blue. Harkaan had to fight to stop himself from choking in the resulting acrid smoke, but both of the old men inhaled it with grunts of obvious satisfaction. Marjooquin then filled an earthenware cup with clear cold water from a larger stone jar and passed it to Conchela, who offered it first to N'Garth, then to Harkaan, and finally to Valda. After the three had drunk, the cup was handed to Exat-Nalan-Ra, who simply set it down in front of him, untasted.

They were handed a plate on which lay five lingor

beans. The lingor was the plant of hidden truths. In the right circumstances, the swallowing of the bean could take a man to heightened realities. In the wrong circumstances, the lingor could drive a man to madness. Each of the three took a bean but made no attempt to swallow it. Quetzyloc placed a bean on the flat of his palm and moved his hand over it twice in a simple blessing. Then he broke the bean in two. He put one half in his mouth and extended his hand for the water. Exat-Nalan-Ra gave him the cup, and the master swallowed, then took the second half of the bean and a second swallow of water. Exat-Nalan-Ra repeated the procedure gesture by gesture. Marjooquin indicated that the three young men should do the same. They copied the blessing as best they could and placed the beans in their mouths; their water was served by the maiden.

For Harkaan, the interior of the lodge seemed to have taken on a golden luminescence. The spirits of the tribe were present in the air. He hadn't noticed before that there were tiny rock crystals sewn at intervals into the beadwork that lined the tent. Each one reflected the fire and the four oil lamps that hung from the roof. It was a moment of magic. He was inside a golden bowl of tiny burning stars.

The euphoria, though, was quick to fade. The fire sank down to an angry red. The air was no longer golden. It was the same red as the light during the battle at Great Maru River. Exat-Nalan-Ra's eyes glittered in the dark as he nodded his head.

"There is no mistake, and there can be no other explanation."

Quetzyloc also nodded, rocking backward and forward on his crossed legs.

"There is no mistake."

"The Gods are coming. For the first time in five generations, the Gods are coming."

N'Garth shifted uneasily, and Marjooquin treated him to a fast look of disapproval. Neither Exat-Nalan-Ra nor Quetzyloc noticed the interchange.

"We cannot ignore the signs, and there is no other way that we can interpret them."

"The Gods are close at hand. We must accept that as fact and act accordingly."

"Everything has come about as told in song and legend, and even as written in the documents."

"The pylon hums louder every day."

"Exactly as it is recorded and exactly as it has been predicted."

"The plains are burned, the hot winds roll the dust clouds before them, and the dust obscures the suns."

"The lightning storm splits the sky."

"It is exactly as it is recorded and exactly as it has been predicted."

"In the final stages, the young men taste of madness and deliver death one to another."

"There is no doubt. It came to pass this way in record, and it will come to pass this way again."

"There is no doubt that the Gods are almost here."

"And we must perform their will in the manner of our ancestors."

"We must perform their will in the manner of our descendants long after we are dead."

"Now and forever, obedience without end."

"So be it."

"I never thought I would live to see this."

In slow unison, the two old men's heads turned toward the three youths.

"Those who kill during the madness go to the Valley of the Gods. That is the law."

Harkaan could feel the other two stiffen. His own shock exactly matched theirs. Was this to be a punishment for having killed? Did they go to the Valley of the

Gods as sacrifices? Were they to be kin to the goats and cranes and oraloos that were sacrificed to enlist the co-operation of the mother spirits?

Marjooquin pointed at the three young men.

"You may speak. You may ask your questions."

N'Garth was the first to find his voice. "Why do the Gods come here? What do they want with us?"

Quetzyloc made the barest of dismissive gestures. "It is not for us to know. They are the Gods. We are theirs, and they will do what they will with us. That is the pre-rogative of Gods. We merely follow the Law and the patterns of the past. By the Law, those patterns must extend into the future."

Valda almost shook his head but caught himself just in time. "I do not understand. I do not understand the mad-ness, and I do not understand why the pylons vibrate."

"It is not to understand. It is only to know. The pylons were given to us in the ancient days. When the Gods left us, they also left the pylons as heralds of their return. When the pylons begin to sing, we know that the Gods are coming. As they draw near, the land is scorched and tormented by wind and storm. Finally the young men become insane, and they kill each other.

"We can only guess, but it would seem that the culling of the young men is important in the Gods' purpose. The law is most exact. The young men who have killed, who have killed in the grip of the madness, must go to the Valley. They and the same number of maidens."

"And what happens in the Valley?"

That was the question in the heart of each of the three. Exat-Nalan-Ra's face was as expressionless as if it had been carved from a block of old seasoned timber.

"Nobody knows. The Valley is forbidden to all others, on the pain of a retribution so severe that it may not even be spoken of."

Marjooquin produced a small bundle wrapped in soft,

heavily embroidered leather. "It is time they were given the stone."

Exat-Nalan-Ra was given the bundle. He unwrapped it with the slow, emphasized movements of ceremony. When the wrapping was smoothed flat on the lodge floor, it showed a representation of the birth of the suns. Inside the bundle was nothing more than a medium-sized smooth black stone, a flattened oval that looked just like a million others that could be found on any streambed. Marjooquin indicated that Harkaan should pick up the stone.

"You will hold the stone between your thumb and forefinger, extend your arm to its fullest, and very slowly move it in a circle."

Harkaan did as he was told, feeling a little absurd. It was something of an anticlimax. After all this talk of Gods, he had at least expected some fiery, magic jewel. And then, just as he was pointing it at Quetzyloc, the tip of the stone suddenly glowed a bright, pulsing red. Harkaan's first instinct was to drop the thing like a hot coal. He quickly realized that this was not what was expected of him. He also realized that even when the stone was glowing at its brightest, it gave off no heat at all. He moved his arm again, and the glow faded. He moved it back, and the glow returned. He looked questioningly at Exat-Nalan-Ra. The old man permitted himself the slightest of smiles. Even in these strange times, it was good to see a sense of wonder in a young man.

"The stone will lead you to the Valley of the Gods. You hold the stone and move your arm as you have just done. When the stone glows, the direction in which your arm is pointing is the direction that you take. It is very simple."

Harkaan put the stone back down on its covering. Marjooquin rewrapped it and then placed the bundle in a leather drawstring bag. Grimly, she handed the bag to Harkaan.

"You will find the way to the Valley," she said.

Beside Harkaan, Valda shifted slightly. "I have one more question."

"So ask it."

"Is there any chance that we might return from the Valley of the Gods?"

Exat-Nalan-Ra shook his head.

"No one ever returns. You belong to the Gods now."

# TWO

It was a perfect day. If it hadn't been for the unknown terror of the Gods, it would have been a dream rather than a nightmare. The air was clear and smelled sweet and clean. There was a cool breeze blowing. They rode their flower-decked mounts at a leisurely pace across a plain that was already recovering from the ravages of the drought. A thin carpeting of green existed where previously there had been only sere brown. After the rains, the grass was already struggling back. But Harkaan couldn't shake the feeling that this recovery was only a lull in a continuing drama. At the height of the previous day's storm, he'd been certain that the Gods had arrived. Now, in this period of calm, he could imagine them in their valley, waiting.

The three had been taken from the Lodge of the Spirits and left in a smaller temporary lodge of their own beside the pylon. Conchela the maiden had instructed them to sleep. Sleep didn't last too long, however, as the drystorm had shortly redoubled its fury. Thunder rolled, the wind shrieked, and the sky was split by bolts of red, green, purple, and orange. They huddled in the stifling lodge and wondered if the world was ending.

17

The rain came like nothing short of a miracle. For a full day, it fell in gray, unceasing sheets. The lodges leaked and smelled of damp hides. Although they had been praying for rain, the Ashak-ai viewed its coming with a good deal of distrust. The omens were so bad that a break in their misfortunes might only be a herald of worse to come. A relief too readily accepted could well prove to be the cruel jest of a malignant entity who would turn on them and multiply their troubles.

The distrust continued during the leaving ceremony that set them on the way to the Valley of the Gods. The ceremony was supposed to be one of celebration. The tribe was renewing its bonds with these mysterious Gods by sending them their young men. Maybe the real cele-bration would come after the three had left. The tribe could rejoice at the departure of the young and the dan-gerous.

After the purification ritual, Harkaan, N'Garth, and Valda were led naked before the tribe. They were care-fully dressed in fringed white robes and brought to their mounts. The three maidens who, by tradition, would ac-company them to the Valley were already mounted and waiting, also dressed in white and garlanded with flowers. The entire tribe watched stone-faced as the six of them walked their mounts out of the village in solemn procession.

The Law laid down only two rules for the journey to the Valley of the Gods. The first was that they follow the path dictated by the stone and go all the way to the Val-ley. The second was that the maidens should remain maidens. To facilitate this, they were charged with trav-eling in two strictly segregated groups. By day, the two groups would ride separately, but in sight of each other. By night, they would sleep in adjoining but separate camps.

The first rule was relatively simple to follow. They

were so steeped in the traditions and superstitions of the tribe that they would never challenge the Gods by succumbing to the temptation to turn away from their destiny. The second was a little less easy. They might belong to the Gods, but N'Garth, Harkaan, and Valda were youths in the first flush of potency. It didn't help that their untouchable companions were three of the most beautiful young women in the tribe. Indeed, they had been chosen for exactly that quality. There was Amsessa, the tall, willowy sister of Ga-Niru who had been killed at the river battle. Her straight black hair fell almost to her waist, and her eyes tilted up at the corners. Harkaan could, if he put his mind to it, make himself ache with the thought of actually lying with her. What disturbed him was that he could ache in the same way for Naio, the witchling from the lodge of Horlem-Fram. She wasn't as tall and straight as Amsessa, but she had equally beautiful eyes and a flashing smile. There were also her ample breasts and the way her hips moved as she walked. In fact, the only one he couldn't feel that way about was the third maiden. Not that Conchela lacked beauty—with her unusual pale gold hair, she was possibly the most striking of the three—but the fact that she had served Marjooquin in the Lodge of the Spirits set her apart. Even this fairly innocent connection with the realm of ghosts and demons made her somehow unsuitable as the subject of an earthy, erotic fantasy.

N'Garth was the first to rebel. In camp, on the second night, he rolled over and propped himself up on one elbow.

"In the end, who would know?" he asked.

"Who would know what?"

N'Garth didn't really have to answer. The other two knew exactly what he was talking about.

Harkaan sighed. "The Law is absolute."

N'Garth lay back and stared at the sky. Pran, the

smallest of the moons, had just risen. All three were silent for a long time. When Valda finally spoke, it was as much to himself as to anyone else. "What are we going to find when we reach the Valley of the Gods?"

For Harkaan, it was frighteningly simple. "We'll find the Gods."

"I'm not sure I'm prepared for Gods."

"We've always been told that a man who comes face to face with his Gods has need of nothing else in his life."

N'Garth rolled over once again. "I'm not sure about that."

He continued to stare at the maidens' campfire.

Every morning when they rose and at intervals throughout the day, Harkaan would remove the stone from its wrapping and scan the horizon. Each time, the glow of the stone indicated that they should continue in the same general direction. They kept moving east, following the course of the red sun.

By the afternoon of the fifth day, the plains started to drop away. On the horizon, there were the purple folds of a low range of hills.

Even though he'd never been there before, Harkaan had a distinct feeling that the Valley of the Gods was somewhere in those hills. These feelings were starting to unnerve him. It was as if the Gods were already reaching out to him. He'd said nothing to the other two, but he'd watched them carefully. They showed no signs of sharing the feelings. Maybe it was because he was carrying the stone and it somehow had an influence on him, or maybe it was because the Gods had selected him for something particularly unpleasant.

On the fifth night, they camped beside a spinney of trees in a shallow, wind-sheltered bowl. N'Garth and Valda were chafing at the confines of the second rule and were about ready to break loose and visit the girls during the night. Harkaan could hardly believe that he was the only one who stood in awe of the Law and who remembered the horror of the killing at the river. His respect for the Law had brought him into conflict with the other two. They called him a prude and an old woman, and probably worse when his back was turned.

"What's the matter with you, Harkaan? You want to deny us what might be a final chance at life? You're as crazy as a Brana-ma."

To avoid an open conflict on that particular night, he elected to take the first watch. They could break the Law on their own; he didn't have to be a witness. He climbed to the nearest high point and settled himself on the short grass, making himself as comfortable as possible. He drew his knees up to his chest and watched the shadows deepen among the distant hills. He was more sure than ever that somewhere in those shadows, the Gods were waiting.

But despite himself, his mind wandered to the young women in the camp below. Were N'Garth and Valda really going to visit them? Perhaps they had already made their move. The idea created a cold hollow inside him. Why did he have to care so much about what was right and wrong that he was prepared to give up a bright fire and a pretty young girl laughing into his face? What was this absurd sense of duty that forced him to sacrifice bright eyes, moist lips, and teasing giggles for a night on a bare hillside?

At one point, he must have dozed. All he knew was that he woke with a jerk as his head toppled forward. He rubbed his eyes. It took him a moment to remember where he was. All four moons were in the sky. The last thing he remembered was Pran shining alone; it had to be very close to dawn. His next reaction was anger. Nobody had bothered to relieve him. He was about to climb back down to the camp when he noticed the tiny spark of light out on the dark plain. Was someone else out there, also camping for the night?

N'Garth and Valda were sleeping beside their own fire, and the women were some distance away. Either they had never gone to the girls or else they had, at some point, returned to their own blankets. He quickly roused them.

"There's a light out on the plain. It looks like another camp."

Valda grunted, coughed, and looked around blankly, but N'Garth was instantly awake, his hunter's instincts straight to the fore.

"Where?"

"It's some distance away."

N'Garth glanced at the embers of their own fire. "Can they see us?"

Harkaan shook his head. "I don't think so. We're far enough down in the hollow to be hidden from them."

"Let's hope so."

"I think we should go and take a look."

N'Garth was already rolling up his blankets. Harkaan turned to Valda, who was slowly coming awake.

"You stay here and look after the women."

Valda stopped rubbing his eyes and scowled. He clearly wasn't pleased to be left out of the scouting party.

As Harkaan and N'Garth crept toward the light, they could see figures moving around a fire. For the last two hundred paces, they wormed their way through the grass on their bellies. The first gray-green of the predawn was streaking the horizon. When they thought they were close enough, they slowly raised their heads.

There were five people, four women and a single man, grouped around what had to be an early cookfire. Two of the women were eating, and the others looked as if they had just finished. Three other men were tending the needs of eight mounts, preparing them for travel.

"They must be making an early start."

Harkaan and N'Garth were too far away to be able to make out any tribal markings, but they could see that, like their own party, the strangers were wearing elaborate costumes and that their mounts' saddles and bridles were decked with streamers and flowers. Also like the Ashak-ai group, they appeared to be unarmed.

"They're going to the Valley."

"It looks that way."

The sky was becoming increasingly light, and Harkaan and N'Garth started to edge away. Again they crawled and then ran doubled over until they felt that they were safe from detection. Back at the camp, there was a single question.

"What do we do about them?"

The others seemed to be looking to Harkaan for some kind of direction. Still very conscious that he alone had spent the night on a bare hillside, he didn't answer immediately. Finally he allowed himself a half smile.

"First we eat, but we make no fire. We don't want to reveal ourselves until it's absolutely necessary."

"And then?"

"We wait until they're on the move. We let them get well ahead of us. If they turn back to confront us, we will have ample warning of any hostile intentions."

They gave the other party sufficient time to move well ahead before they saddled their own mounts and walked them out of the hollow. While they were readying the mounts, Harkaan found himself standing next to Conchela. She looked at him questioningly.

"Why didn't you come to our blankets last night, Harkaan? Are you different from the others?"

Harkaan stiffened. "Someone had to stand watch."

"Is that the only reason?"

"It didn't seem right to break the Law when we're so close to the Gods."

She hooked her foot into the stirrup and swung her leg over her mount's back. "You *are* different."

By noon, it was possible to see a dozen or more groups all riding slowly toward the hills. It seemed that every tribe on the plains, and even those from beyond, were sending their tribute to the Gods. The nearest party was now close enough for him to make out faces and even tribal markings. There were no threats, not even signs of recognition or salute. They simply rode parallel to each other, no party acknowledging that the others existed. That night, the fires on the plain were like stars in the sky. All six of the Ashak-ai stood and stared, overawed by the sheer size of this migration.

Halfway through the next day, there was no longer the slightest doubt that the end of the journey was in sight. Every group of riders was converging on the same narrow pass that wound up and through the first line of hills. There were now so many riders that there was a certain amount of congestion around the mouth of the pass. It was almost the time of single shadows when the Ashak-ai mounts were finally able to start picking their way up the narrow path. The path proved to be little more than a rock-strewn, dried-out watercourse that twisted and turned between steep barren slopes and around folds in the hillside. Dust and the smell of animal apprehension hung in the air. The mounts stepped gingerly on the uneven surface. Both humans and animals felt very close to something infinitely strange and infinitely powerful.

There was an alien sound in the air, a high-pitched hum somewhat reminiscent of the nightwhine of the air beetle. Then the noise grew louder and louder, and it was nothing like any sound Harkaan had ever heard. And then the thing appeared around a turn in the trail, and the noise, frightening as it was, became completely secondary. Harkaan had no word for it. He was sure that nobody had a word for it. It was a red ball, the height of a man across its diameter, and it hung in the air just above the heads of the riders. It glowed, not with the glow of fire but with a steady rhythmic pulse of color that was bright but had no warmth. The only thing Harkaan had ever seen that remotely resembled it was the glow of the stone when it showed the way.

The red sphere came closer, as if to inspect the winding procession of mounts and riders. Up ahead, terrified animals wailed. Necks arched and heads tossed while their fear released a rank, heavy smell. One mount reared, and then another. The red sphere just kept on coming, slow and relentless, riding the air. A mount in the party directly in front of the Ashak-ai bucked and screamed. Its rider tried to rein it in, but it lost its footing and toppled backward with its legs flailing. The mounts around it bucked and plunged. Harkaan had to fight down his own mount and, at the same time, his own fear. Was this a God? Somehow he didn't think so; maybe it was a messenger or a servant of the Gods. Except, if this was a messenger, what were the Gods like? He wanted to turn his mount and crash back down the path. He wanted to run, to flee. He wanted to keep on running until he was someplace where the Gods couldn't find or reach him. And yet he had no will. He couldn't do it. It was as if his arms and legs were no longer his own. He was truly and deeply scared, and there was nothing he could do about it.

The red ball abruptly lifted, rose into the sky, and vanished behind the nearest hill. Harkaan leaned forward and calmed his mount by patting its neck. Its scales were slick with greasy sweat. A strange silence seemed to have settled over the procession, and the only sound was the rattle of the animals' footfalls on the loose rocks. The riders and even the mounts appeared to have passed the point where they could continue to be afraid. Numbness had descended and gripped them. They had no alternative but to continue up the pass and into the unknown.

Nothing in the world had prepared any of them for what they saw when they crested the top of the pass and started down the other side. There was no doubt that it was the Valley of the Gods. The valley itself was a perfect place, long and broad, with a bright stream meandering down its length and a flat, irregular floor covered with a lush layer of meadow grass. It could have been a paradise except for the God that floated above it.

The God was huge. Harkaan found that he simply didn't have the language to describe its size. It shouldn't have been possible for such an enormous bulk to hang there in the air, just at the height of a tree. Its vast pair of shadows covered the whole center section of the valley floor. As far as Harkaan could see, the God was predominantly made of metal—yet that was impossible. There was no way that so much metal could exist in the same place at the same time. The most metal that Harkaan had ever seen were the tiny arrowhead slivers that were kept in the Lodge of the Spirits. It was all the metal that the Ashak-ai owned, and they considered themselves wealthy.

If anything, the God resembled a giant platee. It was roughly the same flat disk shape as the spinning weapon, but where the platee was smooth except for the jagged cutting edges, the God was covered in all manner of blisters and irregularities. Long complex pylons extended from its outside edge, and lights burned on its dark underside. Some shone steadily, while others pulsed in swirling random rhythms. There were a multitude of colors, and some of the beams looked as if they were somehow more than light, as if they were solid.

Harkaan was startled by the sound of impatient mounts; he felt as if he were being jerked out of a trance. The riders behind him were pressing forward. It was much too late to turn back or bolt. He dug his heels into the sides of his mount and started down the track, down into the Valley of the Gods.

# THREE

"POOR little bleeders."

Topman Rance leaned back in the angle of two plasma ducts and braced his foot against a third, making himself as comfortable as possible. Over at the far end of Receiving Hold 3, the first of the new intake were starting to emerge from the lock that led to the sterile area. They looked like corpses in the blue light that spilled out from the lock, and they moved as if, to a man, they were demoralized and completely terrified. Arms were wrapped around chests and hands covered genitals, a few fingered their freshly shaved heads, and all peered uneasily into the shadows as if they expected some new awfulness to fall on them at any moment. Back in those shadows, Rance nodded. He liked them like that. Once the fight and the pride had been juiced out of them and they were about to jump out of their skins, they were also ready for him to rebuild them.

Perhaps the most disturbing thing on any star vessel was the noise. It was never quiet. There was a constant dull cacophony of sighs and booms and deep metallic groans. Discharging energy snapped and crackled, and escaping gases whistled and shrilled. Water dripped, and

totally unknown things grumbled and murmured. Those
who spent their lives on starships never thought of them
as cold machines. It was like being inside, even being a
part of, a vast living organism. Receiving Hold 3 on its
own was quite enough to awe any newcomer. It looked
like a place where gods might dwell, a huge cathedral
space enclosed in a frame of arching power conduits like
giant pillars and the meshed complexity of the plasma
transmission. It was a place of dark, menacing spaces
and mysterious blackness. It was also big enough to ac-
commodate a dropcraft or an e-vac. At the opposite end,
the towering bulkhead doors opened directly onto the
emptiness of space.

"If those poor bastards knew that, they'd probably
shit on the spot."

Rance remembered the first time he'd seen empty
space. It was a moment he'd never forget. He'd been
almost as raw as these suckers.

A plasma throwoff crackled and flowed down the
wall. The whole intake cringed. Rance knew that it was
almost time to show himself, but he held off for a few
moments to give the debris in their minds a little longer
to settle. As if it wasn't bad enough that they'd been
ripped from their families, their culture, and their planet
—from everything that might give them a familiar bearing—they'd also been given the datashot. The datashot
may have been ultimately efficient, a complete education
and military training in a single electric moment, but it
was also ultimately cruel. Even the longtimers didn't like
to talk about their moment of datashot. Men who'd spent
a lifetime in combat and seen a dozen sets of friends
killed, men who needed only the slightest of excuses to
wade knee-deep in blood atrocity, still feared the memory of the datashot. All that one needed to know to be a
ground trooper of the Therem Alliance was fused into
the brain in a single jolting instant. The horror was a side

effect of unimaginable pain. The machines that made the interface and the creatures that operated them had no idea that the agony they caused was quite literally unbearable. The illusion was one of the body being exploded into fragments. The spine would snap in a thousand places, the skull would be shattered, and bunches of nerves would be torn out by the roots as waves of burning images seared the passages of the mind. After the pain there was another horror. Suddenly, there were pictures inside each recruit's head like a new mind. They seemed to come from nowhere, memories in which the rememberer didn't exist, memories to which he had no right. The troopers knew things that there was no reason for them to know. They prayed that they'd go mad and that they'd stop trying to make sense of it all. Rance shook his head. After twenty years, the memory was still too close.

An atmosphere line valved off an excess of pressure with a shriek. The intake moved closer to each other as if looking for some kind of mutual protection. That was also good. It was never too early for them to start banding and forming ties. No one else was going to look after them. They were all out of the lock now, all twenty replacements, shaved and sprayed and irradiated. Even the bacteria of their home planet had been taken from them.

Rance swung down from his vantage point. His boots crashed on the steel floor, and the echoes bounced around the vaulted roof of the hold. The intake started to back away, back toward the blue-lighted sterile lock. What did they think they were going to do? Did they think the lock was the way back into the womb? He rapped out his first command.

"Stand right where you are!"

Without thinking, all of the intake halted. Some even came halfway to attention. The datashot had taken and was already starting to shake down into the normal brain patterns.

"Does everyone understand what I'm saying?"

It was actually too much to expect any of them to answer. They had the new language in their heads, but the use of it would require a little practice.

"If you understand what I'm saying, I want you to raise your right hand. This is a very simple order. If you understand what I'm saying, raise your right hand."

All twenty of them raised their hands. Two, however, raised their left. They would have to go in for testing. If the flip-flop persisted, they'd finish up on disposal. Rance tapped the switchbox on his belt. More lights came on in the hold. It made the place a little less intimidating. The intake still had their arms in the air. They probably wouldn't lower them until they were given the countermand. Rance assumed control. After the datashot, they were like blank slates. He was the first thing that would be imprinted on them. There was nothing like a little discipline to help their minds shake down and start functioning.

"Stand right where you are! You don't have to run away from me. You're going to grow to love me before we're through. And while we're at it, why don't we lower those stupid hands. We don't want to look foolish, do we?"

The hands dropped. Rance gave a satisfied nod. He walked forward and indicated a white line that had been painted across the floor of the hold.

"This is very simple. You will all move up to this line here. You will all face in this direction, and you will stand with your toes touching the line. And when I say touching, I mean touching. I want the toes of both your feet exactly on the line. Not behind it and not in front of it. Now, move!"

They jumped. Rance was reasonably pleased. It

shouldn't take too long to shake this bunch into combat readiness. Rance walked slowly along the line with deliberate steps, his boots ringing on the floor. In every way he was the complete opposite of the dazed naked men in his charge. His black suit was glossy, his harness gleamed, and the steel tips of his boots were buffed until they shone like mirrors. In his twenty years of fighting for the Therem, the life of a ground trooper had thrown everything at him that it was possible to take and still survive. His eyes were hard, narrow slits with deeply etched, humorless lines radiating from their corners. His mouth was a tight-lipped line with few signs that it ever let go and laughed. His hair was cropped short in the style of the longtimers and was rapidly turning to an iron-gray. A network of scars ran from his right ear to the point of his jaw and bore testimony to the ravages of the unending war.

"You are all very confused now, but the confusion will not last. You have been recruited as ground troopers attached to the fifth ship of the *Anah* battle cluster of the Therem Alliance. You are already twelve licks out from your home planet, and you will never see it again. In our language, the enemy we fight is called the Yal. It's doubtful that you will ever come face to face with them. The war in which you are now involved is almost completely fought by proxies. We are some of them. All the information that you need to make the adjustments to your new situation has already been placed in your memories. You simply have to accept it and make use of it. Once you do that, your confusion will diminish."

One man's toes protruded over the white line. Rance paused beside him and brought his steel-shod boot down hard on them. The recruit screamed and fell to his knees. This one would have to be put in for reexamination.

"On your feet, damn you!"

The man struggled painfully to stand. It was likely

that at least one of his toes was broken; Rance had stamped on them with considerable force. It wasn't that Rance was a sadist. It was that he simply didn't have the time anymore. If the individual trooper was going to survive, if the squad was going to survive, indeed, if the whole damned army was going to survive, orders had to be obeyed immediately and precisely. Approximation could mean death or worse. There had been a time when Rance had questioned, when he'd even railed against the system by which the Therem held them all in total bondage. Now he neither raged nor wanted to know why. There was no percentage. He just lived. In a war without reasons or answers or even passion, and certainly without an end, survival became everything. Rebellion had been replaced by a dry bitterness.

"You may be wondering why you should have been snatched up into space from your idyllic and primitive little planet by what you thought of as a god and pressed into service in a war you never heard of. You may feel that it's extremely unfair." Rance looked coldly up and down the line of men. "From this point on you can forget about fair. This is a vastly unfair universe. The best you can expect is a good deal of variety."

Static arced with a sharp whipcrack. The intake jerked. Rance didn't even look around. They were starting to settle down. The sooner the better, as far as he was concerned. His sense of order was offended by their stumbling around like zombies after the trauma of pickup and datashot. He took these details only because pickups were ten times worse. Rance always did his best to avoid pickups, fixing it so that he could stay on the mothership, up in the cluster. Pickups could become messy. Even with the mind control cranked to redline, the primitives could still serk out and cause a great deal more trouble than they were worth. He'd heard that this lot's culture had been based on a symbiosis with some kind of riding lizard. Animals could also be a problem. Apparently a number of these couldn't be driven off after their riders had been taken, and were pulped by the backwash as the pickup shuttle lifted.

It was the eyes that he had to watch. When they came out of the sterile area, their eyes were like those of children, wide and frightened, unmarked and unknowing. It was all too easy to forget the bodies of these men. They were sinewy and lean, hardened by deprivation. some bore the scars of knives or the goring of animals. These men were hunters and fighters. They were able to adjust to the situation and their new, imposed memories with great rapidity. Sometimes the adjustment could be so rapid that more than one topman had lost his life when a recruit used his new skills and knowledge in an attempt at an old-fashioned, take-a-few-with-him kamikaze.

"You may wonder why a species like the Therem should bother with primitives like yourself. The truth of the matter is that our masters find us valuable weapons. And make no mistake, the Therem are precisely that. Now and again, you may hear them referred to as our allies. That's shit. They own us. We're clever violent little monkeys, and we make great planetside shock troops. Why do you think that they'd go to all the trouble of maintaining an accessible supply of us close to all combat sectors? Somewhere in your brand-new memories, you'll find the phrase '*planet forming*.' There are hundreds of worlds just like yours, planned environments to keep you primitive but also to make you tough and resourceful, worlds from which you can be harvested any time they need replacement battle fodder."

Rance halted. He looked up and down the line of men.

"You have been harvested. You're battle fodder, and you might as well make the best of it."

Rance noticed that two of the intake seemed to be

shaking down. Their eyes were starting to harden and focus. It was time to get them under his control before they got ideas of their own. He stood in front of the nearest one, a young man of medium height, in his late teens or early twenties, with the high forehead and the hooked bird of prey nose that seemed to be common to this colony. He looked capable enough, and recent extensive bruising on his left shoulder tended to indicate that he was a fighter.

"You know your name yet?"

The recruit's lips moved awkwardly. "Umm..."

"Come on, boy. You know your name. You can do it."

"Hark..."

"One more time."

"Hark. My... name... is... Hark."

"Very good."

Hark knew that they'd somehow changed his name. They'd also changed his language. The new unfamiliar words felt strange, harsh even, in his mouth, but at least the panic had receded a little. He felt more able to control it. He didn't understand where he was or what was happening, but he found that if he concentrated on an object, the new parts of his mind would tell him what it was and what it was for. When the images had first come, immediately after the pain, they had been so vast that he had felt they were going to swallow him. His identity was diminished almost to nothing. The only consolation was that he could ask questions of the new mind and, at least, he was Hark. There was a number, as well.

"I'm Hark 34103-301782."

"Very good, but don't overreach yourself."

Rance seemed to have lost interest in him. He walked down the line, looking closely at each recruit in turn. When he finished, he stood a few paces back.

"I think you're ready for the first stage."

He touched a control on his belt, and a small port

opened. A number of gray metal cases, one for each recruit, glided through it, floating just a fraction of a centimeter from the ground on a gain-reverse field. Hark was amazed that he knew these things.

"This is your basic kit. Inside it you will find underclothing, multimed—in fact, everything that you need to keep yourself clean and healthy. You will also find that there are spaces to store field rations and ammunition as and when they're issued. The basic kit is your friend. It will follow you anywhere."

Even though the new mind explained that it was a perfectly normal, even mundane, occurrence and nothing compared to what he might see in the future, Hark still marveled when the cases divided, each one floating toward a different recruit to settle on the ground in front of him.

Rance seemed to be amused by their reactions. "Open the cases."

Seventeen of the twenty recruits leaned forward and flicked the red toggle on the top of the case. Seventeen cases flipped open. Rance made a mental note of the three who had failed to connect with the instructions in their new minds. Among them was the one who'd had his toes stomped. Rance knew it was too late for that one. He was beyond reexamination. He'd have to go all the way back.

"You will take out a set of underclothes and put them on."

All of the seventeen seemed to know what to do. They picked out a pair of shorts and a singlet each, but a number, including Hark, put them on inside out at first try. Rance simply pointed at the mistake and, straight away, it became clear. Once they were dressed, even if it was only in drab tan shorts and a singlet, they were invested with a certain minimal dignity. Shoulders were squared, and the terror had gone out of their eyes. Rance was making a final inspection when four other men in suits and harness came through a port and into the hold. Their insignia identified them as overmen, the rank below topman. They were longtimers, and they saluted Rance with an easy familiarity. One of them, a short, thickset man, did all the talking.

"These ready for the messdecks yet?"

Rance shrugged. "Ready as they're going to get. You can berth them down for the throughwatch. Nextday, we introduce them to suits, boots, helmets, and weapons."

"Nextday? Soon as that?"

Rance scowled at the overman. "It's going to bloody have to be, Elmo, my son. They'll need to be jumptuned by the day after. I've heard we gotta jump in three."

"The cluster can't make no jump window in three days, can it?"

"It can if it has to. By all accounts, things are not going as well as they might in the sector."

The recruits were split into groups of five and led away by the overmen, one to each group. Exactly as Rance had predicted, the kit cases followed them, floating neatly to heel, each behind its own individual recruit. Even using the new mind as fully as he could, Hark found that he was totally unable to make any sense of the journey from Receiving Hold 3 to the troopers' messdecks. Hark was in the group led by Overman Elmo, the one who had done the talking. They followed him along a series of passages and companionways that curved and twisted in and out of a much larger and even more baffling system of ducts and grids and conduits that were the bowels of the cluster ship. Much of the interior of the ship seemed to exist in semidarkness with only intermittent red safety lights. Other parts were constantly bathed in streaming and dripping condensation, while still more flashed with dancing static. As well as the steam and electricity, there were also an infinite

number of strange and, to Hark, very alien sounds. They
ranged from a bass shudder that jarred his teeth to a high
metallic whistling that rose beyond the limits of human
hearing. Overman Elmo was short and stocky, with odd,
spiky ginger hair that grew only patchily on one side of
his head. Later it would be told how Elmo had been
badly irradiated at the legendary assault on the Seven
Walls. Overman Elmo didn't waste words and didn't
seem particularly interested in the recruits' awestruck
reaction to their first encounter with the deep interior of
the ship. On the other hand, he did seem to be an individual who wouldn't crack or even waver under pressure. Despite all the strangeness, Hark instinctively
trusted him and wondered if they were to be in his permanent charge.

As with so much else in the ship, the messdeck to
which they were taken looked not so much like something that had been constructed with men in mind but
something that had occurred naturally in the distant past,
dark metal caves with ceilings so low that there were
places where Hark had to duck his head. The messdeck
was sandwiched between two levels of impossible machinery, the function of which, Hark suspected, only the
Gods completely knew. It was Spartan in its simplicity.
On the other side of the central aisle, there were two
lines of what, the new mind informed him, the troopers
called coffins. Each coffin was a container for one man.
There were twenty on each side of the aisle. Every one
had its own transparent cover. When the cover was lowered, it formed a perfect seal around its occupant. Pipes
running into the base of the unit could pump in air in the
event of an atmosphere failure. The coffin also had the
capability of putting its occupant into something called
the longsleep. Surprisingly, the new mind had little to tell
him about the longsleep. It was uncharacteristically

hazy, and he was unable to make it focus. It seemed that the longsleep was something that he would have to find out about for himself. All the coffins except five had their covers raised, and with military precision, they were all at exactly the same angle.

Overman Elmo scowled at the recruits. "Parasites in the belly of the beast, that's what we are. You'll get used to it, though. If you live that long."

He indicated the five coffins with their lids down.

"Pick one each. Their previous owners don't have any use for them."

"What happened to them?"

Elmo treated the recruit who'd spoken to a withering look. "What the hell do you think happened to them? This is a combat outfit. They're dead, and you're their replacements."

Each of the five recruits stood by a coffin.

"Okay, if you look at the base of the unit, you'll see a green toggle. Flip it out and your kit will stow itself in the base of the coffin. You see the slot? That's the place, and the only place, where you keep your kit."

The five recruits did as they were told, and the five cases slid obediently into their slots.

"You will observe, above the head of each unit, there's a rack and lockers. These will take your suit and helmet, your boots and weaponry. You see that one section of your locker space is padded and has an independent environment. You may well be wondering why anyone should go to so much trouble over a locker, particularly a worthless trooper's locker. This section is for your suit. Your suit is your life and your constant companion, and you will cherish it even above yourself. After you have slept through, you will be introduced to your suits. Once the rest of your equipment has been issued, I will show you how to correctly square away your area. I will show you once, and after that, short of actual battle conditions, I never want to see it vary. On this deck, you do things my way or you come to understand grief. I hope you're all taking me seriously."

Just in case they weren't, he allowed them a few seconds of contemplation before he went on.

Inside the coffin was a blanket and a small pillow. These were folded and laid out with an exact regularity. Hark saw how, in this world of machines, the men were made closer to machines themselves. He had a sudden longing to see the sky.

Elmo dismissed them. At the far end of the deck there was an open area where the troopers could spend what off-duty time they were allowed. Though reasonably clean, the area had a certain air of chaos that stood in total contrast to the military order of the coffins and lockers. The chairs, couches, and other mismatched furniture were old and battered. The long table that provided a central focus for the area had been slashed and carved on until hardly any of its original surface was left unmarked. The bulkheads were covered with drawings and pictures almost exclusively of naked women in fanciful and occasionally outrageous poses. Hark wondered what had happened to the women in this strange, enclosed metal world. If this initial experience was anything to go by, he doubted that he would get any immediate answer.

One piece of furniture puzzled Hark. It was circular and plastic, with a slight depression in its middle. As far as he could see, it must have been originally created for a very strange creature and been adapted for human use only by what had obviously been a good deal of applied violence.

A screen that showed moving pictures was set like a window in one of the bulkheads. A scratched and blotchy drama was being acted out by figures in strange armor who fought with swords. Back on his home world, this would have been a magical wonder to Hark; here, the new mind told him that it was only entertainment. There were just three men in the area. Two were staring at the screen while a third was winding tape around the handle of a large and vicious-looking knife. It was the same tape that affixed the pictures of naked women to the bulkheads, and it had also been employed extensively to repair the furniture. Hark, who was the first of the five to enter the area, nodded in greeting and was completely ignored. Finally the man taping the knife looked up and grunted.

"New meat."

Hark nodded again. "We are new here."

The one with the knife spit on the floor and wrapped another twist of tape around the handle. This messdeck apparently had no tradition of hospitality or welcome for new recruits.

These troopers were hardly what Hark had expected. He had started to imagine that their future comrades would all be slick and polished like Topman Rance or Overman Elmo. These three were quite the opposite. They were close to ragged. The trooper with the knife was stripped to the waist, and an oily bandanna was tied around his head. There was a certain logic to that. It was hot on the messdeck. The man's chest was covered in scar tissue from old burns. His uniform pants were equally scrungy and crudely hacked off between knee and ankle. In total contrast, his boots were immaculate. The trooper had stopped winding tape around the knife handle and was now honing the gleaming blade with a small whetstone. His total absorption in the task made it close to an act of love.

Hark looked slowly around the room.

"Is it permitted for us to sit down?"

Again he was ignored. Hark glanced at the other recruits and shrugged. He selected a chair at the head of the big table and sat down. The other four did the same. Their attitude was one of uneasy defiance. What could these men do to them that hadn't already been done? A series of deep, rumbling shudders ran through the ship. The recruits turned to each other in alarm. The old-timers didn't even look up. The tremors subsided, and the recruits attempted to relax. Hark turned and watched the flickering images on the screen. The strange armored warriors were still hacking their way through their bloody intrigues. Unfortunately, when the characters spoke, their language was unintelligible. Even going deep into the new mind, he couldn't understand a word they were saying. After a while, he stopped trying to follow the story and settled into listening to the constant internal noises of the ship.

He was drifting into a half sleep when he heard voices from the other end of the messdeck and five men came down the aisle between the twin lines of coffins. They were an odd mixture. Two were in full harness and bulky black suits and carried black visored helmets under their arms. The new mind told Hark that these were the suits that Topman Rance had mentioned. These were the suits that the troopers wore into battle and into the emptiness of space. The material from which the suits were constructed was like nothing that Hark had ever seen. It was constantly in motion as if it were alive, molding itself to the wearer's body every time he moved. The other three men were dirty and oily, as if they had spent many hours doing hard manual work around machinery. They were dressed in ragged, cut-down dark green coveralls. One of them was a giant, his head shaved and his body such a mass of scars that it scarcely seemed possible that he could have lived through such injuries. Part of his left arm, a section of the forearm between the wrist and elbow, had been replaced by a steel and plastic prosthesis. Despite the fact that the section above it was entirely false, the giant's left hand seemed perfectly natural.

The giant was first into the rest area. He was so tall that he had to maintain a continuous stoop to avoid hitting his head on the ceiling. The trooper with the knife looked up as he approached the table.

"So how goes it, Dyrkin?"

The giant snorted. "How's it supposed to go when you've spent all the watch unblocking a filter in the forsaken twenties?"

The trooper with the knife shrugged. "You shoulda gone sick like me."

Dyrkin scowled. "Still jerking off that knife, Renchett? I wouldn't have thought you'd be so eager to use it again, not after the last time."

Renchett wiped the blade one last time and then slid it into his boot. "I'm in no hurry. No doubt we'll be dropping into some kind of shit soon enough . . . and talking of shit—" He jabbed a bony finger in the direction of Hark and the other recruits. "You see what we got here?"

Dyrkin nodded. "I seen it. I was just getting around to dealing with it."

He suddenly lunged across the table and grabbed Hark by the front of his singlet. "You're sitting in my chair, filth. What you got to say about that?"

Hark's mouth dropped open. "I didn't know—I—"

"Then you ought to have known."

Hark found himself jerked up and out of his seat, dragged across the table, and thrown bodily into a bulkhead. He lay winded for a few seconds, then he started to grow angry. He might have been delivered into this alien place, but he was still an Ashak-ai warrior. He scrambled to his feet and swung his fist at Dyrkin. The blow was stopped cold by a massive hand. The giant twisted Hark's arm, forcing Hark to bend half double. At the same time, he brought the steel forearm down across Hark's back. Hark's knees buckled, and he dropped to the deck plates with the world spinning around him.

# FOUR

HARK woke with a gasp. He was lying in a pool of water. His face was wet, and his singlet was soaked through. For a moment, he had absolutely no idea where he was or even who he was. All he knew was that he couldn't feel his left shoulder. Then he moved his head, and he felt it with a vengeance. Pain surged through him, and for a moment he wondered if his neck had been broken. A ring of grinning faces were staring down at him, hard faces with scars and cold unfriendly eyes. He knew where he was. He was on the Gods' starship. Except all that had changed. The Gods weren't Gods at all, they were creatures called the Therem, and he was part of their army. He groaned. The grins broadened. Dyrkin, the giant with the prosthetic arm, stood right over him. His grin was the meanest of all.

"You learned your place now, new meat, or do you want to go around again?"

Hark tried to sit up. He felt as if he were going to vomit. "I . . ."

Renchett, the one who seemed to be in love with his knife, was holding a plastic container. He must have dumped the water over the fallen man.

45

Hark tried to speak again. "I . . . won't sit in your chair no more."

Dyrkin nodded. "You learn fast, new meat."

Beyond the grinning circle of old hands were the other four recruits from Hark's group. They weren't grinning. Their faces showed an unhappy combination of relief that they weren't the ones who'd been getting the treatment at the hands of Dyrkin and apprehension that they might be next. Renchett turned and glared at them.

"One of you get him up on his feet and into his coffin."

None of them moved. The four stood as if fear had rooted them to the spot.

Renchett scowled. "You hear me, you scumsucks?"

The four looked at each other as if each was unwilling to be the one to draw attention to himself by stepping through the ring of longtimers. Renchett didn't wait for a volunteer. He grabbed the nearest by the front of his singlet.

"You, asshole, get that man to his coffin! Move!"

Renchett assisted the movement with the steel toe of his boot. The recruit leaned over Hark, extended a hand, and hauled him to his feet. Despite the pain in his shoulder and the weakness in his legs, Hark had noticed something. Renchett had referred to him as a man. Not as new meat, scumsuck, or asshole but as a man. He wondered if he'd passed some sort of initial test. Hark swayed, and a second recruit moved quickly forward to support him from the other side. The two of them helped him from the rec room and along the row of silent coffins. As they lowered him down into the one assigned to him, he looked at them questioningly.

"We're all in this together, and we ought to know each other's names. I'm Hark."

"I'm Waed."

"I'm Morish."

Hark lay back with a groan. "It seems like we're going to have to stick together."

Waed and Morish stood in the narrow aisle between the rows of coffins as if they were uncertain whether they should go back to the rec room. Hark dropped the lid of the coffin and pulled the thin thermal-weave blanket around his shoulders. A sense of cold desolation crept over him, a helpless uncertainty as to what was in store for him in this strange, violent, alien place. Despite all his fears, though, within minutes he was fast asleep.

The period of sleep seemed to last no time at all. He felt as if he'd only just closed his eyes when horns started baying and the temperature in the coffin dropped close to freezing point. The lid of the coffin opened of its own accord, and he could hear the hectoring voice of Overman Elmo.

"Up, you scum! Everybody up! You want to die in bed?"

Topman Rance stood back in the entrance to the messdeck. Let Elmo roust them out of their pits—they were his battle unit and his babies. Rance had four units to worry about, and the whole damned combat coordinate. Elmo could scare the hell out of the recruits and take abuse from Renchett and Dacker. Rance noticed that one of the recruits, the one called Hark, was moving stiffly and that there was an ugly bruise running across his left shoulder blade. Dyrkin had been reinforcing the pecking order. Dyrkin had been maingun in this twenty for more than seven standards, and he was possessed of what had, so far, proved to be an unerring instinct. First time around, with a pickup of recruits, he always beat up on the most spirited of the bunch. The one he initially picked on usually rose in the pecking order but never challenged his position. Of course, in the end, there would be a challenger, and the challenger might well topple Dyrkin. Mainguns, if they weren't promoted, always took the fall in the end. There seemed to be a natural rule that ex-mainguns tended not to survive very long in combat after they'd been deposed.

Rance waited until Overman Elmo had run the twenty through the cleanoff and a fast workout on the hexagons. The longtimers were dispatched to their various work details. Keep the bastards busy and they won't have the spare time and energy to start cooking up nastiness. Finally, Elmo paraded the five recruits along the aisle in front of their respective coffins, standing at whatever approximation of rigid attention they could manage. When everything was to Elmo's satisfaction, he took a step back and deferred to Rance.

"Your recruits, Topman Rance."

"Thank you, Overman Elmo."

Rance walked slowly along the line of recruits. He stopped in front of the last.

"Name?"

"Morish 34103-301779."

Rance regarded him bleakly. "I have a name and a title, boy."

"Morish 34103-301779, Topman Rance."

"Just remember that, boy."

He moved to the next man.

"Name?"

"Voda 34103-301780, Topman Rance."

"Good."

"Waed 34103-301781, Topman Rance."

"Hark 34103-301782, Topman Rance."

Rance probed the bruise on Hark's shoulder with his index finger. "Trouble, boy?"

"No trouble, Topman Rance."

The kid was smart. He had a swift grasp of the essentials.

"Name?"

"Eslay 34103-301783, Topman Rance."

Rance faced the pickup. He smiled coldly and rubbed his hands slowly together.

"Well, my children, my poor little lost sheep, now that you all know your name, your number, and, I hope, for your sakes, your place, we come to the most important part of your initiation into the armies of the Therem Alliance." He glanced at Elmo. "Suits, boots, and helmets, Overman Elmo."

Elmo snapped his fingers. "Suits, boots, and helmets!"

The process was taking on aspects of a ritual. Rance was doing this deliberately. He wanted the recruits fully in his grip. There were some who spooked when the suits first touched them. A floating pallet drifted down the aisle. It carried five black and bulbous space helmets, five pairs of heavy-duty combat boots, and five shapeless blobs of what looked like opaque black jelly. Rance hefted one of the blobs.

"Puzzled, are we? Just dying to blurt out, 'But that isn't like any suit of clothes that I've ever seen, Topman Rance'?"

He paused. None of the recruits looked as if he was dying to blurt out anything.

"And you'd be quite right. These suits are like nothing you've even imagined. It wouldn't be putting it too strongly to say that this suit is almost as important as you are. It will be your friend, your partner, and your constant companion, and you will treat it accordingly. When you're not wearing it, you will store it in the specially designed environment in your lockers. You see, my children, these suits are living beings."

He scanned their faces as this fact sank in. Four of the recruits were impassively facing front, but Eslay was looking distinctly queasy. There was usually one. Rance knew that Elmo would be watching him.

"If you delve into your brand-new memories, my children, you will find the term 'symbiotic parasite.' That is exactly what these suits are. They are a form of animal life with their own minimal intelligence. The want nothing more than to guard and protect us. They were genetically tailored and selectively bred by our masters, the Therem, to interact with us humans. They can absorb massive amounts of radiation and impacts that would kill us."

Rance was holding the suit with one hand, and it had started to insinuate itself down his arm. Eslay's eyes had started to bulge. Rance hoped that Elmo had them all well in hand.

"These are our suits. They make us feel good, and in return, we love and cherish them." He tossed the suit he was holding directly at Hark. "Catch it, boy!"

Hark caught the suit and stood holding it awkwardly. The idea of wearing a living thing hardly appealed to him either, but he was doing his best not to show it.

"So put the suit on, boy."

Hark looked down at the blob in his hands. It was gently sliding around his fingers.

"How do I do that, Topman Rance?"

"It's the simplest thing in the world, boy. Strip off those shorts and singlet and stand on the suit."

Hark stripped off his clothes and gingerly placed one naked foot on the blob.

"Don't be shy, boy, stand right on it. It won't bite you."

Hark stepped up onto the suit. His feet sank into it, and it immediately started to flow up his legs, covering them with a thick second skin. Beside him, he heard Eslay gasp. It had reached his knees and was advancing up his thighs. The thing felt warm against his flesh. He almost gasped himself as it flowed around his genitals. As it got to his waist, the feeling subtly changed. The sense of revulsion melted away and was replaced by a pleasant tingling of well-being. Topman Rance was right; the suit was his friend.

"Feel okay, does it, boy?"

Hark grinned. He was close to euphoric.

"Yes, sir, Topman Rance. It feels great."

He was aware that the suit had to be doing something to him, but he didn't give a damn. He was in love with his suit. Rance tossed out the other four blobs of black jelly.

"Okay, the rest of you get suited up too."

Eslay made no attempt to catch the suit that was thrown at him. It thudded to the deck plates at his feet and just lay there. Hark was sure that it was his imagination, but somehow the blob seemed to look rejected. As the suits covered the other three recruits, they all started grinning. Eslay stood stock-still. He might have been afraid of Rance, but he was a lot more afraid of the suit. Rance advanced on him.

"Are you going to put on that suit, boy?"

Eslay looked as if he were about to strangle. "I ... can't."

Rance's voice was hard and quiet. "Put on that suit, boy."

Eslay's mouth worked, but no sound came. Rance glanced at Elmo.

"Let's put him in his suit."

Together, they grabbed the recruit and, before he could put up a struggle, lifted him clear off the ground and dumped his feet into the black jelly. The suit, as if it could sense the urgency, flashed up his legs at high speed. They didn't put him down until it had covered him all the way up to the chest. Eslay swayed and then collected himself. He didn't look euphoric, and sweat stood out on his face, but at least he was calm.

"Do you have a grip on it now, boy?"

Eslay was still sweating, but he had found his voice. "Yes, Topman Rance. I've got a grip on it."

"Then we can move on to the next phase."

Elmo took the floor to explain how to adjust and lock the boots, seal the helmets, and use the tongue switch controls on the air feed, lights, and communicator. As the information was already in the recruits' heads, he had only to go through it once.

"Now we issue your weapons."

The pallet that had brought in the suits and boots was replaced by one that carried a rack of five weapons. Rance removed one and held it up.

"Observe well, my children. What we have here is the standard weapon of the ground trooper. The Multipurpose Energy Weapon, the MEW. Next to your suit, this weapon is your best friend. Its function is very simple. It kills the enemy and, we hope, prevents the enemy from killing you."

Elmo passed out the weapons. The recruits handled them gingerly.

"You don't have to be afraid of them. The power packs haven't been loaded yet."

The MEW was slightly longer than a man's arm. It consisted of four parallel tubes that ran from a hemispherical muzzle shield at one end into a cylindrical trigger control at the other. A folding stock fitted into the user's shoulder.

"All you need to know to operate the MEW has already been implanted in your brains. What we are going to do now is to take you out onto the outside of the ship and shake that information loose by practice."

Hark was surprised at how fast things were going. Rance and Elmo seemed to be giving them no time to stop and think. After less than a day on the ship, the recruits were armed and in full combat gear. They were practically soldiers already. Elmo was marshaling them to move out of the messdeck. As Elmo marched them for the second time through the complex and mysterious bowels of the ship, there was a whole different spirit among the recruits. They had come in as nervous newcomers with nothing but their underclothes to protect them. Now, with the sole exception of Eslay, who still looked less than comfortable in his suit, they were almost standing tall as they walked through the corridors and companionways carrying their weapons and helmets. Their boots crashed on the deck plates, and they no longer flinched at the ship's random groans and booms, the flares of plasma, and the flashes of static.

The spirit wilted slightly when they confronted the large circular air lock that led to the exterior of the ship. Beyond the thick double iris was an unknown infinity that was so awesome that not even the suit-induced euphoria could totally calm their fears. Rance continued to give them no time to panic. At his order, they put on their helmets. He and Elmo carefully checked the seals, then Elmo operated the air lock controls. The inner iris opened with a hollow, echoing sigh. They stepped inside. The iris closed behind them. As the air drained out of the lock, the suits began to alter. They ceased to be a smooth second skin and started to tuck and roll over the vulnerable parts of the men's bodies, providing ribbed protection for the knees and elbows, for the crotch and kidneys and the pit of the stomach.

The second iris opened, and the blackness of space was above their heads. For a few moments, they had no chance to take in the view. There was the instant of disorientation as their horizontal perspective performed a ninety-degree turn, then a clutch of dizziness as they stepped from the floor of the air lock onto the subjectively vertical surface of the ship's hull. In that instant, the pseudograv built into their boots took over from the ship's internal gravity. Everything normalized, and the air lock became a rapidly closing hole in what was now the ground.

For once, Rance didn't hurry them. No one, not even a topman, could bully a recruit through his first contact with the emptiness of space and the different but equally frightening vastness of the battle cluster itself. They had to be given time to stand and stare. Hark and the others did exactly that. Even in the desert, when he had gazed up in wonder at the night sky, he had never felt so completely dwarfed. There were numbers in his head that attempted to make sense of the endless black and the cold light of the thousands of stars, but they didn't help any. There were also numbers for the battle cluster, but those were equally meaningless. Hark couldn't conceive how anything so vast could have been built even by Gods. Thirteen huge ships, each as large as the one on which he was standing and each having its unique if inexplicable design and form, hung together in an unidentifiable configuration, the relationships of which Hark knew that he would never begin to understand. The way the giant ships were clustered together reminded Hark of some strange, exotic flower. The parts added up to a unit that was somehow greater than the sum of the individual parts. Although the ships floated free of each other, there could be no mistaking the fact that the cluster was a fully integrated unit. There were continuous ship-to-ship exchanges of all kinds of raw energy. A faint rainbow aurora glowed in the space between two ships that were long tapering triangles and a third that was a bulky, irregular spheroid. A ship that appeared to be constructed of hexagonal crystals discharged cracks of purple ball lightning into empty space. Three other ships were linked by a vibrating web of plasma pseudopods. The overall impression was one of the battle cluster being so highly charged that it could scarcely contain its own impossible levels of power. All served to reinforce Hark's original feeling that the ship, and now the cluster, was more a living thing than a collection of soulless machines.

Rance allowed the recruits their moments of naked wonder, but eventually he snapped them back to the matter at hand. They were marched across the vast expanse of the *Anah 5*'s outer hull to where the other groups of five that made up the intake were waiting for them along with their overmen. Hark had somehow expected the surface of the ship's hull to be a featureless sheet of smooth metal. If anything, it was quite the reverse. It was covered by a deep patina of fine dust, pebbles, and even small rocks. It was pitted both by numerous small craters and by large washes of fused and blackened metal that were clearly legacies from previous battles. As they marched toward the others, the five passed a team of four humpbacked, suited nonhuman creatures performing a minor repair on the hull with vibrant red lasers. Their suits were jointed steel armor, not the living parasites issued to the troopers.

Waed and Morish paused to look more closely at the creatures, but Elmo chivvied them along.

"Keep it moving. You're going to have to get used to a lot of different species before you're through. There's nothing particularly interesting about the nohans."

When they reached the other squads of five, they were formed into parade ranks. Rance positioned himself in front of the whole intake.

"The overmen will now hand out the energy packs."

Of all the danger spots in the induction process, this was probably the most crucial. The recruits would now be armed and capable of the most terrible destruction if any of them decided to psych or serk. His hold on them had to be absolute.

"Do not load the energy packs until I give the word!"

Each recruit was handed the dull black pod, slightly larger than a clenched fist. It clipped into the underside of his weapon. Each had the specifications of the MEW and its energy source in his new memory, and only the dullest failed to experience a slight thrill of excited fear at the realization of the extent of the power he was holding in his hand.

"Take the energy pack in your left hand. Hold your weapon by its midsection with the underside pointing away from you."

He paused until all of the recruits had it right.

"Place the pack between the guide blocks but do not, I repeat, do not push it home."

Again he paused.

"On the command 'Load' you will load your weapons. At all times, you will keep your hands away from the triggers."

The overmen walked down the rows of recruits to make sure that they followed Rance's instructions to the letter. It was only when they were completely satisfied that the order was given.

"Intake . . . load!"

The energy packs were slammed home. There was no noise in the silence of space.

"Open formation, advance! Keep those hands away from the triggers!"

They spread out into one long, extended rank, each man some two meters from the next one.

"Weapons ready!"

Weapons were pushed forward by nervous hands.

"In this first phase of the exercise, lighted targets will appear in front of you. They will move toward you. The object is to shoot them down before they reach you. You will use all of the functions of your weapons, and I will call the changes of function."

Now that the weapons were energized, Rance was brutal efficiency. All the "my children" mockery had gone from his voice.

"Targets up!"

A blip of yellow light appeared from nowhere and floated a couple of meters above the surface of the hull. At first there was just the one, then it subdivided into a whole line of blips, maybe twenty in all. They advanced on the troopers at about the speed of a man walking.

"Set to blast and fire at will!"

There was a moment of hesitation, as if none of the recruits wanted to be the first to fire.

"The idea is to shoot them down. They're the enemy, and they want to kill you."

The recruits' weapons went off almost as one. A number of the blips vanished, but by no means was every shot a hit. Rance raised his hand.

"Targets down."

The yellow blips vanished.

"That was uniformly pathetic. In combat, you'll rarely have an enemy moving as slowly as that. Targets up!"

For the next four hours, they practiced with their weapons. The speed of the blips increased, and their movement became trickier; they ducked and weaved, and toward the end, they fired bolts of green light that delivered a severe but not incapacitating shock to whomever they hit. Rance had the men constantly switching functions on their weapons. They jumped from lasertracc to blast, from blast to heat ray to concussion, and back to lasertrace. Very early in the exercise, Hark realized that the multiple triggers on the MEW were almost identical to the prayer levers with which he'd worshiped back on his planet. This left him with a growing feeling that his former life had been a cruel deceit.

Rance not only worked the men hard on their weapons, he also pushed them toward the limit of their physical capabilities. He had them running and diving, crawling on their stomachs, all the time firing as they went, beating off the repeated attacks of the blips. He constantly reminded them that it was a matter of kill or be killed. He apparently had an uncompromisingly basic view of warfare.

The disaster didn't occur until the exercise was almost over. Only one recruit from Hark's squad, Eslay, seemed unable either to cop the feel of the MEW or to keep up with the rest of the intake. When the blips started firing shocks, he was constantly being zapped. Finally he gave up and dropped to his knees with a sighing sob that was audible over everyone's communicator. Two blips hovered over him, hitting his body with repeated shocks. He was now babbling in a language that Hark didn't understand. Then, to the horror of the other recruits, the babbling turned to screams that reverberated inside their helmets. The seal between Eslay's helmet and his suit was opening. The suit was peeling back. Blood fountained from the exposed flesh as it went into explosive decompression. More blood splashed the inside of his helmet visor. As the suit retreated toward Eslay's waist, his lungs blew. The force of his chest rupturing lifted him clear off the surface. The suit snaked off his dead legs and, carried by the grav still running in his boots, dropped to the floor. Eslay's corpse, naked except for his helmet, continued to float upward. Rance quickly stepped up to the nearest recruit and took his weapon. He set it to blast, aimed it at the body, and held down the trigger until there was nothing left. He calmly turned and handed the weapon back to its owner, then he faced the stunned recruits.

"Couldn't just leave him to float around, could we?"

Hark was shocked by the blunt callousness. Surely a man's death deserved something, some kind of observation. Rance seemed to be well aware of the feeling.

"Think we should have taken the time to give him a decent burial? Let me tell you something, getting a decent burial can be a dangerous luxury. The first thing you learn is that a dead body is a worthless lump of organic garbage and isn't something you take risks for. Anything else is sentiment, and sentiment can get you killed. You're probably wondering how it was that the suit came off him and could the same thing happen to you. The answer is that it might, but it most likely won't, unless you cave in like he did. Not often, but now and again, a suit turns on its wearer if it feels he isn't giving one hundred percent. Eslay didn't like his suit, and apparently it didn't like him."

Rance made a dismissive gesture, and the overmen began herding the recruits into ordered ranks preparatory to returning to the interior of the ship. Elmo picked up Eslay's suit, boots, and weapon. As they marched away, Rance didn't go with them. He needed a few moments to himself. Eslay's death was a damned nuisance. Now he'd have to make a report to the line officer.

# FIVE

HARK was so terrified that he didn't care who knew it. In fifteen minutes the ship was due to make a jump. His new memory contained only the scantiest information about the jump. He knew that it was what moved the cluster from one point in the universe to another in a matter of minutes. There was the suggestion that it had something to do with the bending of the relationship between space and time, but there was nothing about the actual mechanics of the thing. It was either a closely guarded Therem secret or maybe just something that mere troopers didn't need to know. There was nothing about the terror of the jump in his new memory. He had learned about that on the messdeck during the last three days. Directly the jump had been announced, the whole messdeck had fallen into a deep gloom. Even the normally unshakable Dyrkin was affected. It started to appear as if the troopers hated the jump more than they hated combat. In combat, they were at least partially in control of their destiny. During the jump, they were completely helpless.

It took a while for Hark to find out what exactly was so frightening about the jump. Before the gloom set in,

things had improved a little on the messdeck. The newcomers hadn't been completely accepted, but they were
being tolerated. Toleration, however, didn't extend to
answering a lot of damn-fool questions. A full day had
gone by before Hark got an answer out of a taciturn
longtimer called Helot, who summed it up in just three
sentences.

"It's more pain than it's possible to imagine. You feel
like you're being torn apart limb from limb. The worst
part is that it seems to go on forever."

When Hark had tried to ask more questions, Helot
had cut him off.

"You'll find out."

It wasn't that the previous three days had been spent
sitting around the messdeck listening to scuttlebutt.
Rance had worked them close to the point of exhaustion.
The intake had gone through one more training session
together, and then each group of five, four in the case of
Hark's, had been integrated with the twenty to which
they had been assigned. From that point on, the longtimers and the recruits had trained together as a complete combat team. Working alongside the veterans had
at first filled Hark with a deep depression at how little he
knew. As the sessions progressed he was quite amazed
by the speed at which he was picking up the rudiments of
ground fighting. On the other hand, he still had grave
doubts as to whether he would ever be good enough to
survive the real thing. The recruits' off-duty time was
almost nonexistent, but the gloom on the messdeck was
so deep that it couldn't help but affect them. They
caught the longtimers' dread of the jump and amplified it
with their own fear of the unknown.

About an hour before jumptime, Rance visited the
messdeck. He made a point of always being there just
before a jump. The purpose was to reinforce control and
authority at a moment when the men were at their most

angry. The noncoms in the Alliance were never allowed to forget that the great trooper uprising of a quarter of a century earlier had exploded immediately before a jump. The revolt had spread through almost half the ships in the fleet and had come close to crippling the campaign against the Yal. The presence of the new intake just made the situation more delicate. The longtimers, if they hadn't actually been telling horror stories, would at least have dropped a few sinister hints. He decided that the recruits could probably use a few reassuring words.

"I won't lie to you. The jump is one of the most unpleasant experiences that a man can go through. While it lasts, you may think that you are actually dying. Get one thing straight. You will not die. The jump's awful, but it will do you no permanent harm. It's just one of the things you have to live with. By now, you've probably heard all kinds of wild tales about how bad the jump can be. I want you to put them out of your mind. It's bad, but you'll get over it. Someone may have tried to tell you that men have gone mad during their first jump. That's bull."

A couple of the recruits looked up sharply, Rance cursed himself. They apparently hadn't heard the story. He silently cursed again as Dacker raised his hand. Dacker, along with Renchett, was one of the main troublemakers in Elmo's twenty. He was undoubtedly trying to pull something.

"Permission to speak, Topman Rance?"

When Dacker was polite, it always meant that he was looking to score off a superior. It was a kind of reverse insolence.

"What do you want, Dacker?"

"Begging the topman's pardon, but the stories about rookies going mad during a jump isn't all bull. When I was back on the *Yalna 7*, there was this recruit who—"

"Shut up, Dacker. Whatever you've got in your mind never happened. It's a mess monkey's tall story."

"I saw it with my—"

"Shut it, Dacker!"

Dacker shut up, but the damage was done. The recruits looked green. There was one consolation. The newcomers' fear might provide sufficient amusement to the longtimers that it would take the edge off their resentment. Rance always felt like a fraud after these speeches. He hated the jumps as much as anyone, and he also hated lying to his men. Individuals *did* go mad on their first jump. Some not until their second, third, or twentieth. The idea that the jump was ultimately harmless was a heavily promoted piece of fiction. The truth was that the Therem had been frequently approached to try to get something done to mitigate the pain of the jump. They claimed that it was impossible. The pain was a side effect unique to humans. No other species suffered anything like it, and there was nothing that could be done.

Rance's last job before he sealed himself in his coffin was to check in with his immediate superior, his line officer. If he shared anything with Dacker, it was a distaste for officers. The men despised them because they were almost never in combat. With Rance, who had more contact with them, the hate went deeper. The officers had blended. They were trying to be more Therem than the Therem themselves. At moments like this, just before a jump, there was something that particularly bothered him: The officers showed no sign of agitation. One of the hoariest stories in trooper legend was that the officers did have something to ease the pain, something that was denied to the rank and file. The story might be as old as the jump drive, but Rance had never totally been able to dismiss it.

Line Officer Berref was one of the least appealing of

his kind. There was a condescending limpness about him that grated on Rance. His pale blue uniform was a little too immaculate. The way his blond hair was combed into crisp waves was a little too elegant. The officer's ring that he wore on the little finger of his left hand was just too large and showy. Too much time had been spent on the perfection of his pencil mustache. These, however, were only the external symptoms of what Rance really loathed. Berref and, in Rance's experience, the majority of the officer corps approached the war as an exercise in morbid cynicism. The men were expendable cattle, battle fuel—there were plenty more where they came from. The only thing that had to be preserved was the war. It was inevitable that the two most powerful species in the galaxy should lock in perpetual combat from the moment they discovered each other. The Yal and the Therem existed, and therefore they warred. The officers gave the impression that they considered their duty to be the day-to-day and year-to-year management of that war.

"Men bedded down for the jump, Topman?"

"All in their coffins, sir."

"Any trouble?"

"Just the usual hostility "

"But no actual trouble?"

"No trouble."

"Then you better get yourself sealed in, and I'll talk to you after the recovery."

Rance watched the line officer walk away. He simply couldn't believe that anyone was able to remain so calm before a jump. The bastards had to have something that wasn't being given out to the men. Rance found that he had been gritting his teeth.

"One day, you're finally going to go into combat, and I'm finally going to blow your forsaken head off."

A siren wailed through the messdeck. The coffin lids slowly lowered. Hark found that his fists were clenching and unclenching. How would it start? What would be the first sign? Could it really be as bad as they said? The longtimers on the messdeck didn't seem the kind to exaggerate. Inside the coffin, all Hark could hear was his own breathing. Through the transparent cover, he watched the lights on the messdeck go out. Only small red safety lamps remained. Cold sweat beaded his back. How would he endure it if it was as bad as they said? If he went mad, he didn't doubt that they would dispose of him as arbitrarily as they had disposed of Eslay.

Hark waited, resigned to the coming agony, but for what seemed like an hour, nothing happened. The constant, muscle-tensing fear was exhausting. Let it start. At least end the suspense. Or maybe the jump had been postponed. Did he dare hope for a temporary reprieve? At that precise moment, a vibration ran through the coffin as if the ship had shifted or stretched. He continued to hope, but he knew in his heart that something was starting. For no logical reason, Hark had somehow imagined that the pain would start slowly and gradually increase in intensity. As the first shock seared through him, he knew that he had been completely wrong.

There was molten fire in his bones. At the same time he was being twisted out of shape. It was worse than being twisted—he was losing his shape, he was being spread across space, smeared over the blackness of the void. He was falling and screaming. Every deformed nerve was being tortured; the teeth were being dragged from his gaping mouth. His own screams beat inside his head until his skull started to fragment. His brain boiled over in an eruption of excruciating color. This was worse even than the datashot. His surroundings gone, he was alone, a thing without form, constantly shifting and rending. All that remained was the pain. It was his very being, burning through eternity. The pain defined him.

He was like a star made of constantly exploding and re-generating agony.

To his surprise, he found that he could think inside the suffering. If anything, that made it worse. The capacity to think prevented him from losing himself in the howling hallucinations that racked his overloaded senses. He began to feel how the pain came in distinct phases. There was no respite, and each was as bad as the next. All the change of phase meant was a shift in emphasis. There was the blinding red-gold fire that burned and consumed his flesh. There were the icy razor bolts that ripped and gouged through the backs of his eyes. There was the terrible spatial distortion in which even his identity be-came unrecognizable. Worst of all, the hallucinations re-fused to stop. The cycle of torment went on and on, a spiraling loop on which he helplessly hung, twisted, and turned.

At first, he couldn't believe that it had stopped. It had been everything. He was pressed hard against the side of the coffin, clawing at the lining and muttering to himself. His eyes were tightly shut, and the visions of horror lin-gered like an afterimage while his nervous system cringed, believing in nothing but the next stage in the cycle.

"Let it stop, please. Let it stop! *Let it stop!*"

When the messdeck siren started braying again, he thought that it was still his screaming.

"Let it . . ."

The last word was a sob. He opened his eyes. Every-thing was back to normal. The lights were coming on, but none of it seemed real. The pain—that was real, that was everything. Except that the pain had gone. There was blood on the palms of his hands where his finger-nails had dug in. His right shoulder hurt. He must have been banging it against the inside of the coffin. The cover opened. He experienced a fresh clutch of dread. The unreality was still there. Had he gone mad? There seemed to be something wrong with the light; things didn't look right. The cover was now fully open. Hark tentatively sat up. Immediately, his stomach revolted. He was racked by a spasm of dry retching, and sweat poured from his upper body. He felt dizzy and had to grab hold of the side of the coffin. Strangely, there was a kind of comfort in this violent physical reaction. If he could feel like this, he was probably still sane. The madness that he had felt back on the planet had been nothing like this. There was a certain safety in madness, and the last thing he felt was safe. Reality seemed to be returning. He waited until the spasm passed, wiped off his face, then tried to stand. His legs felt like rubber, but by concentrating hard, he managed it. Others on the messdeck were emerging from their coffins. To a man, they looked as bad as he felt. Most were verging on green, and most had dark circles under eyes that still stared in horror. It wasn't long, though, before the cursing started.

"Shit."

It was Dyrkin, as top man in the pecking order, who led the chorus of complaint.

"I ain't never going to go through that again. They're going to have to burn me first."

"There's got to be some other way."

Renchett, who had recovered faster than most, spat on the deck. "Of course there's a better way. We all know that the officers and medians don't do the jump the hard way. They got something. They got drugs or shielding or implants or something. They don't have to feel it the way we do."

Elmo had come into the messdeck. He looked almost as bad as the men did, but he was doing his best to pull his overman authority back together.

"Curse it up, boys. Get really angry. That's the best way to get over a jump. Anyone in really bad shape?"

Dyrkin scowled. "We're all in really bad shape. What did you expect?"

"Don't get on my ass, Dyrkin. We all went through the same shit."

"Did we?"

Elmo ignored the challenge. He wasn't in any mood to deal with the age-old bitch that came up with every jump.

"If there are no casualties, you better eat and then get suited up."

"What?"

Everyone turned and looked at Renchett. He was a troublemaker and a mess monkey lawyer, but nobody yelled at an overman. His face was a mask of furious outrage.

"What do you mean suit up?"

Elmo was very calm. The aftermath of a jump could also be a potential flashpoint. "Are you talking to me, Renchett?"

"I'm looking at you, ain't I?"

"Under normal circumstances, your mouth would have earned you three days in a pod."

"Under normal circumstances, we'd be getting a down day with all the food and booze we want. After a jump, the messdecks get drunk. That's the rule."

"That's the tradition, and these aren't normal circumstances. We're in an A-plus combat zone, and we got a new intake to bring up to scratch."

"Screw the new meat. Let them take care of themselves. I hurt all over."

"You just ran out of chances, Renchett. One more word and you're in a pod."

Elmo let Renchett glare defiance for a full fifteen seconds, then he gave him a final chance to save face.

"Get your suit on, trooper."

Renchett turned on his heel, ripped his suit from its

environment, dumped it on the ground, and trod on it. The suit, as though sensing his anger, hesitated before climbing up his legs.

"Do the rest of you have any objections to climbing into your suits?"

The rest of the twenty turned away. There was some muttering, but they all started hauling out their equipment.

Rance had decided that he wasn't going to go out on the hull for the training sessions. The new men were getting close to being as ready as they would ever be, and the overmen were more than capable of keeping the men running. The jump had been particularly unkind to him, and he wanted nothing more than to spend the day sleeping it off. Unfortunately, that wasn't going to be possible. The medians would be holding a briefing for noncoms and officers at 0700, and he had to be there. If anything, the medians were worse than the line officers. They'd done more than blended. They'd gone all the way over. They dealt directly with the Therem, and in doing so they had lost all but the faintest shreds of their humanity. They were cold and unworldly, with an attitude that came close to an alien mysticism. For them, the war against the Yal was a holy cause, now and forever, amen. They had become so emotionless that they couldn't even manage the cynicism of the line officers. Rance detested the line officers, but the medians gave him the chills. The single consolation was that a topman had only limited contact with them.

The Therem themselves were comparatively few in number, and they were spread very thinly across the multiple fronts of their endless war. As a consequence, the medians and their equivalents among the other client species wielded considerable power. They were in virtual control of everything except basic strategy. As far as the human ground troops were concerned, they were the ultimate authority, the high priests of battle.

The briefing room was in the upper part of the ship, an area that Rance rarely visited. It was on the very outside of the hull, enclosed in a transparent dome that afforded a panoramic view of space and the two nearest ships in the cluster. They were close to a binary star system, the usual red gas giant and white dwarf. As Rance entered the room, dead on the mark of 0700, he peered out of the dome to see if any of the training exercise was visible. There was no sign of them. They had to be on another side of the ship. He didn't want to look at the stars. They were undoubtedly the next target, and he knew for sure that he'd grow to hate them before the operation was over.

The ship's other nine topmen were already there when Rance arrived. He exchanged curt greetings with them. The topmen on any ship were a tight, if taciturn, club. They were the ones who ran the combat, the real thing, when the troops were beyond the reach of medians and officers.

"Bad jump."

"A swine."

"Anybody get psychs?"

Topman Benset nodded.

"I had one come out mute and staring."

"You keep it from the men?"

"Sure, I gassed them down, disappeared him, and planted the suggestion that he'd been taken in for redataing the day before."

"Anyone else?"

The topmen shook their heads.

"One ain't bad for a jump like that."

The conversation stopped, and the topmen snapped to attention as some thirty line officers filed in. They were followed just seconds later by the five medians. There were no preliminaries. The room immediately came to order. The medians even looked alien. They also looked very much alike. They had been selectively bred to be what they were, and in the process they had lost all vestige of hair. There was almost a luminescence to their polished bald heads, and there was much speculation as to what kind of bodies were concealed under their flowing, dark blue robes. Delarac, the one who did the talking at these briefings, motioned a corpse-white hand toward the dome.

"Dark, please."

The topman nearest the environ panel opaqued the dome. There was a projection pedestal in the center of the room. In the darkness, a miniature of the binary star system floated above it, performing a speeded-up version of the movements of the originals. There was also one attendant planet. That had to be the target.

"Observe the planet."

Nobody knew what the exact relationship was between the individual medians, whether they were all the same rank or whether some were senior to others. Did the fact that Delarac always spoke at briefings indicate that he was the head median? Or perhaps he was the lowliest.

"It is a planet of very little worth. Class G, bad atmosphere, mainly rock and dust, minimal indigenous life, and a potentially unstable system. Normally it would not be worth a second glance except that the Yal have positioned a network of dome batteries in its northern hemisphere, and there will be no hope of clearing them from this quadrant unless it is removed."

There was a narrowing of eyes among the topmen. This was going to be a bitch.

"The Yal installations are shielded against attack from space, and since they can draw power from an entire planet, I seriously doubt that we can break the shields, even with a prolonged bombardment by the whole cluster. We could, of course, continue bombardment until they drained the basic molecular structure of the planet and caused a final disintegration, but planetary annihilation is strictly against Alliance fundamental policy and thus we are left with only one viable option."

The topmen knew what was coming next.

"The strategy is crude, and it may prove costly, but there are no practical alternatives. Simultaneously, we will bombard their screens from orbit and mount a ground attack on their installations. The pressure on their screens should cause them to compress above the batteries and render them ineffective at surface level. Our troops should have no trouble moving through and destroying the domes."

Rance watched the tiny illuminated planet tracing figure eight's around the model of the binary. It always sounded so simple at these briefings. Walk in and destroy the domes, a clean, surgical operation. In the sterile darkness of the briefing room there was no hint of the noise and the fear and the broken bodies.

"The cluster will be in position in two standards. Our dropcraft will launch at 1500 precisely. Our barrage will commence immediately the dropcraft are clear of the cluster. Once our forces are in position on the ground, they are likely to encounter some light ground defenses, but our scans of the Yal emplacements have shown nothing that should cause any major problems. It would appear to be a simple operation, free of any serious complications. You will receive your individual battle orders immediately after this briefing is over. Do any of you officers have questions?"

A number of officers had minor queries for which Delarac had short, summary answers. When they were finished, the median turned his attention to the topmen.

"How about you?"

Benset stiffened. "Yes, sir, I have a question."

"What is it?"

Delarac's expression suggested that he had invited questions from the topmen only as a formal courtesy and had not actually expected any to be asked.

"Sir, it occurs to me that if the Yal screens were to cave in under the fire from the cluster while we were in the middle of the attack on the domes, at least a portion of the force on the ground could be wiped out by our own guns."

It was hard to tell with medians, but from where Rance was standing, it seemed that Delarac's expression has become even bleaker than usual.

"The possibility has been considered, but it would appear to be a low-probability scenario. Of course, as you well know, anything can happen in the heat of battle, and if such a thing did come to pass, it would be unfortunate. It is not, however, anything that merits a change in plans. Any more questions?" The median's tone seemed to indicate that he didn't expect any.

Rance snapped to attention. "Yes, sir, one more question."

"Rance, isn't it?"

"Yes, sir."

"What is it, Rance?"

"Sir, what is to stop the Yal batteries from blowing the dropcraft out of the air before we even reach the ground?"

Delarac looked at Rance as if he were a particularly backward child. "All our evaluations indicate that the fire from the cluster will be more than enough to keep the Yal batteries occupied. The dropcraft may take some hits, but losses should remain within acceptable levels."

"Thank you, sir."

In other words, "We take our chances."

There was something almost uncanny about the way

the news of the impending combat spread through the messdecks. There was no formal announcement, but suddenly everyone knew. They were being dropped onto some forsaken dust bowl planet with poisonous air and were expected to knock out a nest of Yal big guns. The consensus was that it would be bloody. For the soldier, pessimism is a natural state. It makes survival a pleasant surprise. Each man reacted to the news in his own way. Some withdrew, others cursed and complained, a few broke into secret caches of booze or drugs. Some went about their normal routine with a fatalistic resignation. Renchett worked on his knife with a renewed fury. Dyrkin was almost serene, as if he were somehow looking forward to the fight. There was a major outbreak of gallows humor, with jokes about mutilation being particularly popular. The sexual content of many of the jokes started Hark to wondering again about what had happened to the women. On what might possibly be the eve of destruction, though, it hardly seemed right to ask.

Of all the men on the messdecks, the recruits had the most difficulty in dealing with this precombat tension. At least the longtimers could reassure themselves that they had survived before and could conceivably survive again. The new meat had no such comfort. They had no previous experience. They didn't know if they were even capable of surviving. They didn't know how they'd react or whether they'd be able to stand up to combat at all. They were facing the unknown, and like all who face the unknown, they imagined the worst. They waited and nursed their fear. They were quiet and subdued, avoiding each other's eyes and those of the longtimers. They couldn't join in the grim ribaldry; they had no macho swagger to protect them and no knives to hone. All they could do was sit in the background and wait.

Hark, feeling totally at a loss, decided that the last best resort might be sleep. While no one was looking, he retreated to his coffin, stripped off his clothes, lay down, and lowered the lid. Despite the legacy of aching muscles from the day's grueling training session on the hull, sleep didn't come easily. It was the first time that he'd really been alone with his thoughts since he'd been brought to the ship. There was no one yelling at him and no one beating on him. With the lid sealed, he couldn't hear the voices of the longtimers in the downden. All he could hear was the noise in his own head. It couldn't match the voices of the overmen yelling through his communicator and echoing around the inside of his helmet, but it was more than enough of a howl to keep him from immediate sleep. There was so much to absorb, and all of it shaken and stirred by the jump and the datashot. The worst thing that the howl told him was that there was nothing in his mind that he could trust. His current reality was so imposing and so awful that it was scarcely believable, but his previous life, sitting astride a mount in the high desert, had become as tenuous as a fading dream. If he had been in a position to ask a Therem, the Therem would have told him that the howl was a sign that the healing process that followed the datashot was nearing a satisfactory conclusion, but Hark would never in his life be in a position to ask a Therem anything, and Therems rarely, if ever, volunteered information to troopers.

Hark slept fitfully for a time, but the confusion followed him into his nightmares. Finally, he came wide awake and had to face the fact that he was quite incapable of sleep. He popped the seal on his coffin and lifted the lid. The covers were closed on most of the other coffins but not all of them, and a light shone out of the downden. Hark decided that he'd get a drink of water from the spigot. As he walked down the aisle between the coffins, he noticed that a number of the sleepers were tossing and turning just as he had been. Inside the downden, Helot lounged in a deep chair, and a trooper called Wabst, to whom Hark had never spoken, was sprawled out on the strangely shaped couch. Hark didn't pay much attention to the pair of them until he'd drunk a cupful of the ship's metallic water. It was only then that he noticed how both men were wearing their battle suits rolled down to around their waists so their upper bodies were naked. They had their eyes closed and had strange expressions on their faces, and there was the image of an explicitly gyrating naked woman on the wall screen. Hark was shocked. He found that his high desert prudery hadn't deserted him. He'd heard among the young men around the fire that there were women in distant tribes who performed such lewd dances, but he had never seen anything even close to the image on the screen. And yet it couldn't be the image that was making the two longtimers behave the way they were. They couldn't see the dancing woman—their eyes were tightly shut. The realization hit him like a hammer. It was the suits. The suits were doing something to them. Something close to sexual. Hark was in a quandary. What was he supposed to do? He felt that he was intruding, seeing what he had neither right nor desire to see. He was thinking about creeping away unseen, but the steel cup that was attached to the spigot clinked as it dropped to the length of its chain. Both men's eyes snapped open with a killer's reflex. Helot glared at him.

"What do you think you're looking at?"

"I . . ."

"What's your problem, new meat? You got some kind of attitude?"

"No, I . . ."

Wabst started. "What do you think a man's supposed to do when the nearest woman's at least a hundred licks away?"

Helot's face twisted into an unpleasant grin. "This green bastard hasn't made friends with his suit yet."

Hark had a flesh-creep preview of how he'd feel the next time his suit crawled up his legs. By now, Wabst was also grinning.

"Men do all kinds of things when they're kept away from women."

Hark blurted it out before he could stop himself. "Where are the women?"

"Nobody tell you?"

"No."

"Well, kid, the nearest woman is somewhere out on a recstar halfway across the galaxy."

"What's a recstar?"

"He don't know what recstar is."

"Poor bastard's dumber than he looks."

"So what's a recstar?"

"A recstar, new meat, is nothing you need worry about until you've been through combat."

"And he don't look like he's going to get through combat anyhow."

# SIX

"DISENGAGING on my mark!"

"Mark!"

"Everyone stay calm."

There was a series of loud bangs as the drop craft disengaged from the conveyor. It nosed out of the lock and slid into space. Its human cargo, the nineteen troopers and five sappers plus Elmo, Rance, and the pilot, experienced a stomach-twisting lurch as they passed out of the *Anah 5*'s internal gravity. They were falling. The men floated in their seats, pressing up against the lap bars. Their helmets were sealed. They were locked into their seats, their weapons racked beside them.

"Better enjoy the calm before the storm; we'll hit the atmosphere soon enough."

The troopers sat facing one another in two rows, backs to the outside of the craft. Beyond the armored shell, fifty-nine identical ships were falling from the cluster in three distinct waves. The free-fall was comparatively easy to get used to. It was smooth and even. Despite the obvious built-in uneasiness, free-fall did have a certain calming effect. The fear of what was com-

ing was inside each trooper with a dry-mouthed vengeance, but it was being challenged by a mounting excitement. They were fighting men going out to do what
they did best.

"Everyone take it easy. One step at a time."

Hark was surprised at how well he was coping with
his fear. He had imagined that it would have him paralyzed by this point. In fact, it was quite the reverse. He
wanted to go. He wanted to be down on the ground and
getting on with it. His mind kept saying it to him. Yeah!
Go! Go! He could hardly stop himself from grasping for
his MEW.

"Easy."

Rance's voice was in everyone's helmet. He soothed
his troops and held them in check much in the way that a
rider might gentle a skittish mount. Rance knew that his
calming words were pure bluff. He was as scared as anyone, but he had said the words so many times that they
were as good as real.

The pilot's voice cut in. "Atmosphere coming up!"

Unseen by the men—the only vision port in the craft
was in the pilot's cabin—wings extended from the sides
of the dropcraft's needle body, delta, membrane airfoils
that gave the ship both lift and deceleration. They immediately glowed cherry-red; the wings were designed to
recycle the released energy back to the ship's propulsion
plant. The invasion fleet streaked through the upper atmosphere like silent gliding moths leaving trails of fire.
Inside the craft, though, things were not quite as serene.
The ship bounced and wallowed. It shook and buffeted.
The cabin floor pushed up under the men's feet as the
airfoils bit into the planet's thickening air. There were
curses and mutterings all down the lines of men. Rance
quickly stepped on this routine bitching.

"You can cut that out for a start!"

The cabin was filled with noise. The air screamed by

outside. The airfoils groaned and the structure of the ship protested as both were subjected to more and more stress. Then, without warning, the ship was blown to one side by a violent explosion. The first one was followed by three more in quick succession. Fear swamped excitement.

The pilot's voice came on again. "The first wave are taking a beating. There's six of them down already."

"Where the fuck is the covering fire? We're flying into the biggest goddamn guns on the planet, and we ain't got no covering fire!"

"Put a lid on that, Renchett!"

"Signal from the cluster, they're opening up." Each time the pilot cut into their communicators there was a burst of static and the almost unintelligible ship-to-ship cross talk.

Someone cursed. "Will you look at that!"

"Look at what?"

"The whole damn sky's lit up! It's our barrage."

The static in their helmets became deafening. Rance and the pilot were only just audible.

"Hang on tight!"

"There's no more fire coming at us. Some of the first wave are safely on the ground."

The dropcraft continued to bounce, shake, and buffet, but there were no more explosions. Hark was suddenly aware that he was gripping the lap bar so tightly that his hands hurt. The excitement was back.

"Ground coming up."

"Hang on!"

"Here we go! Wait for it . . . *now!*"

The dropcraft hit ground with a bone-jarring jolt. Its wings feathered up. It plunged, bounced, and skidded over an uneven surface. For a moment, it seemed to be slewing sideways, about to roll over, then, at the last moment, it jerked to a stop. There was an instant of stunned silence before Rance started yelling in their ears again.

"Up and out, you bastards! Up and out! Loose those lap bars and go!"

Two ports on either side of the ship swung down. Violet light, punctuated by flashes of brilliant white, streamed in.

"I said let's *go!*"

Lap bars clanged up, and the men were on their feet, heading for the ports. Their boots clashed on the cabin floor. Hark grabbed his weapon and moved with the others. He was no longer thinking.

"Check equipment before you hit the outside."

It was a matter of rote. Helmet seal, energy packs, water bottle, minimed, supply case, trencher. All good. The port was in front of him. Other troopers were pressing behind him, and there was no chance of turning back. Rance slapped him on the shoulder, and he stumbled down the ramp. It was a violet world, a place of violet sky, purple sand, and jagged dark purple rocks. Hark stepped off the ramp and staggered. The sand was deep and incredibly fine. It behaved almost like a viscous liquid. He sank into it up to his knees. Other troopers had also bogged down.

"Cut boot gravity and jump!"

The planet's own gravity was considerably less than either the gravity in their parts of the ship or that generated by their boots. Hark jumped and found that he was immediately free of the clinging dust. A single stride could take him maybe three meters.

"Spread out! Get away from the ship! *Move Out!*"

Out of the cover provided by the ship, Hark saw the four domes that made up the nearest Yal battery. There was so much in this war that dwarfed him. The domes were a line of mathematically perfect Yal-made hills. Brilliant radiation flashed from the apex of each dome, shooting straight up. The sky above was a maelstrom of blinding color, a continuous explosion as the Yal shields fought off the stream of energy from the cluster. The air itself seemed to be vibrating. The glare of the majestically undulating raw energy and plasma field cast distinct shadows and eclipsed the light of the planet's two suns. Even the longtimers were standing and staring.

Rance himself was given a moment's pause. It was one hell of a spectacle. The whole sky was suffused by an instant of iridescent blue. Some trace element in the atmosphere must have burned. At least the median had been right. The shields were so stretched to hold off the bombardment from space that they no longer extended to the ground. He quickly gathered himself. "Don't stand there gawking!"

Dyrkin's voice cut into their helmets. "Incoming! PBA from that ridge at oh-one-five."

"Everyone down!"

As the particle beam accelerator came to bear on them, broken beams of green light sliced through the area. A trooper simply blew apart. Hark didn't know who it was. Something hit him violently between the shoulder blades.

"Get down, you fucking idiot!"

For an instant, Hark thought that he had been hit. Then he realized that Helot was rolling off him.

"Dig in, you dumb bastard!"

Hark grabbed his trencher and twisted the grip, blowing the sand out from under his body. Dyrkin was on the communicator again.

"Confirm PBA on ridge."

"Helot, Hark, work your way over to those rocks!"

There was a spiny outcropping way over on their right. The space in between was crisscrossed by green flashes.

"Can we make it?"

"We can try."

Helot started crawling. Hark followed him with deep misgivings. Behind them, the dropcraft, which had been drawing fire, lifted off in a swirl of dust. The first half of the crawl was comparatively easy, the enemy fire well over their heads, then whatever was operating the particle beam cannon must have noticed their move. Pencil-thin beams blew up dust all around them.

"Dig down! Fast!"

Each trooper carved himself a shallow trench and lay there until the Yal gunner turned its attention somewhere else. Immediately the fire moved away, Helot was up on his feet.

"Run, boy!"

Hark thought that the longtimer had gone crazy, but he still jumped to his feet and followed his mad dash. As Helot ran, he let out a long bloodcurdling scream. Hark found that he was also screaming. Despite the terror that he would be blown to pieces by a particle beam at any moment, Hark found a reckless excitement in the way his blood pounded and his helmet was filled with the clamor of men in battle. Although the voices of his own twenty came through the loudest, there was a constant background of the shouts, orders, and screams of the other groups and the crackling interference from the blaze of energy in the sky. They came under fire again, but they were almost at the rocks. Both men dived and rolled into cover.

"Set to lasertrace—let's grease this sucker!" Helot snapped.

They both fired. Twin streams of colored pulses arrowed toward the source of the particle beams.

"I think we got him vecced. Switch to concussion."

They fired again. There was a massive explosion on the ridge. Helot let out a whoop. Dyrkin was in the phones.

"Confirm PBA out."

He was straightaway followed by Rance. "Move up. Over the ridge."

The troops advanced in an extended line. Fire burst above them, but while they were in the shadow of the ridge nothing seemed able to get a direct bearing on them. They could no longer see the domes, but the violent, angry halo above them was clearly visible. Before the drop, Rance had given them a simple briefing. All they had to do was get the sappers through to the base of the domes so they could place their explosives. He hadn't actually told the troopers that they were expendable, but the message was clear. On either side of them, other twenties were also moving up. They were a grim reminder that only one group had to get through to make the operation a success.

Rance halted them at the foot of the ridge. "There's no knowing what we're going to run into on the other side, but it don't make no difference, we're going anyway. We're going to go up fast. Don't bunch up, and go over the top low. Don't skyline yourselves. Okay?"

Eighteen troopers nodded.

"Let's go, then."

In the low gravity, the ridge was easy. They took it at a run. Near the top, the men dropped into a low crouch. They immediately came under fire again. The crest of the ridge flared and boiled. Hark was once again flat on his stomach, digging into the sand. Waed, who wasn't quite fast enough getting down, screamed and twisted backward. There was a gaping hole in his chest. Hark couldn't quite come to grips with the fact that death could be so sudden. There was something obscene about the way a man could be alive and running one moment and dead meat the next. It was one more underlining of how little they were worth.

"This is going to be a fucking mess."

The growl belonged to Dyrkin. From the top of the

ridge, they could see all the way to the base of the domes. There was only maybe a kilometer to go, but the ground was dotted with fortified gunpits and trenches. There was an odd metallic sheen on some areas of sand. The longtimers knew that this indicated strung molywire. The ultrafine filaments were more than capable of slicing off an arm or a leg, and where there was wire there were usually also mines and jumpers.

"How come we don't get no air cover?"

"I guess they figured gunships would be too vulnerable."

"What the hell are we? Dog meat?"

"If any plane got too close to that burning sky, it'd be fried."

"What about armor? Don't we even rate armor?"

"This wasn't supposed to be a full-scale landing. They're calling it a surgical strike."

"Surgical my ass."

Rance cut through the complaining. "Knock off the crap. We're moving on."

"We'll be cut to pieces."

"Shut up, Dacker. We'll take the two nearest gunpits. Half of you go for the one on the left, the others take the right. Keep firing all the way; we'll make it."

There was still fire hitting the ridge, and the group hesitated. Rance was bellowing in their helmets.

"Move, goddamm it, or I'll burn you myself!"

Suddenly they were on their feet again and running. It was another mad, screaming dash, ducking, weaving, and zigzagging, weapons vibrating in their hands as they fired wildly. It was almost as if something was taking over their will and making them do things that were in direct opposition to all their natural instincts. One man went down, and then another, but they kept on going. They were close to the gunpit, and Hark was amazed that he was still on his feet. He could see the creatures that were manning the Yal PBA. The name "chibas" was repeated in his phones. The chibas were one of the Yal's favorite cannon fodder. Slightly shorter than a human, they were part organic and part robot. Their brains and squat bodies were tank-grown biomatter, but their arms and legs were spindly constructions of implanted metal. They were among the ugliest things that Hark had ever seen.

Two of the chibas were swinging around their tripod-mounted weapon, bringing it to bear on Hark and the men around him. For an instant, he thought that he was dead, then the first troopers were in the gunpit. Renchett was among them, going to work on the chibas with his knife, slashing at the soft, yellow-gray organic parts of their bodies through chinks in their somewhat minimal carapace armor. It seemed that a species that could grow-build its troops as it needed them paid little attention to protecting them on the battlefield. Renchett worked with a savage relish until his suit was slick with the transparent goop that fountained from their wounds.

"I hate chibas, they're an abomination."

He was carefully wiping his knife as he reported to Rance.

"We got the left gunpit secured."

"Right gunpit also secure."

The gunpit provided a brief respite, an interlude with no one shooting at them. Hark hunkered down and leaned against the parapet wall. "What happens next?"

Rance wasn't slow in supplying the answer. "Anyone over there know how to fire a Yal PBA?"

Helot answered. "I've checked out on one of these."

"So stay with it and give us covering fire."

"A-firm."

"Volunteering your way out, Helot?"

"Screw you, Renchett. I don't enjoy the shit the way you do. I'll grab at any chance to save my ass."

There were distant screams in their helmets. Another twenty must have walked into the grinder.

"Okay, let's move out. Keep that covering fire coming."

This time they ran in V formation, with the sappers finding what protection they could in the angle of the V, covering the ground with fast ten-meter leaps. They were flanked by fire from the two PBAs. Once again, Hark had the feeling that some external force had a grip on him—it was akin to the fighting madness that had overwhelmed the young men back on his planet. He was taking risks that he would not normally contemplate. By the time they had overrun two more gunpits, Hark was so pumped up that he almost stumbled into a foxhole containing two chibas. They had light-yield energy weapons fastened directly to the ends of their mechanical arms. Somehow he had the impression that they were surprised. Renchett was right—they *were* an abomination. Fortunately, they were also slow. Hark blasted by instinct before they could bring up their weapons. He noticed that the chibas wore no helmets. The word was that they could breath anything.

"Wirefield ahead!"

The charge halted as the men flattened rather than blunder into an expanse of deadly molecular wire. Blast fire roared over their heads.

"Alternate blast and concussion to plow that wire under."

The massed fire boiled the ground in front of them, and the dust swirled up into a purple storm. There were a dozen major explosions in fast succession, driving the dust even higher. Hark hugged the quaking ground. What had been the wirefield looked like the end of the world. The pale dust even blotted out the light of the blazing thunderhead above the domes.

"That's the mines."

"Stay down, there may be still be jumpers."

A jumper was a saucer-sized disk that, when triggered, jumped to a height of a meter and a half and then sprayed rotating fire through a full 360 degrees. Sure enough, there were flashes of swirling fire inside the dust. When they stopped, Rance ordered the troopers up again.

"Into the dust, it's perfect cover. Watch your step, though, there may still be coils of wire lying around. Take it slow and easy."

They moved cautiously into the dust cloud. They were walking almost blind. One of the recruits turned on his helmet light.

"Turn that damned thing off," Rance ordered. "You want to be a perfect target?"

The light went off. The men pressed forward. The dust was starting to settle. They were all covered with a fine purple film. They were about to get through the wirefield unscathed when somebody began screaming.

"My foot! My goddamn foot! It's gone. The wire got me!"

Again Rance was directly there.

"Calm down! Get a seal dressing on the bleeding and lie down, try and dig yourself in. The e-vac will pick you up. In the meantime, your suit will take care of the pain."

The screaming sank to a drugged whimper as the suit blanketed its wearer with secreted analgesics.

"Move on," Rance told the others. "He'll be okay. Watch your own feet."

The dust had drifted and settled and was no longer any use as cover. There was firing all around, but none of it was directed at them and the majority of it came from Alliance weapons, not those of the Yal. There was a bout of ragged cheering as the first human troops reached the base of the dome. A port in the dome opened, and a squad of chibas rushed out, firing the weapons that they had instead of hands. They were quickly burned down.

"Okay, hold it. We can stop right here. The sappers can move up to the dome. The rest of us will hold this position."

They were standing on the edge of a trench filled with dead chibas. They had been dead only for a matter of minutes, and already they were starting to decay. The yellow-gray flesh was liquefying away from the metal skeletons that had supported it, turning back into the oily protein goop whence it had come. Nobody was in any particular hurry to get into the trench, and fortunately that didn't seem necessary. The only firing still going on was the mopping up of scattered chiba positions. Hark couldn't believe that it had actually happened, that it was over. He felt sick and dizzy—he believed that he would never be able to face food again. His hands shook except when he clutched his MEW, and yet, if anyone had yelled "Run," he would have run with desperation.

"Take the weight off but stay alert," Rance ordered.

Renchett had his knife out. "You want us to go and mop up the stragglers?"

"You've had your share of butchery for the day."

Renchett shrugged and sheathed the knife. The sappers were stringing explosives. Rance looked at the huge bulk of the dome and refused to imagine what might be happening inside the monster. He'd been inside Yal installations a number of times, and they always made him feel bad. They were just too alien. The outside was quite enough. What culture would fashion this gigantic curve of what looked like semi-polished purple stone? They must know what was about to be done to them. How did Yal panic? Rance shook his head and looked away. Hark was staring back in the direction from which they had come. The poor bastard probably didn't believe what had happened to him. The ground around the domes was like something out of a nightmare. There was charred and fused sand; some areas still smoked, others glowed. There were bodies all over, scattered among blackened wreckage from the downed dropcraft.

"Mother of Gods!"

Instinctively everyone ducked. Something was happening in the blazing sky. The halo of warring energy that was now directly above them had abruptly and radically altered. What had once been a glaring white had dimmed to a suffused, bloody red. Rance was one of the few around the dome who knew enough to suspect what might be happening. Was the Yal shield weakening? If his installation was going to be destroyed, it was a logical move for the commander of the battery to try to take as many of the enemy with him as he could. If he dropped his shields, the forces on the ground would be wiped out by their own orbiting guns. The real question was how long it would take him to shut down the shields.

The sappers were through with their work. Rance started waving everybody back. "Back to the assembly points! On the double! We're pulling out!"

He tongued open the long-range communicator. "Bring down the e-vacs as fast as you can."

A strange voice came over Rance's helmet.

"This is Lanza, topman of sappers. I'm staying here with a guard until close to detonation. I don't want any chibas coming out and dismantling the charges."

Sappers were crazy.

"Suit yourself. Don't stay too long."

The whole force was pulling back. The glare in the sky brightened, as if the Yal shields were recovering. Maybe there was time for them all to get out. The glare faded back to an angry red. It was absurd that their survival now depended on the strength of the enemy shields. The men were bunching at the prearranged assembly points. They had the wounded with them. Rance took long leaping strides in order to catch up with them. There was the distant sound of ships coming through the atmosphere. The glow in the sky seemed to be lower than it had been a few minutes earlier. Rance was certain that the Yal screens were about to cave. He hated the idea that his death would be just another cruel joke in a war that was full of them. Where the hell were those e-vacs?

As if in answer, his phones crackled with static. "E-vacs coming in. Watch out below."

The squat circular craft came down vertically with their landing legs extended. The e-vacs had a slab-sided functional ugliness that was a complete contrast to the streamlined winged elegance of the dropcraft that had brought them in. All they had to do was fall fast to a planet's surface and pick up the largest possible number of men. They were the combat workhorses, and the troopers loved them. It was only natural. Other craft got them into trouble; the e-vacs got them out.

"Yo, e-vacs! Get us the hell out of here!"

"What are those damned redballs doing?"

"Who knows with redballs?"

A flight of red spheres was following the e-vacs down. The troopers knew that the red spheres were on their side, but that was about all. The Therem had never seen fit to explain them to the human troops. They were small, little more than two meters in diameter, but they were incredibly fast and maneuverable. They appeared on battlefields, but they seemed to have the capacity neither to inflict nor to sustain harm. At other times, they could be encountered prowling the interiors of the cluster ships. Everything else was speculation. It wasn't even clear if they were machines or beings or just globs of raw energy. They didn't bother the troopers, and most of the time the troopers didn't bother about them, except instinctively to dislike them.

The men at one assembly point had to scatter to avoid the power wash as their ship came too close to the mark. Lanza's voice cut through the noise from the ships.

"We're getting out. The charges are armed, and nothing can stop them."

Five e-vacs settled on the battlefield, each in its own cloud of dust. Wide ramps extended to the ground. The first two men up on each side dragged the others in. The wounded were passed hand over hand.

"Let's go, go, go!"

The ramps started rising before the last men were inside. The final ones stumbled forward, half falling through the ports. There was a lurching confusion of men reaching for any handhold as the e-vac tilted into the air. There were no seats in an e-vac, just lines of grab bars. Rance used his rank to swing up to the overhead crew blister. The darkened cabin was cramped even for the two-man crew, who were secured in contour frames, hunched over multiple control boards. The lights of the panels were reflected eerily in their faceplates. Like the dropcraft, the e-vacs weren't pressurized. The best that Rance could do was to crouch in the hatchway, bracing himself against the top of the steel ladder that led up from the main well of the ship.

"Have the charges blown yet?" he asked.

"Not yet, but the shield's sagging."

Rance craned to see the groundside screen. It was true. From the air, it was possible to see the battering waves of energy that were pouring in from space. The Yal shield had been reduced to a red halo with a definite concave dip at its center. The e-vac lurched, and Rance was almost pitched into the well. There was cursing from below as a number of men lost their handholds and fell into those around them. One of the crew glanced around.

"Sorry about that."

Rance glared into the well.

"Turn up the grav on your boots, they'll anchor you."

Rance looked back just in time to see the charges blow. Rings of small explosions rippled around the bases of the domes. At first, there was no perceivable result. Rance bit his lip. Were they going to have to go through the whole bloody process again? Abruptly, the Yal shield winked out, and in the next moment, the visible world erupted. A huge fireball gathered on the ground. Shock waves spread to the horizon. The fireball started to rise. It was as if a star had been lit on the surface of the planet.

"Damn!"

The crew shielded their eyes. Blinding white light poured through the single armored viewslit. The screen threatened to burn out. The fireball started to rise. The area below it glowed white, a vast sea of liquid rock. The fireball was gathering speed and expanding.

"Hold tight. Here comes the shock wave."

The ship felt like God had kicked it. It was like a living thing. The kick was followed by a spasm of monstrous shudders. They were falling.

"I hope she holds together."

The crew were punching buttons. There was almost a detachment about the way they worked. Panels lit, others went out.

"Here's where we find out."

There was a sickening lurch as the crew tried to power out of the deadfall. There were shouts from below.

"Smoke! Something's leaking smoke!"

The crew was concentrating on coaxing the e-vac to gain altitude.

"Tell them it's nothing to worry about. I'd have worried if we hadn't burst a few seams."

The ship continued to spin and buffet, but they were making ground. There was the pressure of acceleration under their feet.

"The atmosphere is hosing out. We're riding the updraft. It should take us halfway to the cluster."

In the well of the ship, Hark clung to a grab bar, his eyes closed, and prayed for it all to be over, one way or another. He didn't really care. He couldn't take any more. The courage that he'd found earlier seemed to have deserted him. He didn't even care that he'd been whimpering out loud when they'd been falling and that the rest of his messdeck had probably heard him over the communicator. The man next to him turned his head and looked at Hark.

"Suit stopped pumping?"

Hark couldn't recognize him behind the faceplate of his helmet.

"I don't understand."

"They don't tell you, but you find out. It's the suits."

Hark was at a loss. "Suits?"

"It's the suits that do it to us. None of us want to do what we do in combat. We don't want to take the risks. Once the suit smells your adrenaline and starts pumping itself, you don't have a chance. You're blind and crazy. You'll go anywhere and do anything they tell you."

"What does the suit do? What does it pump into us?"

"Who the hell knows. Some endorphin cocktail of fearblockers, ones that can be absorbed through the skin. That's why the trip back from combat can be really rough. The battle's over, the suit stops pumping, and you come down seeing the full forsaken horror of it. At least we get to get drunk when we get back. It helps."

"They get us every way, don't they?"

"You're learning."

Up in the crew bubble, Rance pursed his lips. He preferred that the recruits learn about the suits as late as possible. Doubtless Hark would tell all the others.

# SEVEN

NAKED, they filed into the blue room, carrying their equipment and weapons. The lock sealed. First the water jets came on and washed away the fine purple dust. Next it was the turn of the bright blue lights—the radiation would kill any native bacteria that they might have picked up. Hark noticed that some of the men had brought back small souvenirs of the battle. Helot had the severed metal claw-hand of a chiba gunner. He must have hacked it off one of the corpses in the gunpit while he was manning the captured PBA. It was being decontaminated along with everything else.

Dyrkin looked around at the others. There were thirteen of them. Of the nineteen who had gone down, five were dead; Kemlo, who had been snagged by the wire, had been taken to sick bay to be fitted with a prosthetic foot. They had been less badly hit than some of the other twenties.

"So now we get drunk."

"Polluted. I got to get rid of the taste."

Their ship clothes were laid out for them. They quickly dressed. The lights went out. The lock at the other end of the chamber opened. They filed out into the receiving hold and were somewhat surprised to find that it was a hive of activity. Lights were flashing, and sirens were blaring. Nohan damage-control parties were hurrying to their battle positions. Fault-trace robots, no bigger than a man's foot, skittered about the floor. A gang of human core jumpers, wearing yellow radiation armor, doubled away down a corridor. The PA was issuing orders and bulletins in human, the whistling trills of the nohan, and a wash-of-sound speech that Hark couldn't recognize.

Rance grabbed the first passing human. "What's going on?"

"A Yal battlewagon is closing with us, one of the big ones. We're going to engage."

Dyrkin spit on the deck. "That's all we need."

Rance quickly gathered his men.

"We go back to the messdecks. We're ground troops. There's nothing we can do in a space battle except get in the way."

Dacker grunted. "We can get ourselves killed."

"That's taken as given around here."

Once on the messdeck, there was nothing to do but wait. The thirteen gathered in the downden. Within minutes, Dacker and Renchett had become involved in an argument with Elmo.

"The least you could do would be to issue the booze."

"I can't cut loose a booze issue when the cluster's on full action alert. They'd bust me to trooper or worse. We're going into combat, damn it."

"We've already seen our combat, and after combat, we get drunk. That's the rule."

"And talking of combat, Overman Elmo, we didn't see you down planetside."

"Rance took the command. There was no reason for me to stick my neck out."

"Some of us didn't have the option."

"What are you scum trying to say?"

"Just that we missed you, Overman Elmo."

"You all know that I've seen my share of fighting." He fingered the bald patches on his skull where the hair had long ago fallen out. "I've got a right to sit one out now and again."

Renchett wasn't prepared to let it go. He had absolute contempt for anyone who wasn't always in the thick of the action. It seemed to be the compensation for any second thoughts he might have about his own single-minded bloodletting. "Maybe you've seen too much," Overman Elmo."

"Why don't you just cut loose our booze, Overman Elmo? We're fighting men."

"You two are full of crap, and I'm not issuing booze until we're stood down. If you want to make any more of it, you'll find yourself on a field punishment."

Dacker and Renchett didn't say anything, but they stood their ground and glowered. They seemed to be trying to work out precisely how far the overman could be pushed. It took Dyrkin to step in and put a stop to the war of nerves.

"Why don't we get the screen going and see what's happening outside."

After a few seconds' hesitation, Renchett and Dacker turned their attention from Elmo to the wall screen. The first image to appear was the same naked woman Helot and Wabst had been watching before the drop. This drew a halfheartedly ribald cheer from the men. Hark remembered that Wabst was among the dead. Dyrkin adjusted the single control. The naked dancing girl was replaced by a high-resolution picture of the Yal battleship. There could not have been a greater contrast. Warm, inviting human flesh gave way to cold, deadly alien technology. It was hard to tell from the screen just how big the enemy ship was. Hark had to assume that the many small points of light circling around it were attendant space vessels. If they were only as large as the dropcraft, the Yal ship was very big indeed, larger than any ship in the cluster but not as big as the whole of the cluster together. It was also nothing like any of the ships in the cluster. It seemed to have been constructed from giant hexagonal crystals placed side by side and bonded together. It was not unlike an irregular bundle of translucent rods. Their pointed tips flashed and glittered. To Hark, it was a chill, threatening light. Four of the central rods extended far beyond the others to form a kind of prow, the tip of which glowed with a green light. It was the same green as the fire from the Yal weapons down on the planet.

"Will you look at the size of that bastard!"

"You think we can hold it?"

"The powers that be must, else they would have jumped us out of here."

"Let's hope they're right."

The Yal battleship seemed hardly to be moving. Even Hark realized that this was a matter of its size and the relative distances involved. He could feel, however, that it was bearing down on them. A soft glow blossomed around the ship, a spectral halo that enveloped it from prow to stern.

"Shields up."

The green glow in the prow intensified into a single bright spot. The bright spot moved backward, down the crystal rod, toward the main body of the ship.

"Powering up the forward gun."

There was a slight distortion of the image on the screen.

"That's our shields."

"Are they going to give them the first shot?"

"Looks like it."

The green spot rocketed down the rod. When it hit the

tip, it diffused into a cloudy green energy field that floated directly toward the cluster. Before it even reached the cluster's screens, it dissipated and faded. There was congratulatory noise on the messdeck. Men exchanged handclasps. There was a satisfaction in knowing that whatever was in command of the enemy battleship had miscalculated on its first play.

"It's out of range."

The scanner that was feeding the picture to the messdeck screen must have been in an extreme forward position. The first that Hark knew about the *Anah* cluster firing its own guns was when a stream of white fireballs drifted into the picture. Hark realized that a second or so earlier the lights in the messdeck had dimmed. The fireballs hit the Yal shield. There was a brief flash as the shield was suffused with the sphere's white light, and then it returned to normal. The Yal were powering up again. The green spot retreated down the crystal. This time, the energy field reached all the way to the cluster. For a moment, the screen distorted and snowed, and the floor under their feet trembled. Hark swallowed his heart. They were hit. Then the screen cleared. It was only their own shields deflecting the attack. The lights flickered; the white fireballs came again and again as the Yal shields seemed to cope easily with them.

As time passed, Hark discovered what a ponderous and protracted affair it was when two huge, shielded space complexes engaged each other. The tactic was rudimentary. Each ship or complex stood off, close to the limit of its fire envelope, and pounded the other. Unimaginable amounts of energy were expended on this process, both in firing on the enemy and in maintaining the shields. The loser was the first one to run out of power and drop its shields. Without shields, even something as big as the cluster could be vaporized in a matter of minutes. The moment of truth came when a complex had just enough power left to jump out of trouble. It was always possible that the enemy had lower power reserves, and if the side with greater reserves held firm, it would come out the winner. Wars, after all, were not won by running away. On the other hand, the decision not to jump would be fatal if the enemy proved to have more power.

The pounding went on and on. On the messdeck, the lights dimmed, the floor trembled, and among the troopers, an exhaustion set in. The battle outside was too crucial to ignore, but they were no longer the riveted spectators they had been at the start. Hark noticed that Overman Elmo was among the few who still seemed transfixed by the conflict on the screen. Hark was starting to wonder about Elmo. For the raw recruit, there had been something comforting about the overman's authority, but now that he knew more, it was starting to look as if that authority might be failing. Hark had been surprised that Elmo had needed to resort to threats of punishment in the matter of the booze issue and that it had been Dyrkin who had been the one to defuse the situation. The radiation scars on Elmo's head and neck bore testimony if not to his courage, at least to his capacity for survival. On the other hand, it was clear to a mere recruit that all was not well. Could it be as Renchett had suggested? Were Elmo's nerves really shot?

About 190 minutes into the engagement, the effects of the pounding on the messdeck became increasingly more noticeable. The lights dimmed reducing the downden to almost total darkness each time the cluster powered up to fire. The hits from the Yal ship caused more of a stagger than a tremble. The air began to smell stale and brackish.

"They're diverting power from life support to the guns and the shields."

"We're running down."

On the screen, the Yal battleship fired again. This time the impact was more than just noticeable. The shock was enough to throw a couple of men off their feet. The lights went out altogether, leaving only the red emergency spots. The screen went dead. There was no mistaking the barely restrained terror in the gloom. Hark glanced toward Elmo. It was his place to take control of the situation. No control was forthcoming.

"Why don't we jump?" someone asked.

"A jump would probably kill us, the shape we're in."

Rance would have stomped this kind of talk with both feet. Elmo said nothing. Another Yal energy field slammed into the cluster. To a man, the troopers were down on the deck plates riding the shocks.

"The Yal must outpower us after everything we poured on those domes."

Still Elmo said nothing. There were three muffled explosions from somewhere deep inside the *Anah 5*.

"Something's burned out."

"We're dead."

To everyone's surprise, the screen came on again. The Yal ship was very close.

"Why isn't it powering up?"

There was no green glow in the ship's prow.

"Maybe the bastards are playing with us."

"Look at their shields!"

The Yal shields were a ghostly shadow of their former brilliance. The battleship began slowly to turn away. Thirteen troopers got cautiously to their feet. There was something about the way the room was lit by the screen that made it less than real. The ship was eerily quiet.

"They're breaking off the action."

"Why don't we fire?"

"We've run down. We can't power up the guns."

The Yal ship was shrinking in the screen and turning

faster. The turquoise glow of its impulse exhaust was clearly visible.

"That was an expensive waste of time."

"At least we didn't have to jump."

"We will eventually."

"Yeah, but first we have to lay up for a couple of standards and recharge."

Renchett dropped into a chair. "Yo, Elmo. Think you can break out the booze now? There's got to be a stand-down any minute."

"Yo, Elmo?" That was what Renchett had said. The idea of talking to an overman that way was no longer unthinkable, and in terms of general unit morale, that was bad. Worse was that Elmo merely nodded.

"Yeah, I need a drink myself." He pointed to Morish and Voda. "You can carry it."

Nobody came to bother them, and the messdeck spent the next three hundred minutes or so getting blind and forgetfully drunk. Elmo had taken the full liquor issue for twenty men—ten one-liter containers of clear spirit among thirteen of them. It was traditional to drink up the rations of the dead. Also to eat their food. Elmo had loaded down the two rookies with twenty issues of concentrates. The ship was still uncannily quiet. The lights didn't come back on again, but that didn't seem to bother anyone very much. The booze burned raw, but that didn't seem to bother anybody, either. The first thing to cause trouble was the screen. In a very short time, the troopers proved that they were not the most amiable of drunks. The first argument was over the image at which the majority of them were staring. When the Yal ship had dwindled to nothing, the exterior view remained, facing away from the cluster, an empty and threateningly bleak starscape.

"Can't we get rid of that thing?"

"I don't need to look at naked infinity."

Dyrkin got to his feet. It was the privilege of the maingun to mess with the screen.

"Get some women up there."

"Hell, no. What's the point of looking at women when there ain't none around? There's no use in beating it into the ground."

"We could bring out the suits."

"Give me a break."

"There don't seem to be any women anyway, and not much of anything else either."

Dyrkin was stroking the control surface, but the exterior view stubbornly remained. Finally he hit something. It was a slowly changing and wholly abstract pattern of color.

"What the hell is that supposed to be?"

"Maybe it's supposed to be soothing."

"Maybe it makes perfect sense to some other species."

"It's all we got."

"Shee-it."

Dacker heaved an empty liquor container into the corner. It bounced hollowly and lay on its side. A tiny fault-trace robot scuttled between the twin lines of coffins. It entered the downden, hesitated by the discarded container, and then ran up the wall and across the ceiling. When it was almost over his head, Renchett pinned it with his knife, a fast underhand throw. The robot squealed, a high metallic sound, and shorted out. Renchett reached up, pulled the knife out of the composition ceiling, and the robot along with it.

"Not bad, considering the light."

"What did you do that for?"

"I hate these forsaken things and the way they scuttle about."

He put the fault tracer down and stamped on it, then he dumped its crushed body into the waste hopper. Morish, in what for a rookie was a spectacular display of drunken bravado, wouldn't let it go. "How can you hate a robot? They don't do any harm."

"I can hate anything I want to hate." Renchett's voice was taking on a dangerous edge. He looked to Dyrkin for support. "Can't I?"

"Sure you can. Hate any damn thing you want."

Morish blearily shook his head. "You gotta be crazy to hate a functioning part of the ship."

Renchett was suddenly in front of Morish, the tip of his blade making small side-to-side snake movements in front of the rookie's eyes.

"You want to make something of it, new meat?"

Morish wasn't accustomed to drink, but even he could see that he'd gone too far. He dropped his gaze and mumbled. "I don't want to make nothing."

Renchett backed off. What passed for his honor seemed to be satisfied. Morish reached for a liquor container and took a long drink. When he was through, his eyes were watering.

"I don't think I feel so good."

All through the exchange, Helot had been sitting and watching. He was as drunk as anyone else, but he didn't make a noise about it. He was holding the chiba claw that he had brought back from the mission. Renchett, whose foul mood had in no way dissipated, turned on him.

"What are you doing with that thing?"

"Don't start with me, Renchett. I ain't no rookie."

"I just want to know what you want that fucking thing for."

"I always bring something back from a mission if I can. I got a whole collection. I've even got the ear off a scaly. You want to see it?"

"You're out of your mind."

"That's what the rookie just said about you."

Renchett's hand was on his knife. "You want to say that over?"

"Get off my ass, Renchett. If you go for that knife, I'll break your arm. You know I can."

"And if he don't, I will. You're giving me a headache." Once again Dyrkin was maintaining order. "And stow that goddamn knife. You're too mean a drunk to be waving that thing around."

Renchett had to go on performing. "You going to make me?"

"Don't be dumber than you have to be."

Renchett shrugged. He wasn't going to mess with Dyrkin. He got up and went to put the knife in his kit. His walk wasn't quite steady.

The incident had effectively killed conversation. The thirteen had turned in on themselves. Stress reaction and alcohol had blurred into a somber depression. Some had actually passed out. At least three were staring blankly at the patterns on the screen and might as well have been dead to the world. Hark was somewhere between sleeping and waking. He was no more used to booze than Morish was. Deep inside the haze, he became aware that someone nearby was talking to him. He opened his eyes. He had a difficulty focusing, but after a few moments Elmo's face swam partway into place. His mouth was moving.

". . . and I never saw anything like it. Nothing. That thing today. Right?"

"Huh?"

"That little skirmish you bastards were in."

"What about it?"

"It was nothing."

"Nothing?"

"Nothing."

"You weren't even there . . . Overman Elmo."

"I didn't have to be there. I saw how many of you

bastards came back. At Seven Walls, I was the only one of my twenty to come back. That's how I got to be overman."

A slurred voice came from the other side of the room. "Why don't you put a cover on it, Elmo. We all heard about you at Seven Walls."

Elmo swayed around, peering into the gloom. "Who said that?"

There were a couple of drunken laughs.

"Listen, you slime, the new meat ain't heard it, and they gotta respect me."

"They ain't new meat anymore. They've seen combat."

"They still got to respect me."

Hark was drunkenly horrified. He had always respected Elmo. It was only now that the respect was starting to fragment. Hark wished that the overman would shut up and fall over. He was in no condition for a conflict of original loyalties. Elmo, however, was made of sterner stuff. He put a hand on Hark's shoulder, leaned close, and lowered his voice. Hark could smell the liquor on his breath.

"It was this huge Yal redoubt, see? Seven concentric walls maybe four meters thick. Whole standard of blanketing it with neutrino charges. Thought we were going to go blind from the afterflash. Finally, they sent in us ground monkeys. We were told it'd be a walk . . . a piece of cake . . . right? The walls were breached, and we assumed that it was going to be a fish kill. Some piece of cake . . . We got inside, and they hit us with everything they had. They'd darksided a whole strike force on a moon where nobody had bothered to look. The heavy punishers came in first . . . By the time they hit, we made it down into bunkers. They were full of dead chibas and scalies and some things we'd never seen before . . . the chibas are rotting off their frames while there's an earthquake going on all around us . . . You never seen anything like it . . ."

Maybe it was just that Elmo was one of the first authority figures Hark had seen. Maybe that was the reason for the trust at first sight. Maybe it was just another part of the programming. Was he going to find out that Rance also had feet of clay?

"When I say earthquake . . . I mean a goddamn earthquake. The ceilings are coming in, and guys are getting crushed by chunks of plasteel. I'm lying facedown in a mess of chiba goop and expecting to die at any minute. It's black as pitch, and the noise is like one continuous explosion. There's somebody screaming in my ear, and I don't know if it's me or the monkey next to me."

Elmo was no longer talking to Hark. He was staring blindly into nowhere, reliving the time in the bunker.

"Yeah, and then the pounding stops, and for a few moments, there's complete silence. We're still lying there, not daring to breathe, wondering what they're going to throw at us next. The punishers are only the first stage. We wait . . . and after a while there's this quiet little sound from way down in the tunnels . . . a clicking. There ain't a man down in that bunker that didn't know what it was and what it meant. It's that noise the scalies' exoskeletons make when they move. We lined our redscopes in a goddamn hurry and there they were . . . an assault line of the bastards things . . . with tom-tom guns in front of them . . . coming up through the lower tunnels."

Elmo shuddered at the memory.

"It's hand to hand . . . or hand to tentacle . . . or whatever those things have at the end of their arms. The tomtoms are going off right in among us, and we're falling back from the get go. It's a goddamn slaughter . . . casualties all the way to the surface. We should have known something was wrong when the scalies stopped pressing. Those of us who were left came out into the light and immediately got it by batwings, sweeping us with hard radiation. That's where I lost my hair . . . just one e-vac managed to get in . . . and I was one of the lucky ones."

Elmo leaned forward and reached for one of the remaining bottles. He missed it by a matter of centimeters and toppled over. He had another try for the bottle from a prone position. This time he was a little more successful. He got the bottle to his mouth, and after spilling a good deal, he managed a swallow, only to gag. Hark stared in bleary disgust as Overman Elmo, an individual whom he had previously looked up to, lay on his side with drool hanging from the corner of his mouth.

"Yeah . . . I was one of . . . the . . . lucky . . . ones . . ."

Overman Elmo's eyes closed. Hark was filled with a massive sense of relief.

It was maybe two hours later when Rance came into the messdeck. He had expected to find the men passed out drunk. That was as it should be. They had been damn lucky to get off that battery planet with such minimal casualties. It could have been a whole lot worse. The additional stress of the prolonged exchange of fire must have been close to the last straw. He had half expected to find Elmo passed out among the men, but that wasn't as it should be. Noncoms didn't get falling-down drunk on the messdecks, particularly a noncom who had sat out the mission. He'd been watching Elmo for some time. There was little doubt that the overman had run out of road. By the program, Rance should take the matter to the line officer, but he'd already decided that he'd hold off for a while. It was a matter of loyalty. Elmo had been a good man. Most of the other survivors from Seven Walls had gone crazy. If Rance reported Elmo,

Berref would undoubtedly have the overman termed. It would be better at least to let Elmo keep his dignity. These things had a habit of taking care of themselves. When a man ran out of road, he didn't last much longer in combat.

# EIGHT

THE news was both good and bad. There was a jump coming—but after the jump there would be a stop at a recstar.

"Liberty."

"Women!"

"Give it to me!"

"I'd give up getting laid if I could miss the jump."

"You gotta enjoy what you can get."

"And you gotta suffer to get it."

"That's the way of it."

"You said it."

Just as they thought that they were being accepted, Hark and his intake were once again taking a nervous backseat. The recstar, after combat, was the next great mystery. Hark himself, who had started to feel that he was growing into the role of the fighting man, was pushed back into the shadows of the awkward and nervous semivirgin listening to the others giggling in the darkness on the hillside. What would these women be like? What had the Therem done to them? Had they been as ruthlessly programmed as the men? The longtimers were no help.

111

"Hell, boy, they're just like us."

A day later someone else had told him.

"They're different, real different. Ain't that the point of it all?"

There was the usual, less than satisfactory, consensus.

"You'll find out."

As the jumptime approached an entirely new atmosphere took over the messdeck. There was little of the usual griping and complaining, and almost a lightness in the air. Even Dacker was unusually amiable, and Renchett managed to keep his knife sheathed. The general feeling seemed to be that now that they were going somewhere they wanted to go, they were almost prepared to take the jump in stride. It was something that Hark had never seen before, and it made him slightly uneasy. It was hard to accept that these battle-hardened killers were capable of a juvenile excitement. There were outbreaks of joking and horseplay. Dyrkin actually smiled. The prospect of a respite from the war, no matter how temporary, brought out something else in the men. There was an all around increase in personal hygiene, chins were shaved close to the bone, and troopers even borrowed small mirrors from one another and studied their appearances. The ones who had exposed prosthetics actually polished them to a high, burnished shine. These endeavors caused a good deal of raucous comment.

"Women ain't going to be lovin' up to you on account of your spare parts, peckerhead."

"Getting something replaced is the sure sign of a real man. Women know that."

"Depends on what you got replaced."

"That's mine all mine, asshole."

"I don't know about that, but you still look like a chiba's cousin to me."

One contributory factor to the general levity was the fact that the noncoms were pretty much staying away from the men on the messdecks. It was as though part of the preparation for liberty was a certain relaxing of the controls. Hark had learned enough to suspect that there was a deliberate psychology behind this. Nothing in the Therem Alliance seemed to happen by accident.

It was only in the final hundred minutes before the jump that the more normal gloom reasserted itself. The pain was too close to pretend any longer that it was going to be a breeze. When the alarms sounded, the men went slowly to their coffins, reluctant to face unpleasant reality. Rance hurried them along; it appeared that Elmo was being kept away from the group. As Hark was climbing into his coffin, he found that the topman was standing over him.

"Don't worry, boy, you'll get through it."

"Can I ask a question?"

"If you make it fast."

"How long do we get on the recstar?"

Rance shrugged. "Seven standards, maybe ten if we're lucky. Don't think that our masters are doing this out of the kindess of their hearts. They don't have any. The cluster has to make repairs after that run-in with the Yal battlewagon, and it's easier to off-load the likes of us."

The lid of the coffin lowered, and the waiting began. Hark had expected that this jump would be the same as the last one. Even inside his fear, he was surprised when, right from the start, it proved to be totally different. The only similarity to the last one was the level of pain. It was of no comfort to realize that each jump was unique and that there would be no getting used to them. This one came on slowly, a gradual build that started as a knot in his chest and spread out through the rest of his body. There were vivid hallucinations—monsters and demons from his savage childhood ripped at his flesh and towered over the universe. They tore out his eyes and dragged his tortured body through pits of liquid fire. Encased in his screaming, he had one thing to hold on to, the one thing that he'd learned from his first jump.

*There's going to be an end to this! It's going to end!*

And it did. At the very peak of the pain it was gone. For an instant, he floated in a state of perfect peace, and then he was back in his coffin, soaked in sweat and aching in every part of his body.

"Did we make it okay?"

Immediately the men were out of their coffins, there was a definite effort to reestablish the previous festive mood. Everyone in the messdeck had come through the jump unscathed, and there were no deaths or insanity to cast a pall over the coming liberty. There was very little of the usual groaning and complaining. The troopers had too much to look forward to for them to dwell on the hangover from the jump

After about twenty minutes, Elmo appeared on the messdeck for the first time in days. There were a few contemptuous looks, but nobody said anything. The overman was followed by a small floating pallet loaded with fourteen folded tan uniforms.

"You lucky boys are being issued with new liberty dress."

"New tans?"

"That's right. Somebody up there must like you."

"No kidding."

"So try not to throw up on them the first day."

It was probably a remark that Elmo shouldn't have made. Dacker pounced on it.

"Oh, we can hold our liquor, Overman Elmo."

Elmo ignored Dacker and started handing out the two-piece uniforms. When he was through, there was one uniform left. Dyrkin noticed it and raised an eyebrow.

"What's the spare set of tans for?"

Kemlo, who'd lost a foot to the wire, walked stiffly through the entrance to the messdeck. "That's for me. Think I'd miss the fun?"

He was dressed in a singlet and shorts. His brand-new artificial foot was gleaming stainless steel and made clicking noises as he walked. It was plain that he was still not completely used to it.

Dyrkin grinned. "I thought they'd termed you, buddy."

"I'm too ugly to kill." He flexed the skeletal toes of his steel foot. "Think the girls are going to like it?"

"Gonna knock 'em dead."

Elmo had produced a small plastic folder.

"You three new fish, you're entitled to your combat flashes. Here, impress the girls with them."

He handed red and yellow lightning patches to Hark, Morish, and Voda. Hark scowled. He didn't think that Elmo ought to be calling them new fish now that they'd been in combat. Elmo noticed his expression and looked at him questioningly.

"What's the matter with you, boy?"

Hark made his face a mask. "Nothing, Overman Elmo."

Elmo glanced around at the others with a knowing and unpleasant grin. "Maybe he's worried he won't be able to get it up when the time comes."

The joke was received by blank, stony faces. As far as the troopers were concerned, Elmo had lost the right to insult anyone's manhood on this messdeck. There was a moment of tense silence, and then the overman turned on his heel and marched smartly away.

"Woo-hoo, did you see him go?"

"Showed that sorry sucker the door."

There was more to think about than the humiliation of Elmo. Getting ready for the liberty took on aspects of a ritual, and even the newcomers found themselves caught up in it. Hark carefully dressed himself in the new tan uniform. He couldn't help feeling a swell of pride as he applied the combat patch to the right sleeve. All around him, troopers were primping and preening. Nobody wanted to look anything but his absolute best. Small additions were being made to the uniforms. Some men hung them with pieces of jewelry and small trinkets. He noticed that some of the senior men boasted more insignia than just the single combat flash; he knew that the patches were earned for length of service and acts of outstanding merit. He had the data regarding the exact significance of each individual flash somewhere in his mind, but it was buried deep and he was too keyed up to dredge for it. Dyrkin had more insignia than anyone—his right sleeve was a blaze of glory. Maybe if Hark survived long enough he might get a few of those other patches.

A number of the men, as well as making sure they looked their best, were concealing weapons under their clothes—blackjacks, knives, brass knuckles, and home-made electroguns were strapped to legs and hidden under shirts. When Morish questioned Renchett about it, the longtimer, whose inevitable knife was pushed down in his boot, explained how when different units went on liberty at the same time there was always fighting. It was good to have an edge.

When all fourteen men were dressed to their satisfaction, there was nothing to do but wait. There was no way that they could pretend that they felt like anything but a bunch of kids about to go off on an adventure. The screen in the downden came to life. Once again it was an image fed in by an external scanner. Hark had his first sight of a recstar.

"There she is!"

"Ain't she a little beauty?"

From the outside, the recstar was anything but beautiful. It looked more like another military installation than a palace of carnal delights. Essentially it was a small planetoid, an irregular chunk of slate-gray rock that had been hollowed out, built over, and heavily fortified. Hark could see seven fire domes, and there were undoubtedly more on the far side. Docking spires jutted from the surface like metallic spines. Ropes of tubular moveways snaked across the uneven, cratered surface. There were other installations that Hark didn't recognize. Everything was the same drab gray as the original rock. Morish voiced the three recruits' surprise.

"It's a damned fortress."

Dacker laughed. "What did you expect? That it'd be painted red and gold with a welcome sign flashing? It wasn't put there just for our benefit. It's a regular class-three orbiter. The women were an afterthought. They're down in the interior, down by the core."

The recstar grew bigger and bigger until it filled the entire screen and smaller surface details became visible. It was much larger than Hark had first imagined. Although it hardly dwarfed the cluster, it was possibly as large—the screen didn't make it easy to judge scale. The perspective altered, and the recstar became a vertical horizon. The cluster seemed to be traveling across it. Lights were visible as the scanner tracked the orbiter's darkside. Multicolored plasma pulsed around a discharge stack. In the side-on sky, a small pale sun was visible. It had to be a long way away—it was scarcely larger than the background stars. Hark was overtaken by a lonely desolation that men should have to visit the women of their species in the bowels of this infinitely remote weapons base circling its tiny, distant sun.

Sirens were braying in other parts of the ship, and the

forward motion stopped. A line of surface craft came over the horizon, slab-sided, rust-streaked bucket shuttles headed for the cluster. Elmo was back on the messdeck.

"We better move out if we're going to be on one of the first of those boats."

The troopers didn't need a second urging to start filing out. By the time they reached their designated air lock, an umbilical had been stretched and attached to the first of the shuttles. There were lines of men from other messdecks waiting to free-fall to the surface craft. Elmo's fourteen didn't make it onto the first ship, and there was a delay while a second shuttle maneuvered into the loading position and the umbilical was reattached. Finally it was their turn to swing feet-first into the ribbed tube and float to the entry port of the shuttle. A loading attendant moved them inside. The interior of the shuttle was not quite as Spartan as that of an e-vac. There was atmosphere and even rudimentary berths, gee-frame shocktraps with webbing straps to secure their occupants. The shuttle accelerated hard and fast, and the passengers were pushed back into the frames with their faces distorting. The shuttle also landed hard, but no body cared. They were down on the recstar and out of the war for a short space of time.

There were no humans manning the upper levels of the planetoid. The loading areas and weapon systems were being operated by huge lanteres, bulky chitinous creatures three times as tall as a man. They survived in an environment of methane and ammonia and dim orange light that was as thick as soup. The troopers had to cross their areas through transparent airtight tunnels. It was like walking on the bottom of a dense, alien sea. The lanteres were uncomfortably similar to giant versions of the crayshells Hark had speared and eaten in his youth. When one reared from its hydrolastic control bed to peer

at the humans in the tunnel, he did his best to avoid the
multiple eyes that were clustered between its twin anten-
nae.

A lengthy descent by a cage elevator, mostly through
solid rock, brought them to their own environment. The
humans seemed to have been deliberately isolated from
the military functions of the base. The first thing to hit
the men was the rich and complex diversity of smells.
Cooking food mingled with perfume, alcohol, and a
dozen blends of incense. Above all, there was the warm
funk of humanity. The elevator gates slid back, and the
fourteen stepped out into a crowd that strolled and saun-
tered and aimlessly mingled. It was a shock. After what
seemed like a lifetime of military hurry up and wait,
there was an almost unthinkable luxury in this aimless-
ness and lack of organization. Color was a second shock.
Against the drab uniformity of the messdecks, the riot-
ous color in the heart of the recstar was positively
shameless. It was something that affected even the longtimers. After a couple of paces, the whole group stopped
and just drank in the scene as the elevator gates closed
behind them. There was music in the air that vied with
the shouts of laughter and the general buzz of conversation. The crowd seemed to stretch on forever. There
seemed to be men from every function that humans performed on a battle cluster. A group of drop pilots in mid-
night-blue uniforms leaned on a supporting pillar singing
drunken harmonies. A gang of sluicers in green coveralls
emerged from a booze den shouting raucously. But by far
the majority were in the dress tan of ground troopers.
More important, there were women. There were women
in all shapes and sizes, there were women in feathers and
bright colors, there were women with painted faces and
metallic jewelry, and women who were all but naked.
Hark thought that a short redheaded woman had smiled
at him, but before he could say anything, she was gone.

He was awed. What was one supposed to do in a place like this? Could it really be so easy? Finally Renchett broke the spell.

"So what do we do first?"

Dyrkin assumed command of the group.

"We find ourselves a comfortable place to drink and plan our strategy."

"Why don't we go straight to the knocking shops and get down to it?"

"You have no imagination or finesse, brother Helot. The fighting men of the *Anah 5* deserve better than a twenty-minute knocking shop."

Renchett grinned. "That's the truth!"

In all Therem installations, recreational space seemed to be at a premium, and this was no exception. The overall impression was that an entire town, built from whatever materials were at hand, had been crammed into a system of tunnels and low caverns, but despite what were obviously adverse conditions, an exciting and vibrant humanity flourished in these caves. The elevator gates had opened on an intersection of three fairly wide but low-ceilinged arterial corridors. Each corridor was lined on both sides with booths offering various forms of entertainment for the visiting men. There were drinking joints and places to eat; one sign advertised dancing girls, while another hinted at a more esoteric sexual display. Smaller alleys ran off the main corridors, and these had their own varied attractions. There was something exhilarating about being surrounded by so many people behaving the way humans were supposed to behave. The fighting men of the *Anah 5* advanced down the middle corridor in an aggressively self-conscious group. Dyrkin, as usual, took the point, staring into each booze den they passed.

"The ones right by the elevator banks are strictly for

sluicers and suckers. If you're smart, you press on into the center."

Couples walked by arm in arm and openly kissed and fondled each other. Hark was bemused. Would he behave like that? A scantily clad woman with a butterfly tatooed on her forehead actually beckoned to him. He was about to break ranks and go and talk to her, but Dyrkin pulled him up short.

"Forget it, boy. Only a fool goes with the first one he sees."

Hark shrugged and kept on walking. Dyrkin was probably right. There was also so much to see. It was strange to be once again around human constructions. A side effect of living in a battle cluster was that one started to believe that everything in the universe had been made by the Therem and forgot that humans could also be creative in their own simple way. Each of the booths that they passed was unique. Some were gaudy, others makeshift, even dilapidated, but others were nothing less than works of art. There was a terrible irony, Hark thought, in that the women down here created while the men were off somewhere else destroying. Something had gone terribly wrong with the way human beings existed.

The bulk of the materials from which the booths were constructed had obviously been cannibalized from other parts of the base, but also evident were gems, fabrics, and decorative plastics that had no place in a Therem military installation. They had been manufactured in the women's colony or brought in from elsewhere. It all seemed to point to the fact that the women had organized a fairly complex internal economy and were permitted to conduct some measure of interplanetary trade.

Dyrkin, who seemed to be treating the liberty as if it were a full-blown mission, finally found a drinking booth that met his standards. It was a prime spot on the corridor, situated under a ventilation shaft. The upward shaft gave the place more headroom and brought a constant cool breeze, and the booth's dim, golden light produced an illusion of spaciousness that was a definite plus in the crowded environment. A huge flag with a stylized and exceedingly phallic serpent painted on it hung down from the inside of the shaft and fluttered gently. There was plenty of room for the men from the *Anah 5*. The only customers were three e-vac crew and a woman in a silver tunic that might have originally been cut from a radiation suit. A grade-two armorer was sitting at the same table as the woman, but he was so comprehensively drunk that she seemed to be preparing to dump him. A music unit was pumping muted electronic rhythms.

"This place'll do."

"It's kind of quiet, ain't it?"

"It won't stay that way for long, now that we're here."

"Why don't we go someplace with a bit more life? The big place back down the corridor—that looked okay. At least there were women in there."

"Trust the old master. There'll be plenty of women, and not just thumbprint whores, either."

There was a small sensor pad beside the entrance to the booth, and as they went inside, each man was supposed to press the ball of his right thumb into the pad's receptor. Every recstar establishment—eating house, knocking shop, dance hall—had one of these devices to the right of its door. Each strolling vendor and street-walking prostitute carried a smaller, portable version of the unit hung around her neck on a lanyard. The sensors were the basis of the women's economy. Each thumbprint registered somewhere in the infinite memory of the base's central intelligence. The number of thumbprints credited to a business or individual dictated the quantity of goods and services that could be drawn from the base. If either fell below a minimum quota of prints, that franchise would be revoked, and the vendor would find herself back scuffling in the general population. The advantage of the system, from the visiting men's point of view, was that it created a sense of competition that made for a far higher quality and greater variety of available amusements. It ensured that the recstar offered the fighting men the very best that it could. It also gave the Therem, if indeed they cared, the capacity to monitor the tastes and appetites of every single trooper who took liberty there. At first, Hark assumed that the thumbprint system was yet another example of Therem applied psychology. It was only later that he discovered that the women themselves had been instrumental in devising the system. The competition gave them a certain sense of worth and dignity and, at least in their own minds, made their situation something above a state of enforced prostitution. The distinction was largely illusionary, but in the Therem Alliance, even an illusion was better than nothing.

When the fourteen troopers had seated themselves, a tall, muscular blonde emerged from a room in back of the booth.

"I'm Vana, and I'm going to be your hostess for as long as you're here."

Fourteen troopers stared hungrily at Vana.

"Will you look at that."

"Glad you like what you see." Vana's smile was strictly professional.

Dyrkin immediately got down to business. "So what you got to get loaded on around here?"

"You must be the maingun in this bunch."

"You got it."

"So you know what the deal is."

"We got to like the place first."

"Maybe you should try the special."

"Sure, specials all round."

Hark realized that there was some kind of liberty ritual getting started here. The special came in liter steins, piping hot, heavily spiced, and accompanied by beakers of ice water. Hark took a first experimental swallow, and his head swam. The drink had to contain other intoxicants in addition to the alcohol. Although powerful, the effect was much more subtle than the burn of the raw booze he'd tasted on the *Anah 5*. After three rounds of specials, Dyrkin made up his mind.

"Yo, Vana!"

"You want another round?"

"We want to make this place our home base for the duration."

Vana nodded. "Fourteen of you?"

"Fourteen."

"Ten thumbs per man per thousand minutes. We supply the food, and we invite over some of our friends. Deal?"

Dyrkin looked around at the others. Not all of them looked completely sold on the booth, but they all nodded. They had to concede that Dyrkin knew how to run a liberty.

"Deal."

The grade-two armorer, who had been facedown on the table for a while, sat up with a start. The woman in silver had already begun to exchange glances with Renchett.

"What the hell is going on in here?" the armorer demanded drunkenly.

He got unsteadily to his feet and squinted blearily at the troopers.

"Forsaken ground monkeys."

He had clearly taken leave of his reason.

"I ain't sharing a bar with no ground monkeys."

Renchett was on his feet and coming around the table.

"We got a problem here?"

He slapped the drunk hard on the chest with the flat of his hand. "Because—if you got a problem—" He punctuated his words with further slaps. His voice was flat and unemotional. "—then you—better—leave."

The drunk staggered backward. Renchett was maneuvering him in the direction of the exit. When he had the armorer where he wanted him, he propelled him through the doorway with a practiced kick. This was more than enough for the e-vac crew. They practically fell out of their seats.

"We ain't no heroes. You can have the place."

The fourteen had secured their territory.

Just as Vana had promised, the women quickly began to arrive. To everyone's delight they seemed to have no reservations about getting acquainted with the troopers. A young, very rounded olive-skinned woman who said her name was Zydell had wriggled into Hark's lap after only the most minimal of invitations. The specials had started to make Hark a little dizzy. He'd started to sweat and was seeing the faintest of blurred hallucinations. On the advice of Vana, he'd switched to a pale amber concoction that was called a juliet. The dizzy feeling had abated and he'd stopped sweating, but if anything, the hallucinations had become more intense. After three juliets, and with Zydell smiling, stroking his ear, and running her hands over his close-cropped hair, he felt uncommonly good. Better, in fact, than he could ever remember feeling before. This had to be the real reward of the warrier. Zydell held up her sensor box, and he happily pressed his thumb into it and eased down in his seat, luxuriating in the sense of well-being. Then an unfortunate thought struck him. Maybe this was exactly the way the Therem wanted him to feel. More of their bloody psychology. He was surprised at the strength of his own cynicism.

A trio of dancers in huge painted masks with exaggeratedly full, red lips and heavy sultry eyes swayed into the booth. After they'd completed a complex and highly erotic dance, they went around collecting thumbprints. The other women were vocal in their encouragement to give generously. At this point, Renchett, who had been kissing the woman in the silver tunic, looked around at the other men.

"Think we may be giving a bit freely with the thumbs, my brothers."

There was a chorus of disagreement from the women, but Renchett shook his head and held up a hand for silence.

"The way you have to look at it, my brothers, is that if all of us went sticking our thumbs in every receptacle that presented itself, we'd end up devaluing the currency."

There were shouts of approval from the men and catcalls from the women.

Zydell squirmed in Hark's lap. "That's the most ridiculous thing I ever heard."

Hark grinned. It had to be another liberty ritual, convincing the women that they wouldn't settle for anything less than value for print.

"I heard that if a man makes too free with his thumbprint, the sensors start refusing to accept it."

Vana raised a quizzical eyebrow. "I never heard that."

Zydell nuzzled Hark's ear. "You're not going to stop pressing my box, are you?"

Hark was about to thumb the sensor when a voice in his head warned him to back off for a moment. He held up his thumb.

"You heard what the topman said. Maybe I shouldn't be making too free with this."

Zydell didn't fit quite as comfortably into his lap anymore. "You want me to go?"

Hark didn't even have to summon his courage. The juliets led him smoothly into it. "I thought you and me might go someplace together."

"I'd want double to go to my place. If you're so concerned about your precious thumb, we could do it right here. Some of your messmates don't seem too concerned about privacy."

Hark looked around and saw that a handful of the men had already retired to the shadows and were writhing on the floor with their female companions. He recognized Helot, nearest to the light, but he couldn't make out the features of the others. Hark didn't think that he could handle anything so public.

"I think I'd rather go for double."

At that moment, Vana put another juliet in front of him. He hadn't actually asked for it, but he thumbed her sensor just the same. He didn't want to be too cheap. He put an arm round Zydell.

"We'll go to your place as soon as I've finished this."

"Sure." She didn't sound particularly enthusiastic.

The first fight started before the drink was gone. As liberty fights went, it was a comparatively mild affair. A gang of crawler jockeys, some ten in number and in worse condition than any of the the men from the *Anah 5*, stumbled through the entrance. Clearly they were unaware that the booth with the phallic snake banner had already been taken. Inside the door, they stopped dead, those in the rear stumbling blindly into the leaders.

"What?"

"The goddamn place is full of ground monkeys."

The troopers looked up, but nobody moved.

"Ah, let's get out of here. We don't need no trouble."

For a moment, it seemed as if this voice of reason might prevail and, despite the insult, the intrusion would come to nothing. Then a much more slurred voice piped up.

"Hell, we can take 'em."

Two more equally slurred voices joined in.

"Sure, screw 'em."

"Any crawler hump can take ground monkeys." This one seemed to fancy himself an orator. He glanced at his companions. "Am I right?"

The response was the kind of bravado of which only the very drunk are capable.

"Yeah, right!"

"Screw 'em."

The point of no return had been passed.

Renchett and Dyrkin were on their feet, the woman in silver protesting as she slid from Renchett's lap to the floor. The other troopers were also rising. The women were scrambling for cover. Dyrkin faced the drop pilots.

"You've got ten seconds to get out of here."

"Screw you!"

The crawler jockeys surged forward in a disorganized knot, but they really didn't stand a chance. Their reactions were slowed, and they hadn't had the same basic combat training as the troopers had. They weren't able to operate as a cohesive group. The troopers, on the other hand, drunk as they were, wont to work together like a machine. Boots, fists, and the odd blackjack rained down a hail of blows. Renchett was swinging a chair in a wide circle. In less than a minute, it was all over. Four jocks were unconscious on the floor, and the rest had fled. Vana was inspecting the booth, totaling the damage in her head. The troopers were congratulating each other and calling for more booze. They had come through the incident virtually unscathed. Kemlo had lost a tooth to a wild punch, and Dacker had been kicked in the groin, but that was all. Hark was one of the ones delegated to drag the unconscious jockeys outside and dump them in the corridor. He came back grinning and rubbing his hands with the air of a man who feels he's completed a

well-done job. He had managed to get in a few licks of
his own before the strangers had cut and run. His grin
faded as he discovered that Zydell was nowhere to be
seen. Damn. He'd been about to leave with her. All he
could do was inwardly shrug and call for another drink.
There were plenty more where she came from. At least,
he hoped there were.

The second fight came after about twenty minutes.
The crawler crews returned in force, twenty-five of them
or more, carrying clubs and pieces of broken furniture; it
was obvious that their sole intention was to stomp the
troopers from the *Anah 5*. The fourteen might have been
taken by surprise had Kemlo not been outside the booth
collecting his wits and nursing his bruised jaw. He spotted the gang marching determinedly down the corridor
and darted into the booth to give the alarm.

"Big team of jockeys coming at us!"

Weapons were hastily pulled from their hiding places.
Vana yelled at Dyrkin. "Take it outside, goddamm it! I
don't want the whole place wrecked. There's stuff in
here that I can't replace."

The fourteen troopers boiled out of the booth. The
pilots were almost on them. Renchett's knife flashed in
the dim light. There were shouts and screams as the
noninvolved struggled to get out of the way before the
two gangs ran headfirst into each other. Dyrkin's voice
rose above the general din.

"Flying wedge! Hit it!"

Dyrkin had no intention of running headfirst into anything. They were in combat again and back on their programmed reflexes. They formed a solid arrowhead and,
with Renchett and Dyrkin himself at its point, charged
the disorganized mob of jocks. The crawler crews split
apart, and the troopers waded into them. Hark found
himself in the second rank. When he'd followed the
others out of the booth, he'd had no weapon, but almost

immediately a jock had swung at him with a short length of ceram pipe. Conditioning took over, and Hark chopped down hard with the edge of his hand. He thought he heard the wrist snap. The pipe dropped, and he caught it before it hit the ground. Now he started to swing it. The moment took hold of him. He being was dedicated to knocking over crawler men. Bastards.

At first, it was a surprisingly quiet fight. Nobody yelled or screamed; all that could be heard were grunts, curses, and the sounds of falling blows. The troopers started to fan out, pushing the jocks before them. The nature of the fight began to change. The crawler jockeys wanted to break and run, but the troopers were pressing them too hard, and they were being forced into the surrounding booths. This, in turn, caused a new phase of confusion. The occupants of the booths took exception to a crowd of bruised and bleeding men falling into their parties. Further fights started, with the crawler crews taking the brunt of it. Dyrkin's single sharp burst of organization had been more than enough. He relaxed. The troopers who still wanted to brawl followed them into the booths and added to the mayhem. Others stood and caught their breath and watched as the chain reaction got started.

The fighting was threatening to spread all the way down the corridor. Men were thrown through the flimsy partitions that separated the booths. Crystal screens splintered and fragmented. Curtains billowed into strange shapes, were ripped down, and drunks staggered blindly, wrapped up in their folds. The walls around a jum-yum show collapsed, and the participants scrambled from the mudpit, reaching for their clothes. A sluicer on a private orgy of property damage ran headfirst into a stone column and stunned himself. A number of men were crawling on all fours clutching their heads. Other casualties simply leaned, and still more were stretched

out cold. A small fire had started in a darkened booth.
Somewhere else, a woman was yelling hysterical abuse.
There was the first pop of an electrogun. It was quickly
followed by the shrill of whistles and the crash of steel
feet on the corridors.

"Shore patrol!"

Only the very, very drunk needed a second warning.
Nobody wanted to be grabbed by the shore patrol. Such
an unlucky offender automatically went back to his ship
and maybe a field punishment. The fighting stopped instantly, and, to a man, the brawlers scattered. The sirens
were coming down the corridor. There was no way that
anyone could stand up to the shore patrol. The white-
uniformed women in their heavy-duty servo rigs were
stronger than any man. There were rumors that even
without the rigs, the women of the shore patrol could
incapacitate a man. Once those steel pincers locked onto
one's arm, there was no escape. If the victim struggled,
they'd crush the bone.

Hark took off with the rest. He was running blindly,
straight down the corridor. The sirens trilled, and the
servo feet crashed behind him. He glanced back. The
shore patrol servos were like huge parodies of humans
with hulking counterbalanced shoulders and a flashing
light where the head should logically be. They lurched
relentlessly forward, exactly reproducing the movements
of the small figures inside them. Someone near him was
shouting with laughter. Hark could feel it, too. There
was an exhilaration in the running. People stood in the
entrances to booths and watched them pounding past.
Some applauded and shouted encouragement.

The sirens seemed to be falling back, but still he kept
going. He stopped only when he was far ahead of them.
By this time, he was completely winded. He had to bend
double, hands on his knees, to force air into his straining

lungs. Opposite him, in a similar position, was one of the jocks who had been involved in the fracas. They looked at each other. The earlier fury seemed a little absurd. Slowly they straightened up and went off in different directions.

Hark suddenly realized that he was lost. He turned around twice. Everyone who had run from the shore patrol had zigzagged and turned corners. He had simply followed suit. Now he didn't have a clue how to get back to the booth or to the rest of his messmates. There were people strolling by, but there was nothing that he could ask them. He didn't even know the name of the place. All he could remember was the phallic serpent banner.

A nearby drinking booth looked inviting. It was a low, faceted dome, and a warm red glow shone through the translucent hexagonal panels. He ducked through the low entrance, thumbing the sensor as he moved inside. A couple of people glanced up at him, but there was no overt hostility—in fact, the place was strangely subdued. The patrons there came from all the functions on a cluster and seemed to share two things in common: Almost all of men were veteran longtimers, and a high proportion were fitted with prosthetic limbs. They lounged on cushions that covered practically the entire floor. There was very little conversation, a noise generator filled the booth with quiet ambient sound. There was a drifting dreaminess to the interior of the dome that was like nothing Hark had previously encountered. Drinks were being served from a low half-moon bar, but they were largely ignored. Instead, attentions were focused on the small, pink ceramic cylinders, each about the size of a man's forearm, that were being passed from hand to hand. Each man in turn opened the valve on the neck of the cylinder and drew deeply on the molded plastic nozzle. One lungful seemed to be enough. The valve was closed, the cylinder passed on, and then the man who had just used it flopped back on the cushions. Escaping gas filled the place with a sweet, almost sickly smell that made Hark feel a little queasy.

There were surprisingly few women in the dome, and the ones who were lying on the cushions looked much the same age as the men. They were certainly much older than Zydell and the other women who'd been at the "phallic serpent." The only exception was a very young woman who was sitting on a stool in the center of the floor. Naked to the waist, wearing only a pair of very tight cut-off shorts, she leaned back, one knee raised, arms braced against the back of the stool. She was staring dreamily at the ceiling. Blond curls cascaded down her shoulders. Although the pose was deliberately sexy, the girl seemed totally oblivious to the rest of the room. She looked like a living statue.

Hark squatted down on a cushion next to the half-moon bar. He wasn't sure how one was supposed to behave in this place. He glanced at the bartender.

"Could I get a juliet?"

"What the hell's a juliet?"

"I don't know." Maybe the juliet was something exclusive to the "phallic serpent." "So what's your special?"

A longtimer with a steel hand leaned over and spoke to him. His voice was slow and slurred and grated from deep in his throat. "You're in the wrong place, kid."

"I'm sorry."

"You're too young. You need to be out fighting and whoring. You'll get to be like us soon enough. If you ain't killed first."

"I don't understand."

"Of course you don't. You're too young and green."

"Do you know a place that has a serpent banner?"

The longtimer leaned closer. His breath reeked of the
sweet gas. "Look into my eyes, boy. What do you see
there?"

The eyes were heavy-lidded and bloodshot from the
gas, but there was something else, a deadness that didn't
come from anything but a lifetime of combat horror.

"That's the light-year stare, boy. It means you don't
care no more. All you want to do is blot it out. How long
you think any of us in here has got?"

"I . . ."

"Get out of here, boy. Take all your energy someplace
else and leave us alone."

Hark stood up so fast that he almost hit his head on
the domed roof. He scrambled through the exit with all
the clumsiness of headlong drunken panic. He didn't
want to be one of those old men. Suddenly an idea beckoned. Couldn't he hide out there? Never go back to the
*Anah 5*? The thought evaporated. They'd get him on his
thumbprint. All he could do was go and look for his
messmates. They were all he had. He chose a direction
at random and started walking, hoping to see something
that looked familiar. Nothing did. He knew that he ought
to ask someone, but he held off after his experience in
the dome. More than anything, he wanted to walk. He'd
walk until he found a really rowdy booth, and then he'd
ask someone about the phallic serpent banner. It was
right at that moment that he heard the voice.

"Harkaan? Is that you?"

He turned and faced complete unreality. Her clothes
were black and skintight, her face was heavily painted,
and her hair had been bleached white and fluffed out, but
there was no mistake.

"Conchela?"

Conchela, the witch girl who had ridden with him to

the Valley of the Gods. He looked at what she had become and wondered how he appeared to her.

"Do they still call you Conchela?"

She nodded. "They still call me that."

# NINE

"OF course, they do a job on you. Mindshot, implants, hormone runrounds, and probably stuff we don't even know about. And there's the constant Therem psych. It goes on and on until you can't even think straight. All you've got in your head are the slogans. We are the servants of our fighting men, we're here to please, it's our contribution to the Alliance, our part in the war effort, and all the rest of the eternal crap. From the waist down you're on a perpetual burn, but inside your brain there's this cold, furious knot of truth. We're slaves on this hunk of rock, and there's not a damn thing we can do about it."

Hark ran an uncomfortable hand down Conchela's back. Her skin was so smooth, all he wanted to do was make love to her again. He wanted to repeat the sensation of losing himself in her body. He had no idea how to cope with her sudden anger.

"Come on, now, it can't be that bad."

She slowly turned to look at him. He wanted to put his hands on her breasts, but suddenly he didn't dare.

"It can't be that bad? You troopers are so damned ignorant. It can't be anything but that bad. That's how it's been designed. They keep you stupid, and they seduce you with power, the power to run all over the universe and stomp and smash and blow up anything that gets in your way. It doesn't matter that you die somewhere along the line, you've got to die anyway."

Hark thought of the jumps and the dry, bitter taste of fear going down in the dropcraft. "You don't really know."

"Sure we know. We know better than you do. We've seen thousands of you. We've screwed thousands of you. It's a lifelong line on the old recstar."

Her mood was changing. The anger had diminished to bitterness.

"The only way to keep yourself from the stare is to not see the faces. The men come through, but you don't know them."

She shook her head. "Why the hell did you have to come here, Hark?"

Hark propped himself up on one elbow. He simply couldn't follow her mood swings. "Maybe it was our destiny."

"You men still believe all that. That's what keeps you ignorant. There is no destiny. Our destiny was sold to the Therem Alliance centuries ago."

Bitterness gave way to a terrible sadness. Her arms slid around his neck, and she pulled him to her. His face was between her breasts. He felt her sigh.

"Why the hell did you have to come here, Harkaan?"

Before they made love again, she gave him a small whiff of sweet gas from a tiny vial, only a fraction of the size of the ones they'd been passing around in the dome. It wasn't enough to make him dizzy; it just slowed everything. The previous desperate, rushing need was reduced to warm, easy desire. With so much more time, it seemed that she was able to aid and abet his pleasure in a dozen ways, ways that Hark hadn't imagined were possible. Her hands and mouth played games with his body. His eyes closed, and his breathing became deep and labored. He began to groan. His nerves spasmed. He found that he was talking to Gods that he'd thought were long forgotten. He was perfectly ready to die at any point except that the floods of sensation kept building and building. Why the hell did men have to fight when they could spend their time doing this? She was right. Men were ignorant.

At the finish, they were grunting and screaming and clawing at each other. In the afterglow, they clung for a long time, but eventually they had to fall apart. Hark lay on his back with his outstretched arm under Conchela's shoulders. He opened his eyes. Hers were closed. Could she be asleep? He turned his head and looked at the place where Conchela lived. It was nothing more than a cubicle, but compared to the messdeck, it was a haven of privacy. The bed took up exactly half of the chamber. It was draped with multicolored fabric hangings, irregularly shaped silks and satins that looked like offcuts from the manufacture of flags, banners, and decorative clothing. They turned the bed space into a shadowy, mysterious cave. The other half of the chamber was a complete contrast. It was stark and functional. There was a small workbench with a tiny lathe, a quartz arc, a bench-top anvil, and a miniature welding ring. In addition to her basic duties as a thumbprint prostitute, Conchela designed and made metal jewelry, which she bartered with the other women for clothes, cosmetics, extra food, and small luxuries such as alcohol and sweet gas.

"It's the only thing that keeps me sane," she had explained.

Alongside the workbench there were the survival basics of the Therem system: a water spigot, a diet gooper, and a waste swallow. These, at least, were the same as on the cluster. In a maze of shelves, there were jars and bottles, bunches of herbs, and vials of chemicals. There were the raw materials of her trade, the rolls of metal shim that she turned into small works of art. Hark envied her the ability to direct her own time even in this very minimal way. On the ship and in combat, there was always someone to tell one what to do.

Conchela opened her eyes and looked at Hark. "What are you thinking about?"

"Me?"

"There's no one else here."

Hark stared at the patchwork canopy above his head.

"I was thinking about all the stuff that you've got. We don't have anything up on the cluster, only what we can hide in the cavity behind our lockers."

"You have to remember that I'm so much older than you. I've been here on the recstar much longer than you've been on your ship."

"How can that be? We were picked up at the same time."

"You make the jumps. They do things to relative time. Didn't you think I looked older?"

"I don't know. I . . ."

"You thought it was all a result of the life of degradation I've been leading."

"I knew you'd changed."

"You could lie."

Hark's embarrassment robbed him of words. Conchela leaned over and kissed him.

"You're still such a boy."

The hours passed slowly, and Hark luxuriated in the unique sensation of having nothing do and nobody shouting at him. They ate and drank and made love. In between, they slept. Each time Hark woke, he experienced a moment of panic, sure that he was back on the messdeck and that it had all been a dream. Then he saw that he was still in Conchela's cubicle, and he eased down under the covers with a sigh. He didn't want to think about going back to the ship.

At times, Conchela talked. Along the track of her swings of mood, she seemed to feel a need to explain. She wanted Hark to know exactly what it meant to be a woman and to live on a recstar.

"I guess you could say that we remember. You men see nothing but combat. You're isolated in your crews and your twenties. We see thousands of you guys. Over the years, millions of men pass through a place like this. Each one has his own part of the puzzle."

"What puzzle?"

"Who we are, of course. Where the human species came from and where it's going. It's the one way we can fight against the system, against the Therem, if you like. They've stopped us having children. That's for the primitives out on the planets. All that's left for us is to maintain the memory."

"You mean you remember what the men tell you?"

"That's what they come here for. To get laid and to tell it to somebody. You all have to tell it to somebody. You don't want to believe that after you've gone, nobody will remember. I guess that's what we're doing. We're remembering you all."

"I don't have anything I want to tell."

"Oh, yes, you do. And you will. You'll sob it out to someone before you leave this rock."

Conchela swung her legs over the side of the bed. The flow of words had temporarily halted. The story seemed to be unfolding in fits and starts and snatches. She poured herself dark, amber wine from a stone jug.

"You'd better thumb my sensor a few times. I'm supposed to be working. I don't want to be closed out of this place because I didn't make the norm."

Hark pressed his thumb into her sensor five times. "Is that enough?"

"It'll help." Almost an hour passed before she picked up the story again.

"Bit by bit, we get parts of the picture. It wasn't always like this. That's one thing we know for sure. Before the Yal came, we had our own civilization. We had even colonized the closest planets in our home system."

"Before the Therem came?"

"In the very beginning, it was the Yal that occupied our home world. The Therem took it and us from them."

"You learned all this from listening to the men talk? The men on my messdeck know nothing of these things."

"You have to realize that this knowledge has taken centuries to acquire. Also, there are those of us who go up to the clusters to service the medians. The medians know much more than anyone suspects."

"Have you ever been with a median?"

Conchela laughed. "A median? You're joking. I'm not the kind the medians go for. Something for which I'm profoundly grateful."

"And, according to the medians, it was the Yal that destroyed this human civilization that could travel from planet to planet?"

"The Yal only suppressed it. The Therem, being the Therem, had much more elaborate plans."

"You sound as if you really hate the Therem."

"Don't you?"

"I don't know. We don't get much time to think about that sort of thing. We know we hate the Yal. Most of the time that's enough."

"Doesn't that say it all? The Therem destroy our identity as a species and spread us over the galaxy to be their slaves, and you only hate who they tell you to hate."

"It's not really like that."

"You know it is. Oh yeah, you'll blame it on the suits or the topmen or the officers or something they put in the food, but deep down, you know it's the truth."

Conchela lay on her back, seemingly unwilling to say anything else. Hark put a hand on her stomach, but her body was stiff and unyielding. It was some minutes before she came around and pulled him to her. Sometime later, as they were lying side by side, filmed by sweat, Hark couldn't keep his curiosity to himself.

"What I don't understand is how you women manage to keep all these bits and pieces together."

"That's a question only a man could ask."

"It is?"

"Sure it is."

"So how do you do it?"

"Through the covens."

"Covens?"

"Another man's question."

She spelled it out. "Covens are cells of women. Seven women to each cell. We sift anything that we may have heard and then pass it on to the mother cell. Each mother cell controls seven covens. Beyond the mother cells are the processing enclaves, all the way to the committee of the seven High and Venerable Madames."

Hark was dumbfounded. "There's a whole system?"

"Don't you think women are capable of creating a system?"

"It sounds almost like a religion."

"It does have elements of a religion, but for the most part, they're a cover. It's really modeled on how the thinking machines work."

Hark decided not to ask about thinking machines. The answer would only confuse him. "Why do you need a cover?"

"To deceive the Therem. If they knew what we were doing, they'd more than likely dismantle the whole rec-star system and exterminate us into the bargain."

"Why should they bother? There's no way that your keeping records can harm them."

"The Therem bother about everything. That's what makes them the Therem. It may only be a median's vanity, but there's even a theory that we make the Therem nervous. They may think that we're inferior to them, but we're too smart to be left to our own devices. We did get into space on our own. They don't want humans to have an independent history and culture that they can't control. Besides, they almost wiped us out once, and there's nothing to say that they won't do it again. We have to be careful."

"When did they nearly wipe you out?"

"It was called the Lysistrata Massacre."

"What's Lysistrata?"

"Who, not what. She was a character in a play by a man called Aristophanes."

"Huh?"

"Don't worry about it. The massacre was over a century ago. Unrest was spreading across all the fronts. Needless to say, the recstars were among the most restless. Back then, things were a whole lot more slack but at the same time also cruder, going on bestial . . ."

"Bestial?" Hark wanted to hear about this.

"They were big on orgies back in those days. Piles of naked people, humping and pumping in a cave. It was pretty basic and the Venerable Madame decided that we weren't going to take it anymore. The Madame, by all accounts, was a hell of an orator. We only had the one back then. The committee of seven came later. The plan was simple. We'd totally withdraw our services. Not a man jack was going to have any fun until conditions got better. She believed it would be simplest for the Therem to negotiate. The Therem didn't negotiate. They kept the men locked up in their clusters, and they turned the lanteres and the red spheres loose on us. The lantere execution squads slaughtered over three-quarters of the population before they were called off."

Her eyes were hard, and she quickly took a sip of her wine.

"They brought in new women from the planets to re-populate the place, but there were enough survivors to provide a link with the past. There actually were improvements. The thumbcredit system was introduced. The craftwork was encouraged; the brewing, baking, and distilling; the food production. Our upstart need for an identity was channeled into forsaken basket weaving. There was another side, though. Any keeping of permanent records was immediately stamped out. It was after this that the coven system evolved. As far as we know, the Therem think it's just some witch cult revival, straight out of the planetary memory. They like us to get ourselves locked into that kind of primitive shit."

"Did you ought to be telling me this? I might get drunk or something and blurt it all out."

"Who are you going to tell? Your topman? The top-men know about us. Besides, any woman only knows in detail what her coven or group knows. The thing is the sum of its parts, and they'd have to kill all of us this time. If we ain't a nuisance, the odds are that they'll leave us alone."

She took another sip of wine.

"I can't talk anymore."

Her breakneck emotional cycle seemed to have once again completed itself. She shivered and wrapped a blanket around her body. Hark sat up. He wanted to comfort her, but the way she was holding herself warned him off. As far as it was possible in the intimacy of the bed, she appeared to be shutting him out. He lay down again, suddenly feeling uncomfortable. He waited a full fifteen minutes until he guessed she'd softened enough for him to talk to her.

"Do you think we'll ever get out of this?" he asked her.

"You mean you and me? We don't have a chance."

"I meant the human race as a whole. Do you think we'll ever get free of the Therem?"

"There's always the prophecy."

"The prophecy?"

"You never heard about it?"

Hark shook his head. "No, never."

Conchela glanced at him scornfully. "You troopers really know nothing. It was back before the massacre. The Venerable Madame of the time was Mystic Heda. She had a habit of falling into trances and talking in tongues. Her pronouncements became more and more outrageous, and people began to wonder how long it would be before the Therem did something about her. Finally she went into a trance in front of a huge crowd and announced that sometime in the future, a leader would come who'd free us from the Therem and take us to our own planet."

"Do you believe that?"

"I'd like to, but it's hard. Some of Heda's lesser prophecies did come true, so I try. It's the only hope we've got."

"What happened to Mystic Heda?"

"She was executed."

Conchela stood up and started searching through the clothes that were scattered on the floor.

"It's time we got out of here," she told him.

"What?" Getting out of there was the very last thing that Hark had in mind.

"Did you think that we'd stay shacked up in here, cozy and romantic, until you were called back to the ship?"

"It seemed like an idea."

"Forget it."

"What did I do?"

"You didn't do anything. It's just that we can't beat

the system. The Therem don't like romance. They think it makes you guys hard to handle. They like you to spend your liberty drunk and stupid."

"But who would know?"

"Thumbprints, you idiot. If you keep thumbing my sensor, the big brain is going to notice and we're going to get a visit from the shore patrol. Besides, I'm programmed to get bored with you in double time. It's only the fact that we knew each other back on the planet that's been keeping it in check."

Hark was stunned. It had all seemed so easy. Conchela grinned at him.

"Don't look so desolate. I'll come with you and help you find your messmates. They'll take care of you."

The moment they stepped out into the corridor, they were caught up in an eddying spiral of drunks and women. The recstar never closed. It seemed to be in a permanent condition of roaring night. If anything, the noise seemed louder than when he had gone with Conchela to her cubicle. The booths were humming, and the fighting men were rapidly turning into animals. The light seemed more red than he remembered, bloodshot with anger and alcohol. They had to edge around two men who were head to head, blindly slugging and pounding each other. They also had to skirt a drop pilot who was throwing up on his tunic and stand aside when a shore patrol crunched by. It was the first time that Hark had been able to take a close look at these guardians of order in their lumbering servo suits. They appeared almost indestructible, yellow plate steel with heavy-duty rivets and paint that was flaking to the undercoat. There was nothing comical in the way they rolled and swayed, reproducing the movements of their human operators. The servos were worn and dangerously capable. The giant claws on the ends of their arms could circle a man's waist. They were quite merciless. Despite their crisp white uniforms and hard faces, the human operators seemed almost fragile in comparison to the massive machines that encased them.

"You don't want to mess with those bastards."

"I already learned that."

A troupe of dancers in huge, grotesque masks were coming toward them. The group was a large one, thirteen in all. They were moving slowly, beating on small hand drums, alternately crouching and then stretching up, grasping for the ceiling. They were followed by a large crowd of drunken men, shuffling and stumbling in their wake. Some were aping the crouching and reaching movements of the dancers. Hark and Conchela stood and watched them pass. There was something ponderous and primitive about the ragged procession—almost sinister. Hark realized what was disturbing him. The march reminded him of the way they'd conducted rites for the dead back on the planet. Conchela must have felt it, too. When the parade had passed, she let out a long breath but quickly covered herself by being brisk and matter of fact.

"You said your messmates had taken over a booth with a serpent banner?"

"It was under a vent shaft."

She pointed over to the right. "I think the place we're looking for is just over there."

They cut through a small side corridor and made a left turn. When they came out into the main corridor again, Hark thought that he recognized some of the booths. Then he spotted the air shaft and the serpent banner.

"There it is."

The "phallic serpent" looked a little the worse for wear. A number of chairs and tables had been smashed, and pieces were scattered around the floor. Helot and a woman with short-cropped hair were passed out in the middle of the debris. Kemlo sat at a table with a drink in front of him, but he seemed no more aware of the world around him than those on the floor were. Conchela took hold of Hark's arm.

"I'm going to leave you now. I've got to get back to work."

"Will I see you again?"

Conchela shook her head. "I don't think so. It's better this way. You'll find other women to take care of you through the rest of your liberty."

"Maybe I'll come here again."

"I doubt it. Even if you did, I'd be an old woman by then."

"The time distortion?"

"We can never go back."

"I haven't seen any old women. What happens to them?"

"You don't want to know."

She kissed him quickly on the cheek.

"Good-bye, Harkaan."

She started to walk away.

"Conchela . . . wait."

She didn't stop. Hark's first impulse was to go after her, but he stopped himself. She turned a corner and was gone.

Vana had been replaced as booth hostess by a dark-haired woman with slanted eyes and an ample figure. She stood in the back of the booth, watching Hark.

"You liked her, did you?"

"I guess so."

"And she just gave you the brush?"

"Yeah."

"She's right, you know. You can't fall in love in one of these places."

Hark dropped his gaze to the floor. "I guess you're right."

"Are you one of this bunch from the *Anah 5*?"

A new feeling was creeping over Hark: He was a part of this bunch. And that fact was paramount—because when it came down to the line, that was all he was. He knew that the psych programming was taking over, but what the hell, he was going to let it. It was better than hurt and confusion.

"Damn right I am."

"Then damn well lay some thumb on my sensor. I don't know when your messmates are going to be back. If they get back at all. The mood they were in, they're likely to get shipped out by the shores. The name's Vana, by the way."

"The last one was Vana."

"Everyone's Vana in this booth, honey."

"Mine's Hark."

"I don't remember names, honey. What about the thumb?"

"Where did the others go?"

"Who knows? They were blind drunk and looking for trouble. They could be anywhere by now. If I don't get some thumb, I'm going to have to let the place go to some other outfit."

She held out the sensor. Hark took it, but before he could press his thumb into it, Dyrkin came through the entrance.

"What the hell is going on here?"

"She said she was going to let the booth go."

Dyrkin's eyes narrowed. He glared at Vana.

"I paid you in front, you thieving bitch. And I warned you about clipping the boys."

"You can't blame a girl for trying."

"I just don't want to catch you trying."

"You won't."

"I just did."

"But you didn't do anything about it because you know you won't get another place now that the whole cluster's in. I won't be blatant, but I'm going to make my profit."

Dyrkin shrugged. He wasn't about to waste time arguing with the obvious. He turned to Hark.

"So what have you been up to? I ain't seen you since the first fight. You ain't a loner, are you?"

The word "loner" came out as if a loner was something he definitely shouldn't want to be.

"I met a woman. She came from my planet."

Dyrkin raised an eyebrow. "That must have been weird."

"It was, kinda."

"I don't think I'd fancy it. What did you do?"

"Screwed a lot, and she talked a lot."

"No doubt she filled you up with a lot of witchery."

"She said that they remembered."

"It doesn't do us any good."

"It's good to think you're remembered somewhere."

"When you're gone, you're gone."

Dyrkin didn't seem to expect Hark to argue with the obvious, either. Hark didn't.

"What happened to the others?" he asked.

"Liquored up and crazy," Dyrkin replied.

"How crazy?"

"Crazy enough that the next two hundred minutes will find Renchett and a half dozen others back on the ship in a punishment pod. If nothing else, it's shaping up as a liberty that's going to be remembered."

"What's Renchett up to?"

"Usual Renchett stuff. Some woman told him that the dauquoi had an R&R facility on another level of this rock. He took it into his head to break into this level and see how the dauquoi have their fun. Needless to say, he found a bunch of drunken assholes to go along with him."

"What are the dauquoi?"

"You never came across dauquoi?"

"No."

"Well, they're these big worms. They ain't too smart, and they're mainly used to keep the ducts clear, but they have this real complicated reproductive process, so I guess they qualify for a kind of liberty."

"Shouldn't we do something to stop him?"

"You and me? You want to try stopping Renchett when he's blind drunk?"

"No, I guess not."

"Me neither. I figure if it's anybody's problem, it's Rance's. He can deal with it."

# TEN

"YOU Rance?"

Rance groaned inwardly. A shore patrol squad leader was marching smartly across the topmen's lounge, heading directly for his table.

"Yeah, I'm Rance."

The woman who was with him—she'd said her name was Amansa—looked at him questioningly. "Are you in trouble?"

"Not me, but my men probably are."

The squad leader was typical shore patrol. Her white uniform was crisp and starched, her harness and boots were polished to a high gloss, and she wore a holstered sidearm, complete with lanyard, on her left hip.

"Rance from the *Anah 5*?"

"That's me."

"Some of your men are trying to break into the dauquoi facility."

"I didn't know that this base had a dauquoi facility."

Amansa looked from the squad leader to Rance. "Do you have to go?"

While Rance scowled, the squad leader answered for him. "He can help us sort this out or we can open fire on his men. They're past reasonable restraint, and I can't risk them breaching the dauquoi environment. The Therem would shut us down."

Rance shrugged. Why the hell had Elmo stayed on the ship? This should be his job.

"I'll come with you. I should be able to talk them out of it."

"It'll take some talking. They're crazy drunk, and they got hold of some chemical explosive."

"What?"

"You know, some of the women make it."

"To give out to drunken troopers on a rampage?"

"Some old girls got a funny idea of subversion."

Rance downed his drink in one gulp. He grimaced at Amansa. What could he do? "Maybe I'll catch up with you later."

"You never know."

The squad leader laughed. "There's plenty more where she came from."

"Let's go."

A servo suit was parked in the corridor outside the topmen's lounge. All its lights were flashing. As the squad leader climbed into it, she glanced down at Rance.

"Are you checked out on one of these?"

Rance shook his head.

"That's okay. We don't have a spare, anyway."

Rance had never liked the shore patrol. They demonstrated the same two traits on every recstar: arrogance and attitude.

"Do I follow you?" he asked.

"We can take the emergency chute."

The servo suit ground into action. Jogging to keep up with the hulking metal humanoid, Rance felt like a child who was forced to trot alongside a striding adult. It did nothing for his dignity. The emergency chute brought them to a rough-hewn axial tunnel. The squad leader's suit took a few moments to regain its equilibrium after the jolt of backgrav, but when she had it under control, she gestured with one of the giant pincers.

"The entrance to the dauquoi section that your men are trying to break through is up ahead at the next intersection. It's a secondary air lock."

"Why didn't you gas them down and be done with it?"

"Because I don't want the stuff hanging around in the atmosphere for ten standards or more. It'd be easier to blast them."

"You're all heart."

"I look after my own."

"Then you can't blame me if I do, too."

The area around the air lock was like the aftermath of a small battle. Six troopers were backed up against the air lock, glaring defiance at the same number of shore patrol who surrounded them in a half circle. Back in the corridor, a dozen or more troopers were penned up in mobile holding cages. They were bruised and bloody. The line of shore patrol moved aside to let Rance and the squad leader through. Rance noted, not without a certain pride, that two servo suits had been knocked out of commission. They lay flat on their backs, completely immobilized.

"Your boys have had quite a time at the expense of my women."

Rance did his best not to smile. "So it would seem."

"You've got one shot at getting them to give up. Then I have my people open fire."

Rance took a deep breath and squared his shoulders. Summoning all of his authority, he marched smartly toward the air lock.

"What the hell is going on here?"

"That's far enough, Rance!"

"We bad, Rance!"

Renchett and a trooper whom Rance didn't recognize were in front of the group. They were both holding metal tubes that were obviously homemade bombs. Renchett also had his knife in his hand. Rance halted.

"What are you going to do, blow me up?"

"We ain't going to be taken," Renchett told him.

"You ain't going to get out of here alive if you don't stop this stupidity. You ain't bad, you're out of control."

"We know what we're doing." Renchett's voice was decidedly slurred.

Rance folded his arms and rocked back on his heels. "Yeah? So what are you doing?"

This seemed to confuse the drunken troopers. Renchett and the one Rance didn't recognize looked at each other blankly. Finally Renchett staggered slightly and made a sweeping gesture with his bomb.

"We jus' wanted to take a look at the worms."

"They seem all ready to cut you in half."

"Wha'?"

"Look behind you."

On the other side of a transparent panel in the air lock, there was a line of dauquoi. They all wore silver projector helmets. Since they had no arms or legs, just highly developed telekinetic powers, the caplike projector helmet was the worms' favorite weapon.

"Slimy suckers can' stan' up to us."

"And you can't stand up to a projector helmet. Besides, if you don't give up right now, the shore patrol's going to grease the whole lot of you."

"These shores ain't going to open up on us."

The squad leader's voice came from behind Rance. "Oh, yes, we are. You can count on it."

There was a sullen silence. Even in their condition, it had to be clear to the troopers that they had painted themselves into a corner. Rance relaxed slightly. It was not just a question of giving them a way out. Renchett, at least, seemed to sense this.

"So what happens to us if we give up? What punishment do we pull?"

Rance glanced back at the squad leader. "Can I set the punishment on this, or do you want to turn it into a major beef?"

The squad leader wasn't immediately ready to play the game. "They've got explosives, and they messed up two of my women."

"No real harm's been done. You'll take them in and mess them up a bit and then I'll have them back on the ship in a pod. You don't want to lose me a bunch of my best fighters."

The squad leader was wavering. "I don't know. You know how many times I heard that?"

Rance sighed. "If it goes to superiors, nobody looks good."

"Listen, just get them out of here. We'll pick up the women who sold them the explosives."

"You know who they are?"

"We've got an idea. A cross figure on the thumbprints will confirm it."

The idea that women subversives were manufacturing crude bombs on a recstar was a shock. Even that they were able to manufacture bombs at all. It was also a bad sign. Things had to be deteriorating.

"What will happen to them?" Rance asked.

"They'll be termed."

"It's a mess."

Rance turned back to the troopers. "Okay, here's the deal. Five standards in a pod, even if we jump."

Anyone in a punishment pod during a jump didn't live through it. Renchett was outraged.

"Five standards for getting drunk?"

"Five standards for being an asshole. You can probably assume that the shore patrol will bust you up into the bargain before you get off this rock."

The squad leader allowed herself a grim smile. "You can count on that, too."

Renchett scowled. "I've been in recstar brigs."

"It's better than being greased, isn't it?"

Renchett turned to his companions. There was a muttered discussion.

"So what's it to be?" Rance asked briskly.

"We ain't sure. How do we know you're on the level?"

"Damn it. Renchett, you've had all the chances you're getting. You've got ten seconds to ground those charges and your weapons or I'll let the shore patrol open fire."

He turned on his heel and strolled slowly back to where the squad leader was waiting in her servo suit. His hands were clasped behind his back, and he appeared to have given up on the whole business.

"Fire on a ten count. I can't do anything with these morons."

Renchett quickly called after him. "Hold it, Rance. We'll take the five standards."

Rance looked up at the squad leader and jerked his thumb in the direction of the troopers. "You can take them down."

The men were quickly manacled and led off to the mobile cages. Rance gestured to the shore who had custody of Renchett.

"I want to speak to that one."

Up close, Renchett looked bleary-eyed and confused. Rance shook his head.

"Why do you have to always pull this shit?"

Renchett raised his chained hands in a helpless gesture. "I don't know. I just get drunk."

Rance leaned close so the shore patrol couldn't hear.

"Tell me something. How did you manage to knock over the two servos?"

Renchett winked. "It's easy if there's enough of you."

The cages slammed, and the shore patrol moved out with its prisoners. Rance remembered the one time, as a raw and very drunk recruit, that he'd been in a recstar brig. Those women could be vicious. He'd only been punched around a bit and then left to sleep it off on the hard floor, but one particular troublemaker had been strung up by his wrists in front of the other prisoners and beaten semiconscious with a fiber knout. Rance walked over to the air lock. A shore was collecting the bombs and weapons. She was bending down, reaching for Renchett's knife.

"Mind if I have that?" Rance asked.

The woman straightened up with the knife in her hand. She looked at it.

"I don't know. I don't see why not."

She handed him the knife, hilt first. Rance took it and slid it into his belt. Renchett would be impossible if he lost that knife.

Back at the topmen's lounge, Rance found that Amansa was no longer there. There was, however, a woman sitting on her own at a table. Nobody else seemed to be laying a claim to her, so he approached her.

"Do you know a woman named Amansa?"

The woman, who had very black hair and large, slightly moist eyes, nodded.

"Yes, I know her. She left a while ago with one of you topmen."

"Mind if I sit down?"

"Go right ahead."

Before he sat, Rance pulled the knife from his belt and tossed it onto the table. The woman raised an eyebrow.

"And what's that for?"

Rance realized what the gesture must have looked like, and he smiled a little awkwardly.

"It's nothing. It belongs to one of my men. He was just taken off to the brig, and he'd be lost without it."

"Were yours the bunch that tried to break in on the worms?"

"You heard about that?"

"We've got the best grapevine in the galaxy. Did they really want to see how the dauquoi do it?"

"They were skunk drunk. I doubt they really knew what they wanted. You want a drink?"

"Sure."

Rance took a longer look at the woman. She was no great beauty, but she wasn't as teasingly undressed or as gaudily painted as the regular corridor whores. There was a certain aura of class about her. That pleased him, although he was aware that class was something regularly cultivated by the women who worked the places where the overmen and topmen hung out. It wasn't only a matter of status. There was also an unfortunate reality that an air of distance, mystery, or dark experience could be worn like a perfume to disguise the fact that they were at the wrong end of their youth. Rance considered it only right that this kind were the topmen's women. You didn't make topman in the first year out, either. Of course, there were topmen, and others besides, who compulsively chased the very young, or the illusion of very young. Fortunately, that was confined to another section of the rock.

"What's your name?" he asked her.

"Herma."

Herma drank small, fast shots of clear frozen spirit. She seemed to feel no need to instigate conversation. They sat for a long time just drinking and half smiling at each other.

"You're a very relaxed man, or maybe just detached."

"Either's good when you never know what's going to happen next."

"We always know what's going to happen next."

"Intuition?"

"Inevitability."

Rance laughed. "You've got to keep a loose mind."

Herma peered at him soulfully from under very long eyelashes. "I keep a very loose mind, believe me."

Rance decided that he liked her. "I rented a cubicle. Maybe we should take the conversation over there."

"That sounds like a delightful idea."

There were only two more interruptions by the shore patrol before the recall sounded the end of liberty. Both were minor skirmishes. It was always easier after the major troublemakers were out of the way. Without them, the others, who didn't have the same flair for destruction, were only able to keep up a dull roar. When Rance ran out of time with Herma, who fell victim to the built-in boredom factor, he moved on to Syua. He was just taking his leave of a woman called Mariette and going off in search of a drink when the alarms started howling. Rance was surprised. He had expected the liberty to last at least another standard. The men were surprised, too. There was an angry roar that almost drowned the recall sirens. In that first instant, it seemed that the men would kill before they'd go back to the ships. And then, almost unbelievably, the anger seemed to run out of energy. The roar died away, and a crushing despondency filled the environment like a physical force. The action folded in on itself, and the fun froze and withered in the cold moan of the sirens. It was over. The women were like puppets with their strings cut. The men were zombies, mesmerized by the sirens; they picked themselves up and shambled out into the corridors. Their shoulders were bowed, and they seemed completely defeated. The women simply stood back and let them go. No words or gestures were exchanged.

Rance had quickly inserted a pair of ear filters when the sirens first sounded. The howl was so loaded with control psych that it was only a little shy of weapon level. There was plenty for a topman to do during the pullout from a recstar, and he didn't need to be head-locked by the sirens. Not every man in the environment was completely put under. There were the ones who were too feisty, the ones who were too drunk, and some veteran longtimers who had been through it so many times that they'd built up a tolerance. The shore patrol moved systematically along the corridors, herding the stragglers out of booths and knocking shops. A belliger-ent few had to be incapacitated before they would go quietly.

The horns were now alternating the control howl with a full-load authority voice reciting assembly areas, de-parture gates, and shuttle codes. The men were glumly forming ranks. Rance made his way to the gates where his twenties would form up. It should all run fairly smoothly with his worst assholes already gone. He just hoped there wouldn't be too many unconscious. Those had to be carried by the ones who could walk, and in headlock, the ones who could walk were very badly co-ordinated and tended to drop the stiffs. The stiffs, in their turn, tended to throw up directly they hit free-fall, and the whole outfit had to be hosed down in the blue room. Fortunately, the liberty tans were disposable.

The last thing that anyone expected was an explosion. Just as Rance had started watching the elevator se-quencer with growing impatience, there was a roar from somewhere over on the other side of the environment. For an instant, the lights dimmed. Inside the hollowed-out cavern, the concussion was stunning, but although the men staggered and some would probably be deaf for

the next thirty minutes, the majority took hardly any notice of either the blast or the dusty smoke that billowed
down the corridors a moment later. They simply wandered in confused circles. At the other extreme, the topmen and the shore patrol hit the ground. Protected by
their ear filters, they fell into ingrained battle patterns,
even reaching for weapons that they didn't have.

"What was that?"

"Are we under attack?"

Rance got to his feet again. All his men were still
standing. He yelled and waved his arms. "Get down, you
idiots! Get down!"

They responded sluggishly, but eventually they were
all down flat. Instinctively Rance moved to cover behind
a shore patrol's servo suit. Immediately after the explosion, there was an instant of silence. It was followed by a
long ripping hiss, as if a pressure pipe had ruptured.

"Are we losing the atmosphere?"

"We don't have no helmets!"

"Then we'll find out soon enough."

Shore patrol sirens started up all over the environment. The servo behind which Rance was sheltering
started moving forward. Rance moved with it, holding
on to one of its legs and peering cautiously around the
machine's bulk. There had been no second explosion,
and it was looking less and less likely that they were
under attack. More likely the blast was an accident or an
act of sabotage. The servo's communicator crackled into
life and gave him some minimal information.

"We are not under attack. Repeat, the facility is not
under attack. The explosion was caused by a homemade
bomb, and there are a number of fatalities. There ap-
pears to be no follow-up action, but all shore patrol units
will stand to."

The communicator ran through the message for a second time. Rance straightened up. The shore looked down at him.

"You hear that?"

"I heard it."

"So I guess you can get back to moving your men out."

The full story didn't come out until they were back on the ship. Some of the old-timers, the sweetgassers, had made a pact. Just like Renchett, they had bought a homemade bomb from one of the women subversives. Unlike Renchett, they hadn't used it to try to blast their way into worm territory. One of them, probably a sapper—there were a couple of sappers among the dead—had rigged a situation fuse. After exactly seven minutes of the recall siren, the bomb had blown them all to an afterlife or none, depending on their beliefs. The women in the area must have been in on the plan. There were no women casualties at all. The suicide plot had overshadowed all other messdeck tales of the liberty.

"They must have had earplugs."

"That, or they were gassed out of their minds."

"Had to be gassed out of their minds."

"I wouldn't mind going that way, if the time was right."

"And when exactly is the time right, smartass?"

"They must have known."

Rance, when he heard that, looked around at his men. The topman in him knew that suicide talk had to be squashed, but somehow he just didn't have the strength. He wondered how many of the men around him would even make it to the light-year stare. Would he make it there himself?

The aftermath of a liberty was a topman's nightmare. The men were hung over and sullen. They'd tasted a little of what could be, and they now resented what was with a slit-eyed poison. The suicides and the fact that the liberty had been cut short had wiped out any benefit to morale that might have come from the break. If there needed to be any other reason for resentment, it was the general assumption that a jump was coming up, even though there had been no official announcement as yet. Rance had made a mental note to get Renchett and the others out of the pods if a jump was called. Despite what he'd said, he didn't want to lose them.

He knew that the liberty had done no good, when the time-honored suit-superstition came to the surface. Even though the men were bleary and out of shape when Rance ran them through the first shakedown drill, they blamed everything on the suits. The suits were acting up. The suits were jealous because their men had been with women. Rance had never really made up his mind about the legend. He could remember, as a trooper, how his suit had seemed stiff and unyielding after a liberty. His best idea was that the suits got pissed off at the assortment of poisons that were being sweated out of the troopers wearing them. Rance was ever the realist.

# Eleven

Wʜᴀᴛ was left of the twenty crouched on the crest of Hill 3837. It was the perfect vantage point from which to watch the big push up the Ten River valley, although nobody was relishing the advantage. The valley was a wide sweep, curving north from where the Ten ran into the gulf. It had cut a deep, steep-sided path through a range of young jagged hills. On either side of the slow, passive river was thick fungoid jungle, walls of gray, fleshy growth like luxuriant death. The jungle was so primitively virulent that it had climbed most of the way up even the most precipitous slopes. What was left of the twenty waited on their bare hilltop well above what was loosely called the tree line. As soon as the order was given, though, they'd move on down, burning their way into the dank heat of the pallid leprous jungle that was almost certainly concealing a full menu of Yal rearguard nastiness.

All terminology on this planet was loose. The expanse of brown soup that rolled along down to the equally brown sea could scarcely qualify as water. The men hated this forsaken planet. They had fought in both its major theaters of war and taken serious casualties in each. They'd started out on the permafrost, and now they were in the jungle. Siryn, one of the new intake, had started coughing. The air was also only an approximation.

The troopers now and again cracked their facemasks for a brief respite from the metallic taste of canned air. Siryn had left his mask cracked for too long. The native spores, microorganisms, and all kinds of other unknown crap had their hooks into his lungs. He'd probably get sick. That was the trouble with new meat—they kept finding new ways to act dumb. Hark ignored the kid, who was still having spasms. He'd been around too long to jump each time a newcomer fouled up. There had been so many replacements in this campaign that they had to be with the group for a good while before any of the longtimers even bothered to remember their names. He checked that his MEW was still charging, then he rolled back his suit from the front of his body and lay back on the rocky ground. There was no way anyone could wear a full suit in this heat unless he was actually in the middle of a firefight.

The troopers were dressed in what was known as the dense atmosphere combat suit, the DAC. They were supposed to be lighter than the full vacuum kit, and technically they were, all else being equal, but since dense-atmosphere planets invariably had higher gravity than those with light or no atmospheres, the kit actually presented the men with a greater relative burden. The bulky helmets, although they still contained communicators and brainlink displays, were modified so that they didn't completely enclose the head. The dark visor was only half-face, entending to just below the eyes; the lower half of the face was covered by a transparent breathing mask. In the back, the protective shell extended to the cushioned neck ring but wasn't sealed to it. The backpack was actually larger than that of the full vacuum kit. Since, in this theater, the troopers could expect to be out in the bush for days on end without ever coming in to a service base, the pack had to incorporate air and water tanks, recyclers, spare energy pacs, minimeds, F-rations, and even a deflated one-man bubble environment. The podlike casing of the backpack did come with a small floater in the base that offset the weight, but its bulk and inertia still made it a cumbersome piece of equipment. Most of the men had modified their kits for safety and comfort. The suits themselves had been persuaded to roll back, leaving arms and, in some cases, legs bare. Helmets were decorated with camouflage scrim, decked with fungus and foliage. Some of the troopers had hung small combat souvenirs around their necks. Taken as a whole, the effect, particularly among the longtimers, verged on the barbaric.

Although the medians steadfastly refused to say as much, the Therem troops were bogged down on this planet. They had been on JD4-1A for over two hundred days. It was supposed to have been a relatively simple operation. The Yal had a large ground garrison dug in on various parts of the planet, but they had withdrawn their large battleships and left only satellite weapon systems and smaller interplanetary craft. In the beginning, it had all gone according to the book. The cluster had moved in, and the small Yal space force had been wiped out in a matter of minutes. The larger ground installations had been pinpoint nuked, and Therem troops had gone down to mop up the survivors.

It was at this point that things started to go wrong. More than just survivors waited for the ground troops. The Yal had seeded the planet with every kind of booby trap and sleeper weapon. Large forces of specially adapted chibas had been concealed in the most difficult terrain. Packs of vicious semiintelligent miggies roamed the ice fields and the jungles, making random attacks on the Therem forces. What had looked like a routine occupation quickly turned into a slow, painful planet clearing, a war of attrition that the Therem would win in the end by sheer firepower and weight of numbers but that would cost them dearly before the last Yal surrogates were destroyed.

The suspicion began to spread through the ranks that they had been maneuvered into a trap. JD4-1A wasn't a poorly protected garrison planet but one huge sucker bet, a piece of bait that the *Anah* command had swallowed whole. There didn't seem to be a way out. If the cluster withdrew, the action would constitute a major retreat. The Therem couldn't allow a Yal-occupied planet to remain in a sector that was otherwise under their control. The only alternative to the bloody, protracted warfare was the total destruction of the planet, something certainly within the cluster's power to do. The only reason that the thirteen big ships didn't stand off and pound this world into a brand-new belt of asteroids was that it was against the only basic rule in this eternal conflict: A planet with natural indigenous life must not be destroyed. The rule was a legacy from the early period of the war, when planet smashing had been carried on wholesale. Both the Yal and the Therem had begun to see the eventual outcome of this behavior, and almost spontaneously and certainly without any formal communication, they both had stopped the practice. Even though, on JD4-1A, the Yal were using the rule to their advantage, the planet could not be blown to bits without a major change in policy—and it was a policy that wasn't likely to be changed. Even in this ultimately destructive war, there seemed to be a need for some limit on the destruction. In the meantime, the troopers fought and died.

The twenty had greatly changed. There were a lot of new faces. Dyrkin and Renchett were still there, seemingly indestructible. Helot was still hanging on. Kemlo, because of his prosthetic foot, had been retired to ship duties, but when the losses had started to build, he'd been brought back into the line. Elmo had also been brought back as overman, and he was one old-timer no one was pleased to see. Following the return from the recstar, Elmo's performance as a noncom had gone right down the tubes. The situation had deteriorated to the point where the twenty who were supposed to be under his control simply wouldn't take him seriously. Rance, out of a sense of loyalty, had covered for him as long as he could, but the time had come when it was no longer possible to hide Elmo's mistakes without endangering the men. Rance had organized a little computer trickery, and Elmo had been removed to a post in the supply center where he couldn't do any harm. As the war on JD4-1A dragged on, however, the easy, rear-echelon jobs were eliminated one by one. The fatalities among noncoms were particularly high, and according to the records, Elmo was a perfectly able overman. He was therefore returned to his old unit to replace Overman Macin, who had been killed by chiba fire out on the plains in front of Range 27. He'd arrived only a day or so before the push up the Ten River, and as Dyrkin put it, he hadn't had time yet to foul up. None of the veterans in the twenty, though, doubted that he would.

Renchett walked over to where Hark was lying with his eyes closed. "Taking it easy there, boy?"

"Taking it while I can." Hark opened his eyes and raised his head. "Any sign of the task force?"

Renchett shook his head. "Nothing."

Hark let his head flop back. "I ain't in no hurry."

Renchett didn't say anything—he probably *was* in a hurry. Hark accepted that Renchett was completely unbalanced. He was part of the crew—what, for Hark, was the original crew. A man had to be true to his crew. Besides, Renchett was very good at killing, and the more he killed the enemy, the less enemy there was to try to kill Hark.

"What about goddamn Elmo?"

"What about him?"

"You realize we may have to do something about him?"

"I'm doing one minute at a time, and right now I'm lying down."

Renchett shrugged. "Suit yourself."

Elmo was sitting apart from the others and staring fixedly down the river. Since he'd arrived at the unit, he'd hardly communicated with the men except to give a few curt orders. He looked burned-out.

One of the replacements pointed down river. "They're coming!"

"It's the big dynes," someone said.

Hark pushed himself up on one elbow. The dynes were the biggest land fighting machines in all of the Therem Alliance. He wearily stood up. No matter how many of them he saw, he couldn't help being awed. A dyne was over a hundred meters tall, an ovoid body supported on three long spindly legs and packed with every imaginable kind of weapon. It wasn't clear whether they were composite beings or machines manned by very complex creatures. It was probably an academic point.

"Just look at those suckers!"

There were four of them wading out of the gulf and up onto dry land. Their huge feet effortlessly crushed the fleshy jungle. Hark knew that there were human troops down in that jungle, advancing behind the dynes. He was profoundly glad that he wasn't one of them. It was the worst place to be in this kind of operation. The dynes were preceded by a flight of drone ultralights, which were supposed to trigger any buried Yal weapons that might run on the command of a simple mass detector.

The gunsaucers came next, moving slowly just above treetop level. They tended to stay close to the dynes, floating in among the legs of the enormous machines. Their task was to fire on any movement on the ground. They were supposed to be the first line of spot and destroy, taking care of chibas that broke cover or miggies that started massing for a suicide attack. The problem was their skittish crews, whose fear of a ground blast or a delayed-action mine made them destroy first and spot second. They were notorious for firing on their own infantry.

Simultaneously, four mild explosions erupted out of the jungle directly under the line of ultralights. The drones had triggered a baby mine cluster, probably the kind that crawled blindly around inside deep cover. One ultralight was flipped into a stall and went down like a stone. It was only an opening salvo, but the Therem task force immediately responded. The saucers lifted quickly away from the trees like a flock of nervous birds. The dynes halted. They were powering up. Dyne weaponry was all projected from what could only be described as a ruby-red eye in the front of its ovoid body. The multiple pupils of that eye slowly began to glow. Renchett stood fingering his knife. "Think we're getting under way here."

The electronic chatter of battle started up inside Hark's helmet as the task force moved forward again. The saucer crews were apparently incapable of maintaining communication silence; they continuously yelled to each other, bolstering against their nervousness. There was also a subbass rumble, almost too deep to hear, that some said was the dynes talking. Another series of small explosions geysered out of the jungle. A herd of the big green lizards started bellowing in panic. They smashed their way out of the fungus, stampeded down the riverbank, and splashed into the oily brown water. One of the gunsaucers opened fire on them. Two of the lizards went down kicking and thrashing. Someone whooped. Hark scowled. There were too many assholes who thought it was funny to shoot at the big lizards. Hark didn't think it was funny at all. The green monsters were one of the few things he liked on this goddamn planet.

The next explosion was huge. A broad expanse of jungle seemed to lift straight into the air before it disintegrated into a blazing roar of fire and smoke. Communication was swamped in a howl of static. The twenty scattered, hitting the dust. They knew all too well what was probably coming next. Green fire was flashing from inside the pall of smoke.

"They've sprung a firetower!"

Although the jungle was still burning, the smoke had partially cleared around a cylindrical black tower almost as tall as a dyne. It was a Yal static robot. Until the task force had approached, it had lain dormant in a protective silo under a cover of jungle. It was only when the mines and blastpits that surrounded it had been detonated that it pushed its way upward and started blazing multiple fire. Yal firetowers didn't last long. Even without what was being pumped at it from the dynes' glowing eyes, it wouldn't have lasted more than a few minutes. The firetower was a blaze-of-glory device. It let go of everything at once in the hope of obliterating everything around it. The dynes were big enough to be equipped with rudimentary shields. They didn't have enough power to walk and keep their shields up at the same time, but it was better than nothing. Only one dyne was taken by surprise. It was hit in the knee joint by a blast of accelerator, and in an instant, the whole leg was melting. It stumbled, tried to right itself on two legs, and then crashed down, sprawling like a mighty corpse across jungle and river. The ovoid slowly began to sink. The other three stood their ground and vaporized the tower with a saturation of energy weapons. To the men crouching on the hilltop, it seemed as if the whole river valley had been turned into a caldron of black smoke, colored fire, and pulsing energy. Their helmets were filled with an electronic scream, and the ground shook continuously. Each one could imagine what it must be like to be one of the companies down in the valley, huddling below this battle of the giants, bellies pressed to the soft jungle floor, trying desperately to bury themselves in the fungus mold before they were fried or vaporized. It didn't seem possible that anyone could live through a hell like that—but they knew from experience that men did. That was why the war was still in business.

When the firing stopped, there was a terrible silence, broken only by the patter of falling debris. The men on the hilltop peered into the smoke for any sign of further fire on the ground. It was always possible that the chibas had come out of their rat holes and were engaging what was left of the ground forces. All seemed to be quiet. The smoke was slowly being blown upriver by a lazy offshore breeze, uncovering what remained after the exchange. The firetower was nothing more than a dead melted stump. It was at the center of a burned and blackened area that extended over more than a third of the river valley. Two of the dynes still stood where they had fought. Despite the shields, their outsides were discolored by heat and radiation. The third dyne that was still standing had moved to where its comrade lay, legs stretching out of the river. It had extended a long umbilical into the water and was probing for the body section of the fallen machine. It was the saucers that had taken the worst punishment. Over half of them were history, and the survivors hung back behind the dynes as if unwilling to go on. The twenty were on their feet, staring down into the expanse of destruction. Elmo decided that it was the moment to assert his authority.

"Don't bunch up there. You never know when you're going to come under fire."

Dyrkin rounded on him. "What are you talking about? You think there's going to be a Yal air strike? Or maybe the chibas are going to come boiling out of the fungus and hit us on open ground?"

Elmo went red behind his facemask. "In case you hadn't noticed, there are a whole lot of replacements in this twenty, and I don't want them getting into bad habits."

Dyrkin lifted his mask and spit on the ground. "Most of them've got more on the ball than you."

"You can't talk to me like that."

"Can't I? What are you going to do, shoot me?"

He turned his back on Elmo and deliberately walked away. The overman shouted after him.

"You'll be on a field punishment when we get back to the ship. This is a capital charge, Dyrkin."

"I'll worry about that when we get to it."

The others watched the confrontation in silence. It was the worst thing that could happen to a twenty. A noncom who'd lost it could be a death sentence for his men, and nobody in the twenty was in any doubt that Elmo had lost it. He stayed on his own again until the order came through that they were to move down into the fungus. The twenty fell automatically into single file and started downhill. Elmo didn't have anything to say or do until they came close the edge of the fungus. Their approach to the jungle had become so routine that Renchett, without question, started organizing four of the relacements into the front-line burning party to start carving into the dense, pulpy growth. He was quite amazed when Elmo stopped him.

"No burn?"

"We don't want any chibas knowing where we are."

"They always know where we are."

"We still don't burn."

Renchett shook his head and looked to Dyrkin for support. "You want to check out what's going on over here?"

Dyrkin shrugged. "Whatever the overman says. I'm already on his bad side."

Renchett turned back to Elmo. "So what does the overman say?"

"We move along the line of vegetation until we come to a natural trail. Then we move into the woods."

Renchett put his hands on his hips and looked up at the sky.

"I don't want to be bucking no orders here, but I've been in these woods a lot longer than you have, and one thing I know is that a natural trail is a damn-fool thing to be walking on."

"That's as may be, Renchett, but as of now, and in these woods, we do it my way."

Renchett turned away, spreading his hands in a gesture of helplessness. "You're the boss."

"One more thing, Renchett."

Renchett halted, but he didn't turn. "What's that?"

"Take the point."

"Me?"

"You."

"I don't walk point no more. I did it for too long."

Elmo smiled nastily. "Now you do."

Hark had been watching the exchange. Up until Elmo had smiled, he'd been willing to give the overman any reasonable break. The smile cut it. Elmo shouldn't be enjoying this. Hark wouldn't go against him, but if it came to it, he wouldn't be backing him, either.

They walked slowly along the edge of the fungus. Elmo took up a position back along the line. He seemed to be forever glancing nervously into the jungle. Such behavior was known in the trade as seeing shadows, and it was considered a bad sign in anyone but the most raw recruit. They'd been walking for maybe a half hour, and the single file had started to loosen up. Kemlo fell into step beside Hark. He seemed to be favoring his artificial foot.

"Foot hurting?"

"Yeah, a little. It's the forsaken damp. I ain't as bad as him, though." He jerked his thumb back to where Siryn was having trouble keeping up.

Hark looked back at the new fish. "He looks like he screwed up his lungs back there."

"He ought to be e-vaced out."

"That's Elmo's problem. Nothing we can do about it."

"We ought to say something."

"I don't figure Elmo's interested in anything we got to say. Renchett tried to tell him not to go down a natural trail, and he put him on point."

"So you're taking an attitude, too."

Hark looked sharply at Kemlo. "What's that supposed to mean?"

"You know what it's supposed to mean. Are you going to get with Dyrkin and Renchett and ride him into the ground?"

"I ain't riding no one, but I ain't pretending that he's not a disaster waiting to happen, either. He's the worst. He knows he ain't going to live through this, but he's not quite ready to die. He's likely to take the whole lot of us with him."

Elmo's voice sounded in their helmets. "Cut the gab and get back in line up there."

Hark muttered under his breath. "Fuck you, asshole."

"You say something?"

"Not me, boss."

Kemlo moved into place in front of Hark, and they

walked in silence for a while. When it looked as if Elmo had forgotten about them, Kemlo fell back to rejoin Hark.

"You figure we'll see any chiba action?"

Hark shook his head. "Not yet. Not until we reach the head of the valley. Seems to me that the tower was supposed to slow us in this section."

Kemlo cracked his mask for a couple of seconds.

"If it wasn't for this damn mask, I'd grow a mustache."

JD4-1A had a weird system of night and day. Its natural rotation was 960 standard minutes. It didn't, however, revolve directly around its parent sun. Although everyone referred to it as a planet, it was in fact the largest of the satellite moons of JD4-1, that sun's huge single planet. It took seventy-four of its days to circle the planet, and of those, forty-eight were a sequence of bright sunlit days and a strange half night, illuminated by the light reflected from the giant planet that all but filled the sky on the side that was turned away from the sun. After this cycle was complete, it passed into the sun's shadow and went through twenty-six days of total darkness. The operation on the Ten River was taking place roughly halfway through the light period.

The sun was still high when Renchett called into the communicator. "Looks like we got a trail here, boss."

The twenty halted. Elmo walked up to inspect the opening in the jungle.

"What do you think made that?"

It was Renchett's turn to grin. "It could be a lizard trail, although lizards don't usually come this high, or it could've been cut by the Yal so we could walk down it like a bunch of fucking idiots."

Elmo hesitated, but Renchett offered no further advice. Finally he made up his mind.

"We'll take the trail."

"Do I still walk point?"

"Until I say different."

Renchett raised his weapon and gave the overman a hard look. For an instant, it appeared that Renchett was actually considering shooting Elmo, but then he turned and started down the trail.

"Keep a careful watch on your detectors."

Renchett glanced back. His lip curled. "You're telling me?"

Elmo started moving the other men down the trail.

"Keep a good distance between you. Stick to the edges of the trail."

It was the most obvious advice that he could offer to a jungle patrol and totally redundant for men who had been through it before, but he insisted on repeating it to each man as he passed. The troopers largely ignored him. They adjusted their suits to full cover and ducked grimly under the overhang. Only Siryn seemed unwilling to plunge into the fungus. He appeared scarcely able to walk.

"I . . . don't think I can go much farther."

"You got a problem, boy?"

"I can't breathe."

"Shouldn't have opened your facemask, should you?"

"Couldn't I just stay here? I'll only slow up the others."

"You just keep going, boy. I don't have no cowards in my twenty."

"I'm no coward. It's my lungs; they're screwed."

Elmo gestured with his MEW. "Get walking, boy. I don't want to hear no more out of you."

It was in the jungle that the fear really started. It closed in with the damp heat and the shadows. Very little light penetrated the thick overhead canopy, and heavy moisture dripped constantly from the sweating porous fronds. It was a place of gray monochrome gloom, ideally suited to traps, ambush, and surprise attack. Insects, small lizards, and land crustaceans rustled and scuttled in undergrowth that was festooned with the viscous webs of giant arachnids. The continual small noises stretched the troopers' nerves to the limit. They tried not to look into the shadows—that way led to hallucination and madness. The one thing that they were spared was the smell of fungoid rot. They were protected from that by their masks, but they could still feel its presence. They tried to keep their eyes fixed on the green detector displays that were projected in front of their visors and would give them first warning of chiba movement or antipersonnel devices.

The first leg of the advance down the overgrown hillside was largely uneventful. A replacement almost blasted a large albino butterfly but managed to restrain himself in time. In a small clearing, they stumbled across a dozen of the small, shovel-nosed lizards rooting in the mold. There was a flash of panic as the creatures blundered away into the fungus, but Dyrkin quickly took charge.

"Hold your fire! It's nothing! Nobody fire!"

The company halted. Some were shaking; all could feel sweat running down inside their suits.

"Okay, everybody calm down. It was just a bunch of grunters."

Elmo was moving down the line. For a moment, it looked as if he were going to come down on Dyrkin for taking command, but he must have thought better of it. He simply waved the column forward again.

"Okay, let's keep going."

The trail faded to nothing, and they had to burn their way through virgin jungle. Elmo made no argument when Renchett called up three replacements to do the burning, incinerating the fungus with their MEWs set on low-yield heat ray. Eventually they reached a water course where a tiny stream danced down the hillside in a series of sparkling waterfalls.

As the terrain began to flatten out, the going became more difficult. The ground underfoot, which had previously been dry, turned into semiswamp. The mold now had the consistency of thick, clinging soup, and the men found that they were sinking almost to their knees. Even with the grav in their boots assisting them, progress was exhausting. With each step, swarms of tiny creatures flew up in billowing clouds. They tried to stick to the troopers' suits and helmets. The suits shook them off with spasmodic twitches of their black hides, but the visors had to be constantly wiped, otherwise the displays became distorted and unreadable. There was also another annoyance: The wheezing rasp of Siryn's breathing was audible in everyone's helmet.

"Something should be done about him."

"It looks like the jungle's going to do it."

Siryn had fallen well behind the rest of the column to the point where if he dropped back any farther, he would be out of sight.

"Hey, Elmo, Siryn isn't going to make it."

Everyone in the company heard Hark's voice, and they stopped to see what would happen.

"Shut your mouth, Hark. That fool isn't about to get any preferential treatment. He can hump his pod same as the rest of us."

Siryn chose that moment to give up. He stumbled forward and fell helmet-down in the muck. Elmo slung his weapon over his shoulder and walked back down the line. The column halted, and the recruits stopped burning the fungus.

"You all want to see what happens to cowards in my twenty?"

He stood over the fallen rookie.

"Get up, boy."

Renchett was starting back from his front position. "Leave him alone, Elmo."

"Stay where you are, Renchett."

Elmo bent over Siryn.

"Are you going to get up?"

The rookie's voice was little more than a gasp. "I can't."

"Then take off your helmet. You ain't fit to wear it."

Renchett was on the move again. "You're crazy Elmo."

"I told you to stay where you are."

Dyrkin was also coming down the line.

"You can't kill him," Renchett said.

"I said take off your helmet."

"No!"

Elmo reached down. He was almost gentle as he lifted off the helmet.

"Now the mask."

Siryn didn't say a word. There was a soft sucking noise as Elmo pulled the mask away from his face. He pushed the rookie down and held his head under the dirty water. It was only a matter of seconds before the boy stopped breathing.

"You're insane!"

Renchett was almost on top of Elmo. The overman straightened up. His MEW was in his hands and pointed at Renchett's stomach.

"It'd give me a lot of pleasure, Renchett."

Renchett halted. His own weapon was unslung but not aimed. Dyrkin caught up with him. Elmo continued to hold his gun level.

"You too, Dyrkin?"

Dyrkin also halted. "You didn't have to kill him. He could have been moved out."

"Sometimes there has to be an example."

"We all know what a corpse looks like."

"The new meat have to know that this ain't no picnic."

"Are you just going to leave him there?"

Elmo took a step forward. "You got a better idea?"

Both Renchett and Dyrkin were silent. Elmo smiled.

"Not so brave now? So what's it going to be? Are you going to get back in line or do you want to join this one in the swamp?"

There was a long moment of silent tension, then the two longtimers turned and walked back to their places in the line. Elmo actually laughed.

"Hope the rest of you sorry bastards took a good look at that. There's just one leader in this twenty, and I don't want any of you to forget it."

Hark hefted his MEW. Elmo had made a bad mistake, and sooner or later someone would see that he paid for it.

"Okay, get moving and let's not have any more delays."

The burning started again, and the smoke drifted back down the line. The twenty resumed their slow progress. They moved as if there were an extra weight on them; an ugly sullenness had been added to the heat, humidity, and fear. They continued cutting their way through the jungle for another forty minutes, and then the fungus started to open out a little and there was no longer any need to keep up the continuous burn.

"You can spread out some."

The column, which had bunched up behind the burners, opened up a little. The spaces between the men increased. The resentment seemed to decrease a little as the men became more watchful. This kind of country was a favorite with the chibas. There was enough space for an open order attack but also enough cover for them to lay an ambush. Hark cracked his mask for an instant and breathed out hard. Sweat had started to collect in the base of the mask, and that was the only way to get rid of the accumulation. If it built up for too long, it would start getting in his mouth. He would be glad when this day was finally over. He was tired and hungry and heartily sick of putting one foot in front of the other. When a trooper felt like that, he was no good to either himself or the twenty; he would fall into a dull semi-trance and never sense the danger until it was too late. Hark was close to that state when Renchett's voice rang in his helmet.

"Hold up there! Everybody stop!"

Hark came back with a start, angry that he'd allowed himself to drift. He held his weapon at the ready and quickly looked around, but there was nothing that he could see.

Renchett's voice was immediately followed by Elmo's. "What are you trying to pull now, Renchett?"

"I ain't trying to pull nothing. You'd better get up here and take a look at this."

# TWELVE

THE bodies had been hideously mutilated. Although they were in an advanced state of decay and the mold worms had been at them, it was still all too obvious that they had been skinned by whatever had killed them. It was possible that they had been skinned alive. Their genitals had been cut off and stuffed in their mouths. There was no sign of their suits. They had been arranged in a neat line. It was as if they had been placed there just waiting for someone to discover them. The entire twenty gathered around and stared in silence. Hark sneaked a look at Elmo. He was as green behind his mask as any of the replacements.

"What the hell did this?"

"Chibas?"

"Chibas don't work this way; they just kill."

"Miggies don't have the smarts."

"Unless it's some new kind of psych war programming."

"Designed to get to us?"

"If it is, it's working on me."

One of the new men was gulping and pulling off his facemask. He turned away and vomited.

"Don't breathe in!"

The man coughed twice, wiped his mouth, and put the mask back.

Renchett was staring down at the bodies, shaking his head. "I've done some weird stuff in my time but nothing as weird as this."

Elmo finally found his voice. "Burn them!"

Half the twenty leveled their weapons.

"Stop! Don't fire!"

Dyrkin, who had started walking away from the group, was waving his arms. The troopers hesitated. He started pulling the nearest men away from the bodies.

"Get back! Get away from them!"

Elmo glared at him from behind his visor.

"Have you gone crazy?"

"The goddamn things are quite likely to be booby-trapped. There may even be a proximity fuse. Everybody get back."

Helot was the first to react. He'd been bending over one of the corpses, conducting some kind of morbid inspection. He jumped back as if he'd been scalded.

"Damn! He's probably right."

The longtimers stumbled away from the corpses, pushing the replacements in front of them. This time Elmo didn't argue; he simply moved with the rest. Everyone seemed to be looking to Dyrkin for guidance.

"So what do we do with them?"

"If we're smart, we don't do nothing."

"We can't just leave them."

"That's exactly what we should do. We don't know how the bodies may be gimmicked, and I figure the higher-ups will want to know about this. It's got to be something new."

"We need Rance out here."

Elmo didn't comment on the obvious insult. The troopers didn't even bother to look at him.

"We won't hook up with Rance until we get down to the river."

"So let's press on to the river."

The longtimers finally turned toward Elmo. They were waiting for him to validate their decision with a formal order.

He looked from face to face, and then he nodded.

"Okay, we take a fix on this place and move on."

Renchett helfted his MEW. "Let's get the fuck out of here." It seemed that Renchett was actually volunteering to go on walking point. "Just don't nobody be talking to me."

They pushed on through the forest. A deep gloom had settled over the twenty. They were used to the constant presence of death, and even the idea that any one of them might lose limbs or be blown apart at an given moment. It was part of the function of war, part of their reality. They were so used to bodies twisted into mangled and distorted shapes that the sight of them could even inspire outbreaks of ghoulish humor. This deliberate mutilation, however, was something else. There was a gratuitousness about it that shocked men who thought they were no longer shockable. It wasn't part of the function, it was something extra, and that gave them a chill. This war was no place for extras.

As well as shock and gloom there was a carelessness about the twenty. Men trudged forward with their weapons held loosely at their sides. Some bunched up, and others straggled. The communicators murmured with low-voiced, sullen conversations, but Elmo did nothing to keep them either alert or together. Helot and Dacker caught up with Hark.

"So what did you make of that?" Helot asked.

"I'm trying not to think about it," Hark replied.

"You figure they've built a new kind of chiba?" Dacker suggested.

Hark shook his head. "I don't know. I don't know why the Yal should bother. They kill us, we kill them. Why would they need to mess with us after we're dead?"

"If those guys were dead when they messed with them," Dacker said.

"Goddamm it, don't say that. That's what I've really been trying not to think about," Helot said.

"Maybe it is a psych program," Hark suggested.

"If it is, it's like Renchett said. It's sure as hell working," Helot returned.

"Who do you think those guys were?" Helot asked.

Hark shrugged. "Advance patrol, maybe."

"The whole bloody thing gives me the creeps. I mean, that shit that was done with their dicks, sticking them in their mouths like that, somebody really knew how to get to us. How did some alien know about that shit? Huh?" Dacker shook his head.

"You want to hear something really weird?" Hark said.

"How weird can it get?" Helot put in.

"When I first saw those bodies, this thought came straight out of nowhere. I thought, Men have got to have done this. It was so close to home that it had to be men who done it."

"You're crazy. You saying our own people did that?" Dacker sounded incredulous.

"I ain't saying nothing. I just had this thought."

"You are crazy."

"Who ain't, in all this?"

Helot cracked his mask and spit. "I never thought I'd hear myself saying this, but I'd almost welcome some action. At least it'd be something else to think about."

"And you're calling me crazy?"

Within forty minutes, Helot got his wish. As action went, it was minor. A small gang of miggies erupted out of the ground mold, scrabbling up from where they'd buried themselves or been buried, digging themselves out with their multiple claw-ended legs and throwing chemical fire from the heaters on the tops of their squat disk-shaped bodies. There were twelve of them in all. Miggies usually came in groups of twelve. It might have been because they had twelve legs. Fortunately, there was only one group. Miggies' fire was singularly unpleasant. It didn't simply destroy—it clung and burned, and the suits were able to offer little or no protection. It spread white flame over a man until the body was completely consumed. As the first ones surfaced, Renchett yelled a warning, but it was too late. The two men immediately behind him, both new meat, were hit. The twenty opened up with a roar, blowing the scuttling machine creatures to flying component fragments. One of the recruits was dying slowly and painfully as the relentless flame spread outward from his left shoulder. His screams echoed in everyone's helmet even after they had stopped firing.

The miggies didn't have the intelligence to take evasive action. Their single strategy was a combination of concealment and surprise. They broke cover and they fired, but after that they were almost totally vulnerable. The firefight was all over in less than three minutes with no further human casualties. The last miggie left intact tried to bury itself back in the mold. Hark stood over it and reduced it to vapor with a single extended blast. As he destroyed it, he felt some of the tension draining out of him.

The twenty, now reduced to seventeen, stood whitefaced and breathless with their suit-enhanced adrenaline pumping, turning and staring into the shadows beneath the fungus, looking for a follow-up to the first attack. All too often, a burst out of miggies would merely be the preliminary to a major attack by chibas. But the minutes passed and nothing happened; the men relaxed, and the suits cut back on their output of stimulants. The familiar sense of postcombat letdown started to set in. One by one, they lowered their weapons. The miggies must have been nothing more than an isolated irritant, left behind to slow the human advance. When Elmo gave the order to move on, he sounded exhausted. The dead were left behind. They were mainly ash—there wasn't enough of either of them left to bury or to carry to the next temporary base. Hark hadn't even learned their names.

Light showed up ahead between the growths of fungus in what had to be the burned area where the dynes had destroyed the Yal firetower. The growing babble of other short-range communication in their helmets confirmed it. This was the twenty's rendezvous point with the rest of the task force. Tired as they were, the troopers quickened their pace. Hot food and sleep were almost in sight. In the burned area, they would eat and make camp for the planet's strange half night. It was unlikely that the enemy would attempt anything more than a probe of the perimeter when the whole Therem battle group was assembled in one spot. Of course, the next day they would press on again, back in the stinking vegetation, but nobody thought about that. Out in the bush, they tried to live strictly in the present. A completed day was a completed day. Each man could take some comfort in his continued survival.

As they emerged from the jungle, there was something disorienting about the light and space. The sun was dropping to the horizon, and very soon the huge parent planet would fill the sky. The black charred area was a crowded chaos of activity. Everything was converging on the same point at once. Gunsaucers were coming in to land, throwing up huge clouds of dust like miniature thunderheads. Nohans and human sappers were digging foxholes and bunkers, creating their own dust clouds. Others were rigging the perimeter, the traps and the wire and the disintegration fields. The wounded were being loaded onto e-vacs, and the dead were being incinerated in one huge pit. Above it, smoke mixed with the black dust. The sunlight filtering through was turned a bloody red. The three towering dynes were attempting to raise their fallen comrade, droning at each other in their deep, resonant language. While the twenty had been in among the fungus, amphibious armored crawlers had come upriver, bringing supplies and replacement troops. They had clawed their way up the bank and were now being unloaded. In the middle of it all, two red spheres floated close to the ground, right beside the ruins of the Yal tower. It was just as if they were observing the whole operation.

The combat twenties coming in from the bush seemed somehow out of place amid all these flurries of preparation. They had yet to be told what to do. They crunched aimlessly across the fused earth and black flake ash hoping for a topman to assign them to a bivouac area. Their mood was rapidly deteriorating. The field kitchens, always an obvious goal, were being set up but had not yet opened for business. The nohans seemed to have been quicker off the mark. Lines of the armored aliens were already forming in front of the tall tubular devices that prepared their nourishment. This caused a certain noisy resentment among the troopers. The nohans never actually fought except in the most dire emergency, and the men saw it as a positive injustice that they should get to eat, or whatever they did that passed for eating, before the human fighting men. Elmo tried to stop these complaints in his twenty, but the troopers simply ignored him. Dacker was the first one to lose patience with this purposeless tramping across the assembly area. He threw down his MEW and faced Elmo.

"If you can't find us a place to set up camp, why don't you go look for someone who can?"

Renchett joined in. "Yeah, Elmo, why don't you go find Rance? A report's got to be put in on those bodies. Do something useful for a change instead of busting our chops."

Elmo turned on them. "You two watch your mouths. You're back in the world of discipline now," he snarled.

Dacker waved a dismissive hand at the milling men and machinery. "It looks like it, don't it?"

Renchett shook his head. "One little nuke could take out all of this lot."

"Lucky they don't have any, ain't it?"

"You never know; they might come up with one."

"At least it'd be quick."

"Cut that out!" Elmo tried again.

"Quit trying to prove it, Elmo. We've had enough of your dickhead blustering."

"You bastards . . ." Elmo's voice was shaking.

Renchett pushed his helmet close to Elmo's visor. "What are you going to do, Elmo? Threaten to burn us down again? How are you going to explain it in the middle of all this?"

"Damn you . . ."

There was a familiar roar in their helmets.

"Something going on here?"

It was Rance.

"Tempers getting a little frayed here, Topman," Renchett answered. "It's been a long day."

Rance halted and fell into a parade rest. He looked Renchett up and down.

"A trooper's temper doesn't get frayed with his overman, Renchett. A trooper doesn't have a temper as far as an overman is concerned."

Renchett snapped to an ironic half attention. "No, Topman Rance. You'll have to put it down to combat fatigue."

"Combat fatigue, my ass."

"Yes, Topman Rance."

Rance turned on Elmo. "Do you want to press formal charges against this man?"

"No, I'll deal with him."

"Then let's get the men bedded down."

He faced the twenty and indicated five freshly dug foxholes over on their right.

"Four men to each hole. There'll be an inspection in thirty minutes. Dyrkin, organize a guard rota. Three of you will rotate on the perimeter, and there'll be one area watch. Now, get going."

"There are three dead."

"Then some of you will have more room to roll around in your sleep."

"We'll look forward to it."

"I'm sure you will, Dyrkin."

Dyrkin led the twenty away. Rance indicated that Elmo should walk with him in the other direction. As soon as the men had gone, his whole attitude changed. There was no more grim banter. He became cold and businesslike, a man who no longer had the time to be angry.

"What the hell do you think you're doing?"

Elmo was taken by complete surprise.

"What are you talking about?"

"I told you to lay back on the longtimers and let Dyrkin and Renchett take care of things. They can handle it. It may be news to you, but I want to keep my longtimers alive. We can't clear this forsaken planet with replacements."

Elmo was too tightly wrapped to accept the advice. His jaw set, and he started straight ahead. "I can run my own twenty."

"The hell you can. They're starting to look like walking corpses."

"It was a bad day."

"It's always a bad day in the jungle."

"This was different."

"Damn it, man, you only lost three men. Whole twenties were wiped out in the center section. What hit you?"

"Miggies."

"How many?"

"A group of twelve."

Rance's voice was like ice. "Twelve?"

"Right."

"A dozen miggies don't make a bad day."

"There was something else."

"What?"

"There were these bodies."

As far as Rance was concerned, Elmo was hanging himself out to dry.

"There are always bodies."

"These were different. They'd been mutilated. Deliberately."

"Mutilated? How?"

"The skin had been flayed off them, and their dicks had been stuffed in their mouths. It was disgusting."

"You're kidding."

"I've never seen anything like it. The men took it bad. They've started telling each other that it's some new psych program."

Rance didn't like the sound of this at all.

"Where was this?"

"Back in the jungle, not too far beyond the perimeter. I fixed the spot."

"I'll call it in. Hopefully they'll send out a data team."

Rance touched a stud on the side of his helmet.

"Open a command channel."

He waited.

"Patch me through to Line Officer Berref."

He waited again.

"What do you mean he's returned to the cluster? Yeah . . . okay."

He glanced at Elmo. "You get a dataspot or just a fix?"

"I took a spot."

"The brain wants you to shoot it in."

"On D-four?"

"Code three."

Elmo touched a similar stud on his helmet, activating a direct link facility that wasn't shared by the ordinary troopers. He waited a few seconds and removed his finger.

"It's in."

Rance was briskly final. "So that's it."

Elmo shook his head. "I don't know."

"Whatever they do with the information, you can be assured that you won't hear anything about it."

"That shit was so weird."

Rance nodded curtly. "It's out of our hands."

Elmo looked back at where the twenty were breaking out their environ bubbles. "What do I do?"

"You? If I had my way, I'd have you shipped back to the rear. The trouble is that I don't have my way. It's been decided that you can't be spared, and you have to lead a twenty even if you kill them all in the process. The way things are, I can't get that reversed."

Elmo grunted. "Don't do me no favors."

"I'm not doing you a favor. As far as I'm concerned, you didn't ought to be leading a combat twenty."

"I'm telling you I can handle it."

"And I'm telling you to back off. Take it as an order —don't take out your problems on your squad."

Elmo's face was stiff and blank. "Is that all?"

Rance sighed. "Yeah, that's all."

Elmo turned on his heel and marched away. Rance watched him go. He seemed to be moving like a robot.

The group of men in each foxhole had combined their individual environ bubbles and spread the resulting transparent sheet over the hole. It was anchored around the edge with rocks and dirt. Once in place, the bubbles slowly inflated until they formed a low protective dome. They also took on the coloring of the surrounding ground. The EBs were living entities, biotailored first cousins of the suits. On a planet that was a vacuum or one that had a poisonous atmosphere, the EBs sealed in an environment of canned air. In an emergency, they could also generate oxygen for the men sheltering inside them. On a planet like this one, however, where the air would have been breathable but for the contaminates and the wildlife, they actually filtered the toxins and impurities through their thick membranes.

Structures were going up all over the assembly area. In addition to the individual foxholes, there were larger command posts and supply marquees. Some were inflatable; others were solid domes that were assembled from portable sections. It was all part of the Therem passion for overorganization. Each time the task force paused in its advance prior to the next push, it felt the need to quickly put up what amounted to a small fortified town. When the force moved on, the town would just as quickly be torn down, leaving a tangle of holes, trenches, and debris to mark its passage.

When the foxholes were set up to everyone's satisfaction and the first guard shift was in position, the remainder of the twenty were free to attend to their most pressing personal needs. The most pressing of all was hot food. After days of living on F-rations and concentrates, any kind of cooked meal had to constitute a luxury. The cookhouse was now open, and there was almost a sense of anticipation as the men made their way to the temporary mess hall. As they eased through the bubble lock and pulled off their helmets and masks, they found

that there was already a long line stretching to the serv-
ing area. Among those first on the line were some of the
raw replacements who had come up on the crawlers.
Dacker immediately took exception to this.

"Will you look at this new meat? We've been out in
the forsaken bush getting our asses shot off and they get
to eat first when they ain't done nothing but ride up here
in comfort."

"Ain't that always the way of it?"

"I say make 'em wait."

Some came down on the side of being reasonable.

"Aah, leave the poor bastards be. They're probably
scared out of their minds."

"So what the hell? I've been scared for as long as I
can remember, and with good reason. I'm going to the
front and get myself some food."

Dacker defiantly started toward the head of the line.
After only a moment's hesitation, the others followed,
even those who hadn't agreed with him. As the troopers
elbowed their way to the front there were a couple of
protests from the new recruits, but these were quickly
silenced by glares from the longtimers. One of the mess
orderlies was less easily intimidated. He set down his
ladle and returned Dacker's angry stare.

"You men get back in line or you don't get served."

"Say what?"

"You heard me."

Dacker leaned forward so his face was very close to
the orderly's. "Now you listen to me, dickhead. Not
more than sixty minutes ago I was in combat, almost
overrun by chibas. In another sixty minutes, I intend to
be fast asleep with a full belly. Are you telling me that
I've got to waste my precious downtime waiting on line
while a bunch of pussy-assed new meat get their chow in
front of me? What were you doing an hour ago, watching
the soup on a burner?"

The orderly stood his ground. "The rule here is first come, first served, no exceptions. So you heroes can just get to the back of the line."

"Can you imagine the disaster area we could make out of this place?"

"Can you imagine what will happen to you if you start anything in here?"

"So what can they do? Shoot us? We'll be back in combat tomorrow."

There was complaining back down the line that quickly built in volume to curses and catcalls. No food had been served since Dacker and the others had walked to the front of the line, and the line was getting impatient. A supply overman emerged from the rear kitchen area.

"What the hell's going on here? What's the holdup?" A steel plate that covered more than half of his forehead indicated that he was a wounded combat veteran who had been placed on light duties. The head injury made his speech a little strange, but there didn't seem to be anything wrong with his thinking. "You men just in from the bush?"

"Damn right we are."

He glanced at the orderly. "Go ahead, feed 'em and get the whole bunch out of the way."

The orderly started to protest, but the overman stopped him with a look. "Just get them out of here."

Dacker grinned. "Just get us out of here."

The orderly scowled but started slopping out the food.

As Hawk walked back down the line with his full tray, he couldn't help looking into the faces of the new intake. Poor little bleeders. They were like blank pages waiting to be written on. Sure, they were afraid, but that was it—no marks, no scars. Their skins were smooth and unblemished, and there was nothing in their eyes but apprehension. He thought back to when he had been like that. It seemed like a lifetime ago.

The sun dropped behind the hills, and the river valley sank into deep shadow. The lights came on around the perimeter. The minutes after sunset were the darkest of the whole half night. Then the huge parent planet would start to rise beyond the opposite horizon. At first the giant world was nothing more than a thin luminous band, a second horizon with a slight curve on the leading edge. Rapidly, though, it grew and grew, filling up the sky with its enormous bulk and casting a bright twilight over the jungle that turned the fungus ghostly pale. The planet was an expanse of parchment-yellow banded with strips of red, orange, and purple that slowly twisted and rippled and spiraled into great ponderous vortices as they were driven by the unimaginably violent storms that tore through its deep, dense atmosphere.

The night sounds began, dominated by the booming moan of the big green lizards. The big lizards seemed to make a nocturnal practice of raising their long necks to the sky and baying at the planet. It wasn't an unusual sight to see four or five of them, with necks intertwined and heads raised in unison, moaning together as a group. Above and around their bellows, the smaller creatures shrieked and howled. One particular species—nobody was quite sure which because nobody'd actually seen it—had become a particular favorite of the ground forces. It made a croaking noise that could be approximated by the word "walleye." Isolated troopers had taken to duplicating the cry. With surreal bravado, they'd yell back into the night.

"Walleye!"

"Walleye!"

Already the call of this jungle campaign was echoing around the perimeter.

"Walleye."

"Walleye."

With Dyrkin giving out the details, none of the old-timers had pulled guard duty. When he'd finished eating, Hark found that although exhausted, he wasn't ready to sleep. He wanted to be on his own for a while. That was also something of a luxury. He slipped on his mask, not bothering with his helmet, and wriggled out of the bubble. He felt a little dizzy—Renchett and Kemlo were inside the foxhole sharing a small vial of totally illegal sweet gas. He turned his back on the big planet. It tended to hang over everything like a great psychological weight, and the last thing Hark needed was any kind of additional burden. He walked slowly as far as a parked crawler and sat down on one of its rear treads. To the east, there was a red glow beyond the hills. It might have been an erupting volcano. This young planet was made even more unstable by the clutching gravity of the big mother. On the other hand, it could have been flying wings, firestorming a section of jungle. Somewhere on the perimeter there was a brief chatter of fire. Hark looked around but didn't react in any other way. There had been a time when he would have jumped and grabbed for his weapon. Now he waited until he was called. The hell with it. It was probably just some piece of new meat shooting at shadows.

It was all becoming a matter of time—time in the jungle, time lying in a foxhole trying to sleep but not to dream. The passage of time was marked by the missing faces, all the faces that had started together but had vanished one by one. There was no point in pretending that he wouldn't one day become one of those faces. That was the ultimate matter of time. He wished that some bootleg had surfaced in the temporary camp. Sweet gas didn't do it for him, but alcohol could be trusted to take him away from the war for some unconscious minutes.

"Feeling like baying at the moon?" Dyrkin had come silently around the side of the crawler.

Hark shrugged. "Haven't gotten around to it yet, but there are times when it feels tempting."

The walleye creature croaked, and there was a chorus of shouts from the perimeter. Dyrkin shook his head. "At least you haven't started hollering 'walleye.'"

"I never did think it was a good idea to start advertising my position."

"There are those who just have to do it. I guess it helps convince them that they exist."

"I never had that problem."

"You mind if I sit down?"

"Help yourself."

Dyrkin sat next to Hark on the tread and produced a small metal flask. "You want a belt?"

Hark nodded. "Sure do. You want to step inside? Renchett and Kemlo are getting out of their brains in our foxhole."

Dyrkin shook his head. "We can drink out here as long as you don't breathe in."

In one smooth motion, he flipped up his mask, took a pull on the flask himself, replaced the mask, and handed the flask to Hark.

Hark repeated the process with equal skill; then he swallowed and shuddered. "Bootleg gets worse and worse."

"I hear they're making it from fungus and defoliant."

"It tastes like it."

Hark passed the flask back, and Dyrkin took a second swig. For a while they sat in silence, then Dyrkin passed the flask again.

"You know something?"

Hark shuddered again. "What?"

"You've come a long way since that first day on the messdeck when I beat you up."

"I guess I have." Hark thought for a moment. "I've wondered about that. How come you picked on me?"

"I always have to beat up one of a new intake. It's part of the system. It's called imprinting."

"But why me?"

"You looked like you could take it."

Hark laughed. It wasn't something that he did particularly often.

"There's plenty of taking it in this game."

"That's all there is."

The two men sat in silence again, just drinking and staring into the night. Finally Dyrkin coughed.

"You still seem pretty good at taking it."

"Don't have too much choice."

Hark found that he was copying the topgun's slow, economical speech pattern. Dyrkin didn't show that he noticed.

"You don't even seem to be letting Elmo get to you."

"If you want my opinion," Hark said, "I think he's going to kill us all."

"And it don't bother you."

"Sure it bothers me. It bothers me a lot, but since there ain't a forsaken thing that I can do about it, I try not to let him stress me out."

"Back when I was new on the *Hyma 1*, the old-timers used to talk about what they called learning the calm. I guess that's what you've done. Learned the calm. Only you call it not letting it stress you out."

Hark didn't say anything. Dyrkin had to be leading up to something even if he was taking his sweet time getting to it. Dyrkin looked up at the sky and then directly at Hark.

"We may need a whole lot of calm pretty soon."

"You figure it's going to be hairy tomorrow?"

"I not only figure it's going to be hairy tomorrow, but I also didn't like those bodies today. They could be the start of something new and bad." Dyrkin paused. "That's not all, though."

"I kind of thought it wasn't."

"If something has to be done about Elmo, we're going to need all the calm we can get."

"Are you telling me something?"

Dyrkin looked Hark straight in the eye. "Just making an observation."

He rubbed the steel prosthesis between his hand and elbow.

"Still have feeling in the damn thing after all this time." He stood up. "I'm going to get some sleep. Like I said, I have a feeling it's going to be hairy tomorrow."

As Dyrkin walked away, Hark was grateful for the alcohol that was warming his system. There was a chill coming down.

# THIRTEEN

THE Yal forces hit them well before the sun was due up. The first sign of attack was a glowing green energy cloud that rose at the head of the valley and then drifted slowly downriver. Its appearance threw the base into alarm and quite a degree of panic. When it sank to the ground, it would vaporize anything beneath it—and it was coming straight at the base. Some men ran to their battle stations, and others just ran. Still more merely stood and stared at the deadly cloud as if mesmerized by it. Inside the domes and the foxholes, men were struggling into their equipment. Anti-Air Defense was hastily readied. Noncoms bellowed and screamed at their twenties. A handful of recruits threw themselves flat, trying to dig down into the burned earth. Everyone who had a helmet on was deafened by a cacophony of cross-communication and the roaring static that was generated by the approaching cloud. A number of gunsaucers were burning fuel, warming up prior to lifting.

The AADs opened up, splitting the sky with violet streaks of fire. The dynes were also coming alive. Their eyes glowed as they powered up their weapon systems. The cloud was getting close. The dynes also started firing. Multiple energy flares flashed from their eyes and ripped into the cloud. It seemed to slow as every heavy weapon on the base poured fire into it. A ragged cheer from the men followed a series of explosions inside the cloud. It started to fragment. Portions of it sank down into jungle that was immediately consumed by blinding white light. Other parts touched down on the surface of the river and were transformed into roaring gushers of superheated steam.

The outpouring of fire from the base wasn't, however, completely effective. A small green fireball from the heart of the cloud, probably the fragment that contained the motivator, plunged on, losing height but making directly for the base. It hit at the very edge of the perimeter, and the white fire blossomed upward. Men on the extreme margins of the blast staggered away screaming, their backpods melting and their bodies trailing clouds of smoke from their charred suits. Others were blown apart when the energy packs on their MEWs exploded. A squad of nohans were cooked inside their armor. First one and then two more gunsaucers blew up where they stood. One managed to get into the air before the fireball hit, but the shock wave caught it and flipped it over. It crashed into the jungle and started a fire of its own.

The white fire on the perimeter seemed to have been the signal for the chibas. They came in their thousands, wailing the nerve-jangling chorus of high electric trills that always accompanied their mass attacks. Their losses were horrendous. Without hesitation, the first wave plunged straight into the mines, the wire, and the fixed line autos. They were mown down in their hundreds. Some lost limbs to the wire and continued to drag themselves forward, firing as they went. When they finally failed, the ones behind charged straight over them. The chiba bodies were piled up so high in front of the buffer fields that they simply shorted out and collapsed. There was no instinct of self-preservation in the goop that passed as chibas' brains, just a relentless, almost mindless hostility that kept them coming and coming, breaking out through the fungus, pounding across the open space beyond the perimeter with their strange mechanical run and then hurling themselves into the defenses. They must have been massing under cover of the jungle all through the night. The longtimers couldn't believe that there hadn't been patrols sent out. Were the medians really that confident? Not that the longtimers, or any of the other troopers, had much time to ponder tactics. To the last man, they had their hands full holding back the onrushing lines of chibas. Even the cookhouse help and the walking wounded found themselves with weapons in their hands, formed into makeshift combat teams and pushed into foxholes. Their only hope of saving their lives was to keep up a withering stream of fire until their weapons threatened to melt.

The hot spot was where the energy fragment had burned a gaping hole in the set-piece defenses. The chibas had moved directly up to the still blazing fires. Briefly, they'd halted. Specialists had come forward, spraying the molten ground with liquid nitrogen until all fires had gone and it was black slag covered with a thick layer of frost. The defenders had picked off dozens of them, but the enemy seemed to have an inexhaustible supply of every variety of chiba.

"Where the hell did they get these numbers?"

"And how did they assemble them without us hearing them?"

"The bastards can be quiet as the grave when they want to be."

As the first horde of chibas came streaming through the gap, Rance had led his twenties in a fast flanking movement against them. It wasn't that he had any desire to be a hero, but he was in the right place and the breakthrough had to be halted. If the chibas weren't stopped, they'd be all over the interior of the base, and everyone in it would be cut to pieces. He knew how deadly a chiba horde could be when it got in among a disorganized and uncoordinated enemy. His first objective was a system of shallow trenches on the right of the gap. There was no one in them, their original occupants having burned, but they had remained largely intact. They were an ideal position from which to direct fire at the chibas coming through the gap. There was one snag. Between his men and the trenches, there was an open expanse of bare ground that was being raked by a PBA that the chibas had brought in with them. He could make it to the trenches okay, but he'd certainly lose up to a third of his men in the process. That was hardly the object of the exercise. He looked wildly around for another solution. The big planet was setting and soon the sun would be coming up, but for the moment, it was getting darker. The irregular green flashes from the PBA and the multicolors of the scattered return fire seemed doubly bright. He spotted a crawler some distance behind them, maneuvering aimlessly. He prayed that his communicator could cut through all the conflicting noises.

"Crawler nine, crawler nine! I need your help to plug that hole in the perimeter."

After a short but agonizing pause, there was a voice in his helmet. "This is crawler nine, we hear you."

"This is Topman Rance. I have my twenties up ahead of you. I need you to give me cover across that open space."

"We have you on scope, Topman Rance. We're moving up."

The armored hulk grated toward them on its huge treads. Rance waved his men back.

"Fall in behind the crawler! Use it as cover."

The men didn't need urging more than once. Crouching low, they bunched up behind the big machine as it moved into the open space, dragging its bulk laboriously forward like some monster metal crustacean. One man wasn't fast enough. He was caught in the open by chiba fire. The top half of his body was smeared over the side of the crawler, while his legs and hips, quite untouched, fell back, still kicking. The crawler immediately came under fire from the PBA. Where the particle beams hit, spots on its high-density armor briefly glowed red, but it suffered no other damage. Its prow guns opened up, and the PBA was silenced. The chibas started to fall back, retreating through the gap. Rance's twenties were now level with the trenches.

"Quick! Move it! Get down in that trench system."

Some of the men were reluctant to leave the shelter of the crawler, but with Rance behind them they had no choice. Quickly, a hundred men were down on their bellies, worming their way along the trench system. The crawler commander's voice crackled over Rance's communicator.

"I'm going to pull back. If they bring up a punisher, I'm dead meat at this range."

"Thanks for the assist, crawler nine."

"You're welcome."

Rance gripped his weapon and slid into the trench. If they brought up a punisher, everyone in the area would be dead meat, but presumably a piece of heavy armor was worth more than his men. Certainly his men were more replaceable.

"Look alive! Spread out along the trenches! The chibas will be pushing back again as soon as the crawler pulls out."

"Why the fuck can't it stay and give us covering fire?"

"Shut up, Renchett."

The chibas were streaming back into the gap, but the fire from the trenches at least temporarily checked them.

A gunsaucer ran fast and low along the perimeter line, strafing the attackers, but then it flipped up as it ran into return fire from the ground. The dynes had also moved into action. Towering over the base, they were unable to do anything about the intense fighting around their feet. The risk of hitting their own men was too high. Instead, they pumped fire into the surrounding jungle in the hope of destroying any Yal reserves that were still waiting to move up. Although temporarily taken by surprise, the Therem forces were quickly responding. The perimeter was holding, and the chibas were taking terrible losses. Then the ground around the trenches began to shake violently.

"Motherfuck, they're pushing a thumper at us!"

There were muffled screams in everyone's helmet as a section of trench collapsed and five men were buried alive. Rance was immediately yelling into his communicator.

"Don't panic! Breathe normally and dig yourselves out."

Three men struggled out of the loose dirt. Two didn't. They had either panicked themselves into shock or lost their masks in the cave-in and suffocated. The ground shook again. Another section collapsed, but this time no one was buried. The longtimers had their trenchers out, ready to dig if necessary.

"That thing's got to be stopped!"

Rance opened a command channel. "This is Topman Rance requesting an air strike."

"State your position, Topman Rance."

Rance's voice was calm and by the book. "I'm at the gap in the perimeter. I have the enemy contained, but they're using a thumper against me, and my trenches are collapsing."

"Your air strike is being ordered."

The ground vibrated for a full five seconds. The

tremor was more intense than the previous one. The firing faltered as dozens of men were freeing themselves from the loose earth that was cascading down all along the complex of trenches.

"Please make it fast."

A dozen or so chibas were through the gap and racing toward the trenches. They were cut down only a few meters from the first trench. Rance quickly scanned the sky. Where the hell was the air strike? Had the goddamn saucer jocks chickened out on him? A couple more tremors and the chibas would be in among them. Finally he spotted the aircraft. Two saucers were running fast from the other side of the base with sunguns blazing down at the ground. They swept over the twenty's position and out beyond the perimeter, then they turned and came back. They made two more passes before the command channel came alive.

"Rance, we've pinned your thumper."

There was the sound of engines in the background.

"Taking it out now."

The saucers halted in midair and started pouring fire directly at the ground. There was an explosion. The saucers peeled away.

"There you go, Rance. Don't say we never do anything for you ground monkeys."

"Many thanks."

The chibas withdrew as fast as they had come. It was as if a sudden loss-cutting decision had been made by the Yal generals. Some alien calculation of cost-effectiveness seemed to have indicated that the chibas would not be able to overrun the base and stay within some strange limit of acceptable losses. The engagement had simply been terminated. Looking at the piled heaps of dead chiba wreckage, though, it was hard to imagine what those limits could possibly be. There was an eerie unreality to the way the fighting abruptly stopped. It was

intensified by the fact that the contact was broken off at
the very moment that the sun first showed over the hills.
As the light filtered into the valley, casting the first long
shadows of dawn, the chibas fought a swift rearguard
action and melted away into the jungle, leaving the fallen
behind them. A terrible silence settled over the base as
the firing stopped. Here and there a wounded man was
screaming. The jungle animals appeared to sense that the
fighting was over, and their dawn cries filled the thick,
sluggish, smoke-filled air as if it were any normal day.
The men on the ground stayed exactly where they were,
expecting a trick. The gunsaucers silently pulled back
and regrouped, hovering over the center of the base. A
dyne took a pace forward and sprayed the jungle with a
final sweep of fire. The dawn chorus faltered. The ports
of a crawler clanged open, and its crew climbed wearily
down the cabin ladder. When they reached the ground,
they simply dropped to the dirt and sat with their heads
between their knees. The communicators were a level
hum with just the faintest undertow of heavy breathing
and muttered curses. One man straightened and clam-
bered out of his foxhole. A second followed. A third
took off his helmet. All over the base, men were standing
up as the realization spread that the firefight was really
over. There was little conversation. Men looked around
at the whole picture, shaking their heads and grimly mar-
veling that they had survived yet another one. They in-
spected the wreckage and the dead, and a few cautiously
walked to the perimeter, toward the tangle of chibas'
frames and the goop soaking into the scorched earth.
Some even broke into their ration packs and started eating. All over there was the lethargy and depression that
was left behind as the suits stopped their chemical mas-
sage.

The calm didn't last very long. The noncoms started
yelling, pushing men into exhausted, round-shouldered

ranks. They called the rolls and tallied the missing. The complaining had started. Bitching was the second stage of reaction.

"I gotta tell you all, I thought we were going to hear the fat lady singing back there."

"How the hell did they get so close to us without us knowing? That's what I want to know."

"We don't never get to know nothing, asswipe."

"I just want to sleep for a couple of days, that's all I want."

"Don't it bother you that the medians are screwing up?"

"Sure it bothers me, but what the hell do you want me to do about it?"

"The medians always screw up."

"That's the whole story."

The earth shook slightly as all three dynes started to move forward. The conversation stopped dead. Crawler crews were reluctantly saddling up again. Sappers had begun to dismantle the temporary structures. Helot looked at Hark. His face was a mask of disbelief.

"We're going after them?"

"You got to be kidding."

The longtimers confronted Rance.

"Is that it? Are we going after them?"

The dynes had waded out into the river and were striding upstream. The gunsaucers were making a wide formation pass across the valley. The crawlers were pulling into line. Rance didn't have to nod.

"Those are the orders."

There was a storm of protest, but even the men doing the protesting knew that it was futile.

"At least you're among the lucky ones," Rance said. "You're all going to ride a crawler up the river."

Elmo's twenty was assigned to crawler 3—except that there was no sign of Elmo. They straggled toward the machine and swung themselves through the port, only to discover him waiting inside the passenger bay.

"What fucking hole were you hiding in?" Renchett snarled.

Elmo's face was as blank as his visor. "I don't know what you're talking about."

Renchett made a disgusted gesture. "Forget it. I ain't got the strength."

The amphibious crawlers slid down the bank and nosed into the water. The overhead compartment covers started to close. The last thing Hark saw before they closed completely was a dead, bloated lizard floating belly up in the shallows of the opposite bank. The covers sealed with a hiss. The lights came on. The compartment was pressurized. The troopers started taking off their helmets and masks. Rations and water were broken out, but a lot of the men just sat hunkered down, backs against the wall, too tired to eat.

Crawler 3 moved smoothly up the river. The majority of the troopers slept. It was an uneasy, uncomfortable sleep, cursed by dreams. Elmo just stared straight ahead in a semitrance, as if he didn't even have what it took to make nightmares anymore.

There was only one incident during the trip upriver. After seventy uneventful minutes, the craft lurched and there was a series of loud bangs. The troopers grabbed for their masks, helmets, and weapons. They had to be taking fire from the bank. A section of the hull was warm to the touch. The crawler's own guns opened up. Inside the passenger bay, the lights flickered. Everyone was crouching on the steel floor, ready for anything. There were two more series of shocks, and then the crawler heeled over in a sharp left-hand turn. Moments later, it did the same to the right. After it straightened out, the men braced for the next shock, but nothing happened. The crawler remained on an even keel, and the guns stopped. Nothing else hit the craft, and the incident seemed to be over. Confirmation came from a voice in their helmets.

"Hope that didn't shake you up too much. We had a bit of nastiness from the bank, but we seem to have nailed it. We're proceeding on course."

Things had only just settled down when there was a new voice in their helmets.

"All ground troops will hear this."

"It's a forsaken officer."

"That's got to mean trouble."

"Our long-range scouts have discovered an enemy tunnel system that covers most of the upper parts of this valley and extends through the hills. This has to be the means by which they were able to mass so quickly last night before attacking the task force. Accordingly, we have been given the responsibility of clearing and destroying these tunnels."

"What do you mean 'we,' asshole? You won't be in the goddamn tunnels."

"You will be issued with your individual orders as you disembark from the transport. It only remains for me to wish you luck with this mission."

The men were silent. What they had heard was close to a death warrant. The longtimers had encountered Yal tunnels before. Tunnel clearing always involved severe casualties.

"I hate tunnels."

There was unashamed fear in the voice. It belonged to Tabor, who had been with the twenty for some forty days. Nobody seemed to have anything to add.

Something grated under the crawler's hull. It lurched as it reared up onto its treads and started to climb the riverbank. Finally it leveled off and stopped. The original voice was back in their helmets.

"You can all relax. As of now, there's no one shooting at us."

When the ports were opened, the first thing they saw as they came down the ramp was Rance. The topman was standing waiting for them.

"I don't want to hear any complaining. I'm no more pleased about it than you are."

The crawler had halted on a flat area of river beach. Beyond it, the side of the valley rose sharply. Sappers had already burned away a large section of jungle, revealing the mouth of a large, previously hidden tunnel that was driven horizontally straight into the hillside. Rance pointed to it.

"That's your one. Take a good look at it."

Take a good look because the odds are that you will die in there, he thought.

"Nothing happened when we opened it up, so we can probably assume that the first stretch is empty. It may well be gimmicked, though, so be exceedingly careful."

He glanced at Elmo, who was staring transfixed at the tunnel entrance.

"Are you netted into the schematic?"

Elmo didn't answer.

"Do you hear me, Overman Elmo?"

Elmo twitched and then looked at Rance. "What did you say?"

Rance's voice was acid. "I asked if you were netted into the schematic of the tunnel system."

"Yes ... yes, I'm getting it in my visor."

"Then why don't you take your men into the tunnel."

"You're not coming in with us?"

Rance shook his head. "I'm coordinating this one."

Elmo took one more long look at the tunnel mouth, and he seemed to pull himself together. He faced the men.

"Okay, let's get moving. The sooner we get in, the sooner we get out."

"If we get out."

Elmo ignored the remark. Behind them, the crawler was up on its treads and easing back into the river. The thirteen men, all that were left of the twenty, started up the slope toward the tunnel. They halted again before actually going inside.

"Check your redscopes."

Each man turned on the heat vision option in his visor. Where the interior of the tunnel had been pitch-black, it was now a threatening red. There were no more excuses for delay.

"Okay, let's do it."

They moved cautiously into the darkness, as if they were treading on glass. The tension showed with every pace. Kemlo took the point, with Dyrkin right behind him. Elmo stayed well to the rear.

Dacker, who was seventh in line, craned up to look at the ceiling. "I never did like the idea of having a whole goddamn hill over my head."

"Cut out that talking."

They moved on in silence. Behind them, the sky was nothing more than a small disk of brightness beyond the tunnel mouth. The redness in Hark's visor created the illusion that he was walking through the intestines of a giant. The datashot hadn't included much information about anatomy, but he'd learned more than enough on the battlefield to feed the fantasy.

"Hold it back there," Dyrkin barked.

The thirteen halted. Dyrkin, walking point, was in effective command of the squad. It was the way everyone, with the possible exception of Elmo, wanted it. Dyrkin would take no chances. There was an opening in the left wall of the main corridor. It was the first one that they'd encountered, and for all they knew, it could be full of chibas just waiting to boil out all over them. In these kinds of situations, chibas seemingly had infinite patience. Dyrkin waved his arm in a low sweep that everyone understood. The column moved away from the center of the corridor and pressed against the wall. Dyrkin had stopped a few meters before the opening. He spoke softly into his communicator.

"Elmo, any sign of this on the schematic?"

"No, there's nothing. This is supposed to be a straight corridor with no turns or intersections."

Elmo seemed content to let Dyrkin run the squad. Dyrkin waved up the next man in line, a recruit with the minimal name of Kov. He indicated that the man should get in front of him. The routine was simple. They edged their way along the wall with weapons at the ready. When they reached the entrance, Kov ducked briefly and adjusted the grav on his boots. When he'd straightened, they both took a deep breath that was audible in everyone's helmet. Kov made a grav jump straight across the opening. At the same time, Dyrkin spun around and fired from the corner. Immediately afterward, Kov fired from the opposite side. The concussion blasts were like hammer blows in the confined space. Although their helmets protected their ears, their bodies were kicked by the shocks. Their lungs felt as if they were suddenly being hugged by a huge constrictor. Dust cascaded down from the roof of the tunnel.

The firing stopped; Dyrkin stepped back from the opening, putting up his MEW and letting it rest against his shoulder.

"Ain't nothing in there."

The others moved up and peered into the opening. Dyrkin had been right. There was nothing in there except a pile of dark blue hexagonal cargo containers and a rack of gleaming new chiba frames, presumably waiting to have the sacs of intelligent goop fitted to them. Glowing scars of residual heat from the firing crisscrossed the walls. One of the containers had fallen and burst open. Its contents, a kind of gray packing fiber, had spilled out and were burning, giving off oily smoke.

"Don't touch any of that stuff. It's probably booby-trapped."

Two explosions came from somewhere else in the tunnel system. Some of the men ducked. More dirt fell from the tunnel ceiling. A meter-square section detached itself and crashed to the floor. Everyone froze. In tunnel clearing, the other hazard, apart from the enemy, was cave-in. This planet was so young and unstable that tunneling into it was a dubious business at the best of times. The constant low-level quakes meant that the best reinforced tunnel was prone to collapse even without a firefight inside it. The men waited tensely. There were no further rockfalls.

"Did anybody think that the Yal's best bet would be to wait until we were all inside and then blow the whole system?"

"I don't want to hear that talk." There was no authority in Elmo's voice. It was pure fear.

Dyrkin slung his weapon over his back. "You want that we should move on?"

The squad pressed on deep into the hill. There were sounds of firing and more explosions from other parts of the system, but nothing engaged them except a handful of miggies that dropped from the ceiling and were quickly dispatched. At regular intervals, wafts of scalding hot air washed down the tunnel. These only helped to accentuate the feeling that they were parasites in the bowels of some monstrous beast. Every step was racked with tension. Just because nothing had happened so far didn't mean it couldn't happen at any moment. The troopers, particularly the new recruits, flinched at every sound and movement. Already frayed nerves were being stretched to their limits. The prolonged stress involved in a search-and-destroy mission was bad enough in the open. In these claustrophobic tunnels, it was close to unbearable.

Dyrkin called another halt. Up ahead, there was what looked like a yellow glow in their redscoped visors. As far as they could see, the tunnel was opening out into a larger lighted space. The air had become very warm, so warm that it was starting to interfere with the function of the redscopes. The walls were now pulsing with a blood-red light, and the men were pouring sweat. The yellow glow seemed to be the source of it all. Nobody had any particular desire to be the first to find out exactly what it was. Finally, when Elmo offered no suggestions, let alone orders, Dyrkin beckoned to Hark and Renchett.

"Okay, let's go and see what we got here."

The three of them walked slowly forward, silhouetted against the yellow glow. Their weapons were held in front of them, away from their bodies, ready to fire at the widest possible sweep.

"When the tunnel opens out, keep on going. Hark, go to the left; Renchett, you go to the right. Look for cover and hit it. Best cut out your redscopes; that yellow light's going to blind us."

For a moment, the three men couldn't see, but then their eyes adjusted to regular light. Now that they weren't looking at heat, the yellow was little more than a suffused purple glow.

"That's plasma."

"It must be a main energy interface."

Renchett halted. "Then it's got to be defended."

"So let's go in and find out," Dyrkin said.

"Do we have to?" Renchett said.

"You got a better idea?"

"No."

The spectacle that greeted them was little short of

awesome. The tunnel had opened out into a wide, high-ceilinged, roughly circular cavern that seemed to be at least partly natural. The centerpiece was a tall translucent column that rose for the full height of the cavern and then vanished through the roof. A massive charge of plasma was pulsing up it. This was the source of the purple glow. In addition to the channeled plasma, white flares of secondary energy flickered on the outside of the power stack. The base of the column was a large containment sphere of dull black, extradense metal. It was supported by five heavy-duty grav pumpers. Without their aid, the sphere would simply have sunk into the ground and gone on sinking until it reached the center of the planet. The sphere had to be unbelievably massive. It contained what was, in effect, a miniature sun. It was banded by an intricate system of interconnected subducts. Below the sphere, the ducts ran out and away, across the floor in a sunburst that extended all the way to the walls of the cavern. These were also attended by outward ripples of dancing static. As Dyrkin had guessed, it was a major energy interface.

"Mother! It's big!"

"This sucker could power a couple of firetowers."

"Move it!"

There was no time to stand and stare. Renchett and Hark peeled off as they came out of the tunnel, just as Dyrkin had instructed. Hark spotted a pile of the hexagonal containers that seemed to be a standard item with the Yal. He ran for them, jumping the ducts as he went. When there were no more ducts, he dived and rolled. So far, there was no one shooting at them.

In position behind the containers, Hark tentatively called out to Dyrkin. "Nothing so far. You think this place is empty?"

The plasma was crackling in their helmets.

"Seems hard to believe they'd just leave it."

Renchett came in. "I don't like it."

Hark carefully studied the cavern. Other tunnels ran into it at regular intervals all around its circumference. The spaces in between them were taken up with racks of what, alien as it was, had to be control and monitoring equipment. A gantry, constructed from one molded piece of an ultrahard ceramic, ran around the containment sphere, some three meters above the ground. A broad ramp of the same material ran down from the gantry and into the mouth of the widest of the intersecting tunnels. Where the ramp and the gantry joined, there was a huge black chair. It appeared to have been contoured for some large, angular multilegged creature.

Renchett hissed in his helmet. "You know what that is? That contour chair?"

"What is it?"

"It's Yal. It was built for a Yal. There's been a Yal here."

There was almost reverence in his voice. Most humans never so much as came close to a Yal. To be where one might recently have been was sufficient to inspire awe.

Hawk whispered back to him. "You never told us you saw a Yal."

"I never did. Never saw a Therem either, for that matter. I heard plenty, though. Big black bastards, all legs and joints with a dark energy shimmer around them like they weren't completely in the same dimension as us."

"I heard the Therem were—"

"Knock that off." Dyrkin didn't seem to be as impressed as Renchett or Hark. "You sound like a couple of recruits."

"There's been a goddamn Yal in here."

Dyrkin ignored him. "I'm going to move forward. Stay put and cover me."

He ran alongside one of the floor ducts toward the center until he found shelter behind one of the gantry supports. Still nothing happened.

"I'm going to take a look into that wide tunnel."

"Is that a good idea?"

"Somebody's got to."

His suit had to be pumping.

"You want us to back you up?"

"Stay put. I'm just going to take a look. If anything happens, get the hell out of here."

"You can bet on that."

Dyrkin ran in a low crouch, keeping well under the cover of the ramp. Still nothing. He reached the mouth of the tunnel and flattened against the wall beside it. Slowly, he craned forward and peered up the tunnel.

"Not a damn thing. Just another tunnel."

"You think we should bring up the others?"

"Not yet. I want to check out a couple more of these."

"Okay."

Dyrkin moved from tunnel mouth to tunnel mouth.

"The whole area seems deserted."

"Let's call up the others."

"Yeah, screw it. We can't do nothing more on our own. Yo, Elmo, can you hear me?"

"I can hear you."

"What we have here is a major energy interface, and it's secure as it's going to be. I got to warn you, though, it could be a trap. It don't feel right that a thing like this should be left unguarded."

"Maybe we should hold back here for a while."

"Why? If there're chibas waiting to jump us, they would have done it by now. If there is a trap, it won't be sprung until we've all moved up here."

"All the more reason to stay where we are."

"You chickenshit bastard, Elmo. You expect us to sit around here waiting for the axe to fall?"

"I don't have to listen to your shit."

"Move up, damn it!"

"I don't have to take orders from you."

It was at that moment that the chibas hit. They came out of one of the tunnels that Dyrkin hadn't examined. Hark and Renchett opened fire, giving him a chance to scramble into cover. Hark noticed that when he fired past the energy stack, the fire from his MEW was noticeably deflected, bending around the curve of the containment sphere. He had to aim accordingly. Dyrkin, who was now on the other side of the cavern, also started blasting at the chibas. The three-way cross fire managed to keep the chibas at bay in the tunnel. Dyrkin was yelling into his communicator.

"Elmo! Move up, damn it! We're under attack!"

"What sort of numbers?"

"Fuck the numbers, just get up here and bail us out."

"How many enemy are there?"

"I don't know! We've got them bottled up in a tunnel, but we can't hold them too long."

"I'm holding this position."

"Damn you, Elmo."

There was a confusion of shouting in the communicators, then Helot was yelling.

"Hold on, I'm coming!"

Helot, Kemlo, and two others came out of the tunnel mouth, immediately drawing fire from the chibas. They all scattered for cover. Kemlo wasn't fast enough. He was hit square in the back. Blood fountained. There was no way that he could only be wounded. The chibas were now pressing forward. A squad was crawling across the floor, using the power ducts and even their own dead as cover.

"Elmo! Bring the others up here!"

There was no answer.

Dyrkin rose from cover, sprayed the crawling chibas with a long blast of lasertrace, then ducked down again. Enemy return fire spattered all around his position.

"I'm out on a limb here . . . Hark? Can you hear me?"

"I hear you."

"Can you get back to the rest of the squad?"

Hark looked over his shoulder. He didn't fancy breaking cover and running the gauntlet of chiba fire back to the original tunnel, but it was no time to argue.

"I guess so. It'll be hairy, but I can try."

"Get back and convince Elmo to send up the rest of them. Make him get on the command channel. We need reinforcements here."

"Suppose he don't want to?"

"Just convince him."

Hark looked carefully around. There were no chibas near him. Crouching low, he left the cover of the hexagonal containers and sprinted. Sporadic fire flashed at his heels, but he reached the tunnel mouth unscathed. Elmo and the remaining troopers were waiting some distance down the tunnel, hugging the walls, weapons at the ready.

"Move the goddamn men up. Those guys in there are going to get creamed." Elmo shook his head. His voice was flat. "Nobody's moving anywhere. We're outnumbered. The only thing we can do is pull back."

"Dyrkin, Renchett, and Helot are in there. Kemlo's been killed already."

"They're expendable."

"You bastard."

Elmo tapped his weapon. "So are you, for that matter."

Hark slowly raised his MEW until it was pointed straight at the overman. "I'm not leaving my friends to die."

"So what are you going to do? Kill me?"

"If I have to. I want you to send in the rest of the twenty and then get on the command channel and call up reinforcements."

"And if I don't?"

"Then I'm going to spread your guts all over this tunnel."

"You're not going to do anything to me, boy."

There was a flurry of weapon fire from back in the cavern. Hark knew that time was running out.

"Just do what I say."

"I'll tell you why you won't do anything to me. It's called imprinting. Apart from Rance, I was the first thing you saw after you came out of the datashot. I'm like your mother, boy. You can't do anything to me."

"I'm going to count to three." Hark took a deep breath. "One . . ."

He was very aware that everyone was watching. It was possible that Elmo was right. Maybe he couldn't kill a noncom. Maybe his programming wouldn't let him, or maybe he didn't have it in him.

"Two."

Elmo slowly turned away. He faced the others.

"I've heard enough of this crap. Start moving back down the tunnel."

Hark didn't bother to count three. He touched the firing stud and blasted Elmo. As the MEW bucked in his hands, there was a sense of complete unreality. The overman staggered forward and fell. His body was all but cut in half. The others were staring at him openmouthed. Hark rounded on them with a snarl.

"Get into that cavern and help the others. Dacker, you're in charge."

"Me?"

Hark knew that he was near the end of his rope. "Just do what I say, damn it!"

Dacker recognized the desperation in his tone. "Okay, okay." He waved the troopers ahead. "Let's get in there and see what we can do."

Hark waited until the others had moved up the tunnel, then he knelt down beside Elmo's body. He took off his helmet, placed it on the ground, and reached out for Elmo's, the noncom model with the command-channel link. He stopped; he didn't want to touch the dead man's helmet. He closed his eyes, fumbled for the facemask, and ripped it loose. He opened his eyes again and took a firm grip on the helmet. At first it resisted. He tugged harder and twisted. It slid off the head. There was blood coming from Elmo's mouth. The dead face looked tired and old. The spell was broken. Whatever hold Elmo might have had on him was gone. The overman was just another body. Hark placed the helmet on his own head, checked the twenty's position on the projected schematic, and opened the command channel.

"Twenty at coordinates 435-623-678, we have run into a large force of chibas around a main energy interface. We need reinforcements urgently."

"Relaying."

The brain voice was replaced in the helmet by that of Rance. "Elmo, what's going on?"

"This isn't Elmo, this is Hark."

"Where's Elmo?"

"He's dead."

"How bad is it?"

"It's bad. Half the squad is pinned down in the cavern that houses this big plasma unit, and the other half is trying to get them out. If we don't get help, we're going to be overrun."

"How did this situation come about?"

"Dyrkin went in ahead, and then the chibas hit. Elmo wanted to pull back. The twenty was split in two."

"And now Elmo's dead?"

"Right."

Hark was certain that Rance had guessed what had happened. The question was, What was he going to do? What happened to a trooper who killed a noncom? Rance gave no clue. The topman was all business.

"Try and hold on. Help's coming."

Hark ran back to the cavern entrance. There were chibas everywhere. The troopers had formed into two defensive positions which they were managing to hold despite the overwhelming odds. Dyrkin was no longer out on his own. Renchett was beside him. Between them, they were laying down a withering fire. Somewhere along the line, Renchett had lost his MEW, but he was doing just as well with a chiba handweapon.

"Rance is bringing reinforcements."

"About time."

At that moment, Tabor tried a shot at an advancing chiba, but he stuck his head out too far. Instantly, his helmet exploded and he died without a sound.

They had to hold for another seven minutes before Rance turned up with a reserve twenty. Three more men were killed in those final minutes. Then the fresh troops poured into the cabin, and the tables were turned. The chibas fell back under concerted fire. The survivors fought a brief rearguard action and then fled into the tunnels. The fresh twenty seemed inclined to go after the chibas, but Rance restrained them.

"The other groups will catch up with them."

The remnants of Elmo's twenty climbed out of their makeshift cover. They seemed dazed and uncertain, as if they could hardly believe that it was over. There were just six of them left. Dyrkin and Renchett, Hark, Helot and Kov, and a recruit called Tain. The men gathered around the base of the power stack.

"What do we do about this thing?"

"Are we supposed to blow it?"

Rance shook his head. "Not a chance. If we messed with this baby, it'd vaporize half the valley. We'll get sappers in here to shut it down slow and easy."

He looked around the group of survivors, spotted Hark, and beckoned to him. "I want to talk to you."

Hark walked over to where the topman was standing. He was too tired to be afraid. Whatever was going to happen would happen.

Rance pointed to his helmet. "Is that Elmo's?"

Hark nodded. "I didn't take it off after I used the command channel."

"Troopers aren't supposed to use command channels except in the most dire emergency."

Hark looked him straight in the face. "It seemed pretty dire at the time. We were losing the whole twenty."

"So where's Elmo?"

"He's back down the tunnel."

"Let's go take a look."

Rance turned on his redscope and started down the tunnel. Hark followed. Without a word, Dyrkin and Renchett fell into step behind them. Rance glanced back.

"So the whole gang's coming, too?"

"Just want to see what happened to Elmo," Dyrkin said.

The overman was sprawled facedown where Hark had left him. Rance took his time inspecting the body.

"Shot in the back."

Dyrkin shrugged. "It happens." His voice was studiedly neutral.

"If I didn't know better, I'd say that those burns came from an MEW set on blast."

Renchett hefted his chiba weapon. "It's hard to tell for sure."

Rance glanced at Hark. "You have anything to add?"

"Nothing. I found Elmo dead and used his helmet."

"And what were you doing back here if all the fighting was in the cavern?"

"I was looking for Elmo."

Dyrkin stepped in. "I sent him back. To look for Elmo. We needed to get word through."

"So what was Elmo doing back here?"

"Who knows with Elmo? He'd gotten pretty strange."

Rance walked slowly around the body as if a different angle would give him some new insight.

"A rerun of the helmet conversations during the engagement might give us a clearer understanding of what went on."

Hark knew that he was dead. Even if the conversation between him and Elmo hadn't already been noted by the command brain, it would certainly come out on any rerun. He wondered if he simply ought to confess.

"It's a pity that we can't do that."

What was Rance talking about?

"The conversation couldn't be datastored. There was too much static from the interface."

"There was?"

"We'll just have to assume that Elmo died a hero, won't we?" He gave Hark a long, hard look. "We all want to be heroes, don't we?"

# FOURTEEN

"I hope you know what you're doing, Rance. There's chaos going down all over. If this ain't on the up and up, we could all be shot out of hand. There's headhunters all over the embarkation sites," the gunsaucer pilot said.

"Field police always show up when the fighting's over."

"That's as may be, but they still have weapons and the authority to carry out summary executions."

"I told you when we took off. I'm going to the nearest embarkation point to smooth the evacuation of my combat group."

"You're only a topman, Rance. You really think you've got that kind of clout?"

"We'll find out, won't we?"

"I guess we will."

"All I know is that I'm not going to be stranded on this ball of mud."

"And what about these other guys? How do we explain them?"

"They're my best longtimers. I need them with me."

The gunsaucer pilot shook his head. "I hope you know what you're doing."

"So do I."

The big trap had been sprung. Word had come through the command channel immediately after the tunnel clearing had been completed. What everyone on JD4-1A had feared all through the long and grinding campaign was now coming to pass. The Yal were returning in force. Five huge enemy battleships had appeared out of jumpspace and were heading for the planet. They would be in operational range within a matter of planetary days. The *Anah* cluster, which had been majestically orbiting the planet for so long, was already powering up to jump for safety. It would be touch and go as to whether the now heavily outgunned complex of ships could get clear in time. On the ground, there was a sense of scarcely controlled panic. Those who were able to make it to the cluster in time would be safe, but there would be no waiting around. The ones who couldn't be evacuated would simply be left behind. Nobody knew what the Yal would do with a whole army of prisoners, but there were few who didn't fear the worst.

Rance had acted immediately. While everyone else was still in the grip of the initial shock and confusion, he had gathered Drykin, Renchett, Dacker, and Hark around him.

"I don't intend to be left here for the Yal."

The longtimers had been a little surprised that the topman was putting self-preservation over duty. In a situation like this, they would have expected him to be one of the last into the lifeboat, not the first. He must have sensed what they were feeling.

"Don't get me wrong, I'm going to get out as many men as I can, but I'm also getting myself out if I possibly can."

The four longtimers looked at each other.

"So where do we figure in all this?" Dyrkin said finally.

"I'm taking you with me."

"I ain't going to argue with that. What do we have to do?"

"Hill 4078 is being set up as an embarkation point."

"Where's that?"

"About two hundred klicks to the north."

"What are we supposed to do, walk there?"

"We're going to commandeer a gunsaucer."

"We're what?"

"I'm calling in all my favors."

Dyrkin scratched the back of his neck. "Can I ask you a personal question?"

"Why am I doing this?"

"That's the one."

"Because a lot of good men are going to be left stranded on this forsaken planet, and there's nothing I can do about it. That's it. I'm damned if I'm going to be one of them. Besides, most of the people I feel I owe my loyalty to have been killed."

"It finally got to you."

"It finally got to me."

Renchett had grinned wolfishly. "So let's get ourselves a saucer and get the hell out of here."

Calling down the saucer was a simple matter of putting a request through the command channel. Convincing the pilot, a hard-eyed individual called Maso, had been a little more difficult. It had taken fifteen minutes of hard talking by Rance and a considerable trading of obligations before Maso finally agreed to fly them out.

"Just so long as me and my crew go out on the same e-vac as you," he said.

"What about the saucer?"

"Forget the saucer. There's going to be a hell of a lot of material left behind before this scramble's over."

Beneath them, Hill 4078 came into sight. Its cleared top stuck out of the surrounding fungus jungle like a bald head. On one side, sappers were still burning off the vegetation. Clouds of black smoke rolled into the air and were driven away from the site by a brisk wind. A number of e-vacs were already on the ground.

"I bet the bastard officers are getting away first."

Warning lights started flashing on the saucer's control panel.

"We're running into ground fire!"

Maso glanced swiftly at Rance. "You didn't tell me that we'd hit enemy fire."

Rance's expression was bleak. "What did you expect? The Yal are going to use every last chiba on this rock to slow us up."

Pulses of green energy arced lazily up from the fungus. Crew and passengers were pushed down into their couches as the saucer accelerated and banked steeply.

"I'm turning back."

"Back to what? There's going to be enemy around any place that e-vacs are jumping off."

"Dear God!"

The craft rocked and rolled as an energy pulse burst beside them. Maso's fingers danced over the control keys. The saucer lifted vertically.

"I'll try and get above the flak."

There were two more explosions, but neither was as close as the first.

"Body gunners stand by for manual override."

"Check."

"When we're over the hill, I'm going to drop fast. I want blanket fire on the surrounding jungle. Anything to make those Yal gunners keep their heads down."

"Check."

"Comm here, chief. I'm getting a demand for identification from traffic control on the hill."

Rance spoke into his communicator. "Tell them we got an A-thirty priority clearance."

"But we don't."

"If it's as much of a mess up down there as we think it is, they ain't going to know. Try and sound like an officer."

"Okay, I hope you're right."

A few seconds later, the comm operator came back on. "They seem to have bought the story. We're cleared to land."

"Dropping on my mark."

The ship fell like a stone, decelerating only at the last, bone-wrenching moment. Halfway down, the guns opened up with a shuddering roar.

"Torquing up here, Chief."

"Don't worry about it, I don't intend to take this thing off again."

The saucer hovered as its landing legs extended, and then it touched down. The passengers and crew unstrapped and stood up. Rance looked all around the cabin.

"If we run into a problem, let me do the talking."

The port opened. The saucer had set down some distance from where an e-vac was running its drive prior to a fast lift. The e-vacs, too, were drawing fire on the way in and out. The squat ugly ship was vibrating hard enough to pop its seams, and the noise was deafening. When it finally rose into the air, it went up screaming like a banshee, cramming on every last measure of speed. The backwash produced an instant dust storm all across the embarkation area. The men leaned into the hot wind as they climbed out of the port. The sound of the climbing ship died away, to be replaced by yelling in their helmets.

"Get down! Incoming! You by the saucer, get under cover."

Rance looked quickly around. There were some half-finished slit trenches on their left. The digging equipment seemed to have been abandoned by its crew.

"Run!"

They sprinted and dived. Orange fireballs streamed from the jungle below them in a lazy curve that ended in a tight group of explosions. A ground transport blew up. Pieces of metal pattered down around the crouching men.

"I've had better welcomes."

"No shit."

"This is a place to get out of."

The firing ceased. There were three other figures also sheltering in the trench. The trio were all sappers. They had to be the digging crew, and they were probably the ones who had shouted the warning. Rance called out to them.

"Is that the end of it?"

"Stay down. There's likely to be a second burst. They mostly dust us off after a ship gets away. The bastards usually do us a second time to see if they can catch us creeping out of our holes."

In absolute confirmation of the sapper's words, a second burst of fire hit the area. Again it stopped. The sappers left it a couple more minutes before they raised their heads.

"Looks like they've given it a rest."

"How long have they been out there?"

"They started last night."

"Have they been hitting the perimeter?"

"Not yet. So far they've just set up a couple of firing positions."

"Who's in command here?"

"There ain't nobody in command. The officers are all too busy getting their ass off planet. The closest thing is the field police who are going around shooting everyone they don't like the look of."

"So where do I go to hook up with my ship's e-vacs?"

"You could try the traffic control dome. That's the big one over in the center. I doubt you'll get too far, though. We heard that they had just two standards to get everyone off this rock."

"Two standards? Is that all?"

"That's when the cluster's supposed to jump."

There was less time than even Rance had imagined. The sappers were climbing out of the trench and remounting the digger.

"Keep your heads down. And watch out for the headhunters."

Rance turned to the troopers and the saucer crew. "You all heard that. We're going to go to this dome and see if we can bullshit a line to our own battle e-vacs."

Dyrkin and the others climbed out of the trench. The saucer crew seemed unwilling to leave its shelter. Maso was about to say something, but Rance cut him off.

"Did you think it was going to be easy?"

"We're going to get ourselves killed here."

"So what else is new?"

"You conned me, Rance."

Rance turned to go. "Take it or leave it. It doesn't matter to me. Now you've got us here, we ain't going to sweat it if you don't go the rest of the distance."

He started walking away. The troopers fell into step behind him. The saucer crew reluctantly followed. In the open spaces, people moved very fast. They tended to congregate in areas of cover. Most seemed to have little to do but wait. At regular intervals, a steamer would drop into the area. Their detonations had produced an acne of craters between ten and fifteen meters across. There was a burned-out digger beside where two craters overlapped. It appeared to have been bulldozing the first crater flat when the second missile hit. The field police, identifiable by the gray tabards that they wore over their suits and the starbursts on their helmets, prowled in groups of five or six. They were constantly stopping and questioning individuals. Rance and his party moved from one piece of cover to the next, doing their best to avoid them in a way that didn't appear furtive. While they were taking a breather in the shadow of a crawler, they saw their first execution. Seven men, naked except for their facemasks and placards that hung around their necks and proclaimed them to be deserters, were forced to their knees around the rim of a crater. The head-hunters stood behind them and burned each man in the back of his head. The bodies toppled forward into the crater, and a digger moved up to fill it in.

"Deserter seems to be the key word."

"We better make sure that we don't qualify."

Dacker opened his mask and spit. "Lucky we got our topman with us."

They reached the dome without drawing the attention of the police. The pressure lock was guarded by two troopers. Rance saw this as definite good luck. Troopers he could handle.

"Topman Rance. I'm here to collect my orders."

The guards treated him to a look of battle-tired irony. "You ain't going to find out no orders in there."

"I've got to give it my best shot."

"Suit yourself." The guard nodded toward the others. "Just you, though; the rest got to stay outside."

Within, Rance found the expected chaos. Riggers were still working on the main status board, and nothing was netted. Some equipment was functioning, but some still had to be unpacked. As far as he could see, there was some communication with the cluster and with the various main units down on the planet. Controllers were monitoring incoming flights, but nothing was coordinated. Unless they quickly got into the brain net, the evacuation would turn into a locked backup and nobody would get off JD4-1A. An overman in dress tans held down a first-line information desk just inside the entrance. He looked too young to be a combat noncom; he was probably some rear-echelon jerkoff. He regarded Rance with an expression of resigned boredom.

"You want something?"

Rance pulled off his mask. "I want to get on an open line to my ship's e-vacs."

"You and everyone else. You got authority?"

Rance lied without hesitation. "I got my orders over the command channel. I was to pull out and get here as fast as possible to bring my e-vacs down."

The overman half smiled. "Your e-vacs?"

"My e-vacs."

"Who gave you these orders?"

"How the hell should I know? I was in the middle of a firefight at the time."

"I'm afraid that won't be good enough. Without tangible authority from an officer, you ain't going to get out of here at all."

"So check on my orders."

"Check?"

"Get on to the Ten River task force and confirm my orders."

"You're out of your fucking mind."

Rance placed his hands on the desk and leaned forward. "Watch your mouth, sonny."

The overman wasn't intimidated. "For a start, nobody's getting anything confirmed right now. And if that ain't enough of a problem, we ain't heard from the Ten River task force in over a hundred minutes. For all we know, there may not be a Ten River task force. The enemy are popping up all over. They must have been waiting for this."

"So what am I supposed to do?"

"Hope the field police don't take a dislike to your face."

Rance took a deep breath. "Let's look at this another way. How many officers are there in this area?"

"There may be a couple of parties waiting for a ship, but most of them have lifted out."

"So there may be no officers at all in the area?"

"No functioning officers, that's for sure."

"And we're virtually cut off by the enemy except in the air?"

"Whatever you're thinking about, forget it. You won't get out of here without authority."

"Are there any other topmen here?"

The overman sighed and jerked his thumb toward the other side of the dome. "Yeah, there's a bunch of them over there making a nuisance of themselves."

"Just like me?"

"You said it."

"Is anybody going to stop me going over there?"

The overman shrugged. "Not me."

Rance walked past the desk. A group of five topmen were gathered around a communication console, arguing with the operator. From their expressions, they didn't seem to be getting anywhere. Rance recognized two of them. There was Benset from the *Anah 5* and Kalgol from the *Anah 2*. They both turned as Rance approached the group.

"Hey, Rance, what's going on?"

"Just trying to get myself off this forsaken planet. Everyone I talk to seems to be a complete asshole."

"So what else is new?"

"I don't intend to get stuck on this rock."

"The Yal are going to slaughter everyone who's left behind, and that's a fact."

"There's going to be plenty left behind, too."

"I take it that none of you have any kind of authorization?"

"There ain't no authorization."

"You got any ideas?"

Rance lifted off his helmet and ran his fingers through his close-cropped hair. "It seems to me that since the officers have all run, we should be technically in command here."

"Chain of command, right?"

"Right."

Benset rubbed his chin. He hadn't shaved in days. "The field police may not see it that way."

"They've pretty much taken over this evacuation," Kalgol added.

"Bastards."

"Maybe we should go talk to their commandant."

"We could just get ourselves shot."

"What other choice do we have?"

Kalgol looked at Rance. "You got any men with you?"

"Four of my longtimers. They wouldn't let them in here. I've also got the crew of the saucer we rode in on."

"Saucer crews ain't worth spit on the ground."

"I got some old boys outside dodging the headhunters," another topman said.

It turned out that all but one of the topmen had each brought a handful of men with them.

"If push came to shove, we could take an e-vac by force."

"You got a point there."

A topman with *Anah 7* patches looked thoughtful. "I think we should talk to the head cop first. Between us, we've got enough muscle to stop them screwing with us."

Benset nodded. "So what are we waiting for?"

The group of topmen replaced their masks and helmets and headed for the dome's pressure lock. Outside, they discovered Dyrkin, Renchett, Dacker, and Hark standing guard along with the two original troopers. There was no sign of the saucer crew.

"What's going on here?"

Renchett looked mock rueful. "We lost the flyboys."

"How?"

"The headhunters came calling."

"And?"

"We told them that we'd been assigned here. These guys—" He pointed to the original troopers. "—didn't say anything to contradict us. The flyboys weren't as fast on their feet, so the headhunters took them away. They were muttering something about desertion."

"And you didn't do anything to help them?"

"What could we do? We'd come up with a plausible story. It wasn't our fault that they couldn't."

One of the topmen grunted. "I said that saucer crews weren't worth spit on the ground."

The other topmen started gathering up the men they'd brought with them. Dyrkin and Renchett looked questioningly at Rance.

"What's going on?" Renchett asked.

"We're going to see the field police commandant."

Dacker scowled. "From where I'm standing, that sounds like a bloody silly idea. We just had a run-in with those pigs."

"We've got to start taking control around here."

The other troopers started joining the group by the dome. All had the battered equipment and closed faces that were the hallmarks of the hardened longtimer. They gathered silently; there was little unnecessary conversation. When everyone had emerged from shelter, there were eighteen in all. Benset nodded grimly.

"This should be enough to make an impression. You want to tell them, Rance? It was your idea."

Rance nodded.

"Okay, listen up," he said. "The object of the exercise is to get off this planet and back to the ship while we still can. What seems to be stopping us at the moment is that the headhunters are in practical control of the field. Our objective is to take that control for ourselves. Or at least enough of it to get us all onto an e-vac and off planet. You follow me so far?"

There were a number of reluctant nods. Nobody looked happy.

"The central police post is in a bunker across the area, due north. We've got the firepower of almost a full twenty and the experience of a whole combat group between us, and we have to demonstrate that no one can push us around. We'll go to the police bunker in force. When we get there, we'll give their commandant one chance to cooperate. After that, we start leaning. We are going to get off this planet, and nobody is going to stop us. You understand me? Nobody. If we have to, we'll use any force necessary. If we are forced to fire, we won't hesitate. A lot of men are going to be left behind for the Yal, and we are not going to be among them."

Though the men weren't exactly standing tall, tired but fatal belligerence had taken hold of them. They knew that they were an elite, and they were tired of being messed around. Rance wished that he were as confident as he sounded. There were enough headhunters crawling around the area to be a real problem.

They started across the area in a tight skirmish formation. Men actually came out of cover to look at them. Field police groups followed them at a distance, but none approached. Rance glanced across the cleared hilltop. There were storm clouds gathering in the east. There would be rain soon. The spectators ducked as a streamer exploded on the other side of the field. The troopers went right on walking.

The police bunker was almost completely underground. There was just a low hump where a buried dome had been covered with banked and fused earth. It was the standard practice for quickly creating a protected command center. The police commandant had taken much more care with his lair than anyone had with the actual evacuation center. Four armed guards stood at the top of the steps that led down into the bunker. They stiffened as the troopers approached but seemed unsure of how to respond. They were heavily outnumbered even though more of their kind were within shouting distance.

Rance continued to assume command.

"You troopers fan out and cover our backs; we don't want any of those cop units coming over here and interfering. Topmen, we'll go talk to the guards."

The troopers walked slowly backward, their guns pointed at the following police. The topmen marched directly up to the four bunker guards.

"Step aside, we're going in."

The center guard, the tallest of the four, shook his head. "I can't allow that. I have orders not to admit anyone but police personel."

Rance pushed his face very close to the guard's and stared into his visor.

"And I'm countermanding those orders. Do you know who I am, boy?"

"No, Topman, I don't know who you are."

"I'm your new commander, boy. Now that there are no officers left, we topmen are in charge."

"I don't know."

"What do you mean you don't know?" Rance roared in the man's face.

"I . . ." The guard faltered.

Rance gestured to the other topmen. "Disarm them."

The guards hesitated for a fraction too long before they raised their weapons. That was more than enough for the topmen. They had the MEWs out of the head-hunters' hands in one smooth, concerted movement. Rance peered down the stairs.

"Kalgol, take ten men and secure this entrance. I don't want anyone getting in here."

"Check."

"The rest of you follow me inside. It'll be a classic bunker clearing. They've probably seen us coming, but I doubt they'll expect a frontal assault. Benset and Dyrkin, I want you both up here beside me. I'm taking the point."

Instantly they were a team. They exchanged glances and plunged down the stairs. They went into the bunker fast, peeling off in twos into each room and passage. The men inside were calmly going about their routine duties. Most were in shirtsleeves, totally unprepared for being suddenly engulfed by armored troopers who wouldn't take no for an answer. It was hot in the bunker; there had been no time to install a cooling system. Six head-hunters, clad only in their underwear, were actually hustled from their beds and lined up against the wall with their hands above their heads. The only token resistance came in the main control room when a subkapo tried to draw his sidearm. An MEW was thrust into his face before he could clear the weapon from its holster.

"Shall we all relax?"

Rance looked slowly around at the faces of the occupants. Most of the field police in the nerve center were bunched around the central plot dais. None of them seemed inclined to make trouble. He spoke into his communicator.

"Area secure. How are things on top, Kalgol?"

"Everything's quiet. The headhunters are keeping their distance. It looks like it's going to start to rain any minute."

"Just hang in there."

The field police commandant pushed his way to the front of the knot of men by the plot dais. He was a portly individual clearly not recently accustomed to action. His head was shaved, and a livid scar ran down his right cheek. A tag on his tabard stated that his name was Maltov.

"What is the meaning of this?" he demanded.

"I'm Topman Rance from the *Anah 5*. I am one of a group of topmen who have assumed command of this e-vac area."

"On what authority?"

Rance was getting tired of telling the story.

"Simple chain of command. We're now the senior combat noncoms on this base and therefore in command. We have come here to see if we can count on your cooperation."

"You know damned well that in any withdrawal situation, the field police have jurisdiction. What you're doing is little more than armed insurrection."

"The most important thing is that we don't like the way this operation is being conducted." He motioned to the armed men behind him. "We do have the upper hand right now."

"I suppose you want to get e-vaced out."

"Not only that, but we also want to see the evacuation speeded up. We want to get off as many experienced fighting men as we can."

"Then you'd be better off guarding the perimeter. The enemy are bound to stage an attack before too long. Why don't you get out of here and let me get on with my job? Nothing's happened here yet that can't be forgotten."

"I could simply shoot all of you out of hand."

"You'd probably live to regret that."

"You seem to have grown fat on it."

"Suppose we could reach a compromise?"

"Keep talking."

"You might be surprised to learn that my job here is to slow down the withdrawal."

"What are you talking about?"

"You must realize that most of the ground troops on this planet have been written off. There simply aren't enough ships to take off even a fraction of the forces committed here before the cluster jumps."

"We already figured that out for ourselves."

Maltov looked at Rance coldly but carried on. "As more and more units come in here looking for a way out, this area and the others like it will turn into a bloody nightmare with men fighting each other for places on the last ships out. I have to hold off that degeneration for as long as possible."

"By mass executions?"

"Terror is a most effective method. The rank and file might as well stay more afraid of my men than they are of the Yal for as long as possible."

Rance didn't like the way he used the term "rank and file." "So what's the compromise?"

"That I let you onto one of the next e-vacs out, you topmen and the longtimers that you brought with you. In return, you let me run things my way."

Rance had known that it would probably come to this kind of deal.

"We need to get out as many of our experienced men as we can."

"You already brought your longtimers. They're the ones you need. They'll be the foundations on which you'll build your new battle groups."

This last remark caused Hark to start paying attention. He'd been one of the men who had followed Rance and Dyrkin into the control room, but up to that point he'd been standing in the background, not altogether grasping what was going on. After Maltov's remark about foundations, it had all fallen into place. Rance's

abrupt departure from the battlefield and the fact that
he'd taken the four of them with him hadn't been a matter of either self-preservation or mutual respect. He
hadn't been bucking the Therem. Quite the reverse, he'd
been acting exactly according to his programming. He
was getting out his best men. After the Therem had gar-
baged one army, these survivors would be the seeds from
which a new one would be created. If Hark was angry at
anyone, it was at himself for believing that anything
could happen at random. Everything was planned.

Rance and Maltov were still in confrontation. Despite
the armed men all around him, Maltov seemed to be getting the edge.

"So, do we have our compromise?"

Rance slowly nodded. It was probably the best deal
that he'd get. The longtimers would certainly hate him
for selling out the bulk of the men, but they'd have to
share the guilt. They were getting out, too—if Maltov
didn't double-cross all of them.

"Yeah. It's a deal. When do we get an e-vac?"

"We'll go to the command dome and find out."

"Together?"

Maltov reached for his helmet. "Right."

Outside, Kalgol and the ten troopers were still holding
the entrance to the bunker. A heavy tropical rain was
falling, and the men were up to their knees in a mist of
spray. Water was streaming from their suits. The hilltop
landing area was rapidly turning into a desolate sea of
mud.

"This ain't going to help matters any."

There was a brief conference between Rance and the
other topmen, and then the whole party of troopers, plus
Maltov and an escort of six field police, set off for the
command dome. As they splashed their way through the
mud, Rance kept everyone bunched up. If they were

close to the commandant, they were probably safe from a sneak attack by the headhunters.

They were almost exactly halfway between the bunker and the dome when the alarms went off.

"Enemy in the wire, third quadrant!"

The command channel suddenly came alive with voices.

"They're throwing everything at this one point! We can't hold them; we're spread too thin."

"What is it? Chibas?"

"I can't take no more! I can't take no more!"

"Cut that out!"

"There's men in among them!"

"It must be some of our boys making a break for it!"

"They're in gray camouflage armor, and they're firing at us."

"What the hell is going on over there?"

"There's men! Men fighting with the enemy!"

There was the sound of an explosion, and the shouting stopped. The troopers had halted. Rance was looking at Maltov.

"I suppose you expect us to go charging over there and plug the hole."

"If we're overrun, nobody will get off."

"Are you sending in your men?"

Maltov spoke into his communicator. "All available men! Go immediately to hold that breach in the third quadrant perimeter!"

He actually smiled at Rance. "Your move."

"You're right, goddamm it!"

Rance turned and faced the men. "Okay, you heard it. Let's shag it! Let's secure their forsaken perimeter for them. I want to see these men that have gone over to the enemy."

There was a good deal of cursing, but no one disobeyed the order.

"Come on! At the double! Fan out and don't bunch up. You all know the routine."

The men struggled through the quagmire, heading for the smoke and steam that were already billowing up from the firefight on the perimeter. They came under sporadic fire but kept on going. A man was hit and went down. Rance was glad that it wasn't one of his. He didn't want to lose any of his longtimers in these last minutes.

"They're hitting on a very narrow front. Maybe there ain't too many of them!"

"Don't count on it."

Rance didn't push his men too hard. There were a number of other squads converging on the same point. He didn't see why they should be the first to get there. The odds were that the first to arrive would be slaughtered.

"Easy now! Don't get crazy."

There were figures coming toward them out of the rain. Visibility was so poor that it was hard to make out exactly who or what they were, but they seemed roughly human in shape. Then they started firing. The flashes were those of Yal weapons. So these were the renegades. Another man went down. It was Dacker. Rance cursed. The troopers were returning fire. The human figures were halted in their tracks. One by one, they were cut down. At least Rance had the satisfaction of knowing that his longtimers were better than whatever these things were. A voice from the wire came over their communicators.

"They're pulling back! The chibas are pulling back!"

Just then the rain stopped. The troopers walked slowly forward. The mud sucked at their feet and ankles, and moisture hung like a hot shroud. Rance stopped beside Dacker. The trooper was quite dead. Half his chest was missing, and his suit was slowly curling away from his lifeless flesh. As Rance watched, the suit stopped moving. It, too, had died. There were bodies all over, but everyone was making for the ones in the now mangled, fungus-gray armor. Everyone wanted to know who they were. Men bent over and pulled helmets from these strange corpses.

Renchett was the first of the squad to reach a body. "Hey, Rance, get a load of this."

They were not renegades. There were marked differences between the men who fought for the Therem and these creatures. Their skins were close to orange, and their eyes had a strange slitted configuration. Either they used some sort of depilatory or they had never grown hair on their heads. They were obviously human, but equally obviously they were a different race.

"Where the hell did they come from?"

"The Yal must have bred them."

"Yeah, but why?"

"Why do the Therem use us?"

Renchett was silently shaking his head. "Maybe they captured one of the home worlds and used its inhabitants."

"Surely they'd look more like us."

Hark had a thought. "Maybe the Yal took them from the Earth when they were first forced to leave it."

"The Earth?"

"The original world. Our original world."

Rance walked slowly over to where Hark was standing. "What do you know about the Earth?"

Hark gave a slight shrug. "A woman told me."

"You shouldn't believe everything women tell you."

It was the worn-out topman response, and the moment Rance had said it, he felt a little stupid.

Hark just looked away. "I believe this."

Renchett was bending over one of the bodies. "You know what I think?"

"What?"

"It was probably these assholes that skinned those corpses back in the jungle."

Renchett had his knife out. He was about to carve off an ear. Rance stopped him.

"There'll be no more mutilation."

Hark was still deep in thought.

"You all know what else this means," he said slowly. "It means that we've started fighting our own kind. There are men on both sides in this damned war. Men are fighting each other for aliens that most of them will never even see."

"It sucks."

Hark was suddenly deeply angry. "Goddamn right it sucks. It makes it all totally meaningless."

The thought was still sinking in when the sky was lit by a blinding flash on the horizon.

"Nuke!"

"They don't have no nukes left!"

"That's a fucking nuke."

They all threw themselves flat. The fireball was climbing into the air like a fast-rising sun.

"They must have had some stashed."

"Maybe the men were stashed, too."

"That was probably another e-vac area."

A voice from the command dome came into their helmets. "It was in the right direction for the Fourteen River base, the one that the dynes were shipping out from."

"How soon will the shock wave hit?"

The minutes passed agonizingly as the base waited for the shock. When it arrived, it came with the force of multiple hurricanes. Eddies of debris, dust, and smoke sped across the cleared ground like twisters. Men clung to the earth as the wind threatened to lift them clear off the hilltop. The shriek of static in their helmets threatened to deafen them. The ones who had remained on their feet either were whirled into the air or rolled through the mud. A gunsaucer was turned over, and panels were torn from the control dome. There was panic inside as the pressurization was lost and the men grabbed for their masks. The fury passed as swiftly as it had come, leaving behind a strange battered calm. The white mushroom cloud stood on the horizon like a terrible epitaph to the whole doomed, fruitless campaign. Nuclear weapons, although crude and ancient, were still viewed with fear and awe. Their destructiveness was so all-encompassing that their use remained a matter of desperate last resort. Touching off what amounted to a small sun on the surface of a planet was a frightening gamble.

Men readied their weapons, fully expecting an enemy ground attack. When none came, there was a distinct feeling of unease. It wasn't like the Yal to pass up any opportunity.

"If they can nuke that base, they can nuke this one."

An e-vac came down with is retros screaming. It looked as if it, too, had taken a beating from the nuclear shock wave. As soon as its landing legs touched, Rance sprang to his feet.

"Everybody up! Let's go! We're getting on that crate, and nobody's going to stop us."

# FIFTEEN

THE *Anah 5* felt as if it were being torn apart, and maybe the whole universe along with it. The shields had already failed on two of the ships in the cluster, and those two were being battered to pieces by the guns of the Yal. The coordination that made the cluster a single entity had been lost. They were now thirteen solitary ships fighting for their individual survival. The Yal battleships had arrived ahead of schedule and before the cluster could jump to safety. The *Anah 12* was slowly and majestically being turned into a shapeless cloud of gas and debris by a chain reaction of explosions. The shocks were felt on all the other ships. It was unlikely that there were survivors of any kind, but even if a few unfortunates remained drifting in space, nothing could be done for them. The green clouds of Yal fire came on relentlessly, and only three of the cluster ships had sufficient power to fire back.

None of the surviving troopers had thought much about what would happen when they actually arrived back on board. As they'd stormed onto the e-vac, gunning down three field police in the process, simply getting off the planet in one piece had been the all-consuming goal. It had remained so during the go-for-broke takeoff that had them running the gauntlet of a sudden storm of enemy ground fire. It was only when they were in space and could see the dozens of tiny craft shuttling in between the thirteen big ships that they started to remember that they might well have jetted from frying pan to fire. Collectively, the shuttles seemed to be moving with such a desperate frenzy that it was obvious that the cluster was in the throes of a major alert.

The bombardment began while Rance's troopers were just emerging from the blue room decontamination process. The ship shuddered, and the floor tilted. A number of men fell on their faces. There were muffled explosions in another part of the ship. Farther down the corridor, a duct burst and superheated steam roared from the breach. This in turn caused a short in a power transfer, and a shower of blue sparks cascaded through the clouds of swirling vapor. The ship lurched again, and there were more explosions. Smoke billowed down the corridor. Fire alarms were ringing. Rance clung to a doorjamb and tried to organize the men under his command. Their equipment was still on the conveyer, coming out of decontamination. Without a helmet, it was hard to make himself heard.

"Everyone suit up!"

The ship now seemed to be tilting steeply toward the bow. Rance knew that this was probably a localized illusion. The floor grav control in this sector had probably been jarred off line, and no one had yet managed to reset it. The knowledge didn't make the experience any easier to stand.

Dyrkin crawled up the sloping floor, dragging himself with one hand. His suit and helmet were tucked under his other arm. "So what are we supposed to do?"

"Get into your suit. The ship's going to jump before

too long, and we've got to get back to our coffins. If we don't, we're going to be pulp."

Most of the survivors were at the bottom of the angled corridor, piled against an emergency bulkhead that had closed immediately after the first series of shocks. They were grazed and bruised, and a couple had been scalded by the steam, but otherwise the men seemed to be more or less intact. Rance clawed his way to the conveyer offload. He grabbed the first suit to emerge, slapped it against his chest, and let it crawl over his body. He fitted his helmet and then started sliding the rest of the suits and helmets down to the men.

"Dyrkin, get up here and help me!"

The floor righted itself, but the lights went out. A half dozen helmet lights came on in the gloom.

"Get that bulkhead open."

"Controls don't respond. It must have shorted out."

"Somebody rig a bypass."

Hark's voice came over the communicator. "I got it."

The bulkhead rolled back. There were still lights in the next section of corridor. A public address was trilling urgently in nohan. The ship slammed sideways as if it had received a blow from a giant hammer. The men were thrown up against the left-hand wall. Those who were still struggling into their suits were thrown down on the deck.

"That's got to be a direct hit."

"You wouldn't know about a direct hit."

"The screens got to be buckling, though."

Rance hurried them along. "We've got to get back to the coffins if we don't want to make the jump on bare floor."

The men reached the next safety bulkhead.

"This one's fused, too."

"Hark . . ."

"I got it."

The bulkhead opened on a sheet of flame that billowed out at them. It engulfed the trooper next to Hark. His suit was only half on, and he staggered back screaming with his underclothes on fire. Benset grabbed him and rolled him on the deck. Rance was yelling.

"Back! Back!"

The fleeing troopers ran headlong into a nohan firefighting crew in red ceramic armor. They were whistling in what sounded like the alien equivalent of panic, but at least they were headed for the fire.

"This way!"

They ran in single file down a narrow companionway. All around them, sirens were blaring, signifying widespread damage. There was a confused babble in their helmets. They came up against a third closed safety bulkhead. This time, the manual bypass refused to work, and Hark and Renchett had to crawl into the mechanism before they could get it to open. The others waited tensely.

"We ain't going to make it."

"Come on, you guys!"

"Will you shut the hell up and let us work? We're troopers, not riggers," Renchett called back tensely.

The bulkhead creaked open. It led to a free-fall shaft.

"If I remember right, this is the emergency shaft to one of the dropcraft bays," Dyrkin said.

As he spoke, the sound of the alarms changed.

"That's five minutes to jump."

"What do we do?"

"Into the shaft," Rance ordered.

"That's not the way to the messdecks."

"Don't argue, I got an idea."

The men ran to the end of the companionway and jumped. Even in their armor, they floated lightly down to a kneebend landing on the dropcraft launch deck. There were only two ships in a bay designed for five, but they had been locked down in preparation for the emergency. Rance pointed to the nearest craft.

"Inside, as fast as you can!"

"We can't fly that thing!"

"We're not going to fly it. We going to rack ourselves in and hope we can survive the jump in there. At least we'll be strapped down."

The ship reeled as it was hit repeatedly. Plasma cascaded down the far side of the bay, burning through anything it touched. There were more internal explosions.

"Are we capable of a jump?"

"Everybody inside! Now! There's no way we can make the coffins."

Dyrkin fell into step beside Rance as they ran for the grounded ship. "Is this going to work?"

"Your guess is as good as mine."

Training took over, and the troopers went to their places as if they were going on a mission. The restraint cages were snapped into place, and then the men waited. Renchett tried to strike a positive note in the terrifying communicator silence inside the ship.

"This may be almost as good as a coffin. At least we can't thrash around, and the suits should help some . . ."

The calming voice was stretched out into an inhuman scream. The damaged ship had gone into the jump.

The hallucinations were jagged and metallic, no doubt a result of the surroundings. Razor-sharp shards sliced through tiny vulnerable figures as they scuttled through towering mazes of incredible pain. Steel jaws snapped and snarled and tore at naked flesh. Iron claws gouged and ripped, spikes impaled, and needles slid through genitals and eyeballs. All the time they were falling, down toward other waiting rows of knives and teeth. Perhaps it was the noise that was the worst. A screeching, ripping scream, surface against surface, that constantly rose in pitch and volume assaulted the ears and seared through the mind. Where the surfaces touched, sheets of flame and burning gas spiraled upward, broiling flesh and brain into red, raw, blind horror. The universe was a hollow steel drum being constantly pounded by some hammer of the gods. Metal. Metal. The prisoners of the hallucinations were chained to the interior of that drum. The vibrations rattled loose their teeth and caved in their chest cavities, shaking apart their very molecular structure. Ears and eyes and noses were bleeding. Blood ran down between their legs. It was oozing from their every pore. Hot blood was everywhere. They could taste it, boiling and angry against the background of the ever-present metal. As they drowned in blood, a terrible laughter started, a laughter so angry and mocking that it seemed to be a summation of all previous pain.

"At least it was a short jump."

Hark opened his eyes. He was no longer one with the pain of everyone around him. He was himself again, strapped in, inside the dropcraft. There was acrid smoke in the air from fires that flickered somewhere outside, but everything was real. It was Renchett who had spoken. He had unsnapped his restraint cage and removed his helmet. He was standing in the central aisle with a look of pure madness on his face. Abruptly, his eyes rolled back into his head, his legs gave way, and he crumpled to the deck. The laughter was still going on. That, too, was real and right in the ship with them. Hark unsnapped his own cage and tried to stand. His legs threatened to let him down, but he willed them to work for him. He tongued a whiff of pure oxygen from his helmet, and he felt a little better. He walked unsteadily to where Renchett had fallen. He knelt beside him, feeling his suit for some sign of life.

"Is he breathing?"

Hark looked up. Rance was standing behind him. The

topman had also taken off his helmet. He looked green, and there was blood caked around his nose.

Hark shook his head. "I can't tell."

"Take off your helmet; the air's okay."

Hark put his ear to Renchett's mouth.

"Yeah, he's breathing."

"Okay, we'll see about his sanity later. Let's take a look at the others. Who's doing that goddamn laughing?"

"It's down that way."

The laugher was clearly beyond help. His eyes had the vacancy of someone who had retreated into his own distant world and was never coming out. Hark wondered if the trooper was doomed to go on living in the hallucination for the rest of his life. Or maybe he had just seen the whole terrible joke. Hark was relieved that the man was a stranger to him. The next man was quite dead. His helmet had filled with blood. Hark started in momentary horror at the dark red faceplate. Had they been sharing a collective hallucination? How was that possible? Some of the others were coming to life. Cages were being unsnapped, and men were trying to stand. Most were going through the angry confusion that followed any jump. Renchett opened his eyes. He looked as sane as he had ever been.

"We made it?"

"We made it so far."

The final total of casualties was two dead, one insane, and one catatonic. Rance ordered them left where they were.

"We've no time to bury the dead. First we have to find out what our own prospects of life are."

Once all the survivors were back to normal, Rance led them out of the dropcraft. As they emerged onto the hangar deck, the *Anah 5* let out a rumbling roar that ended in a drawn-out sigh. It was as if a part of the ship had just died.

"We'll head into the interior of the ship and try and hook up with whoever else is left. I don't have a clue what we're going to find."

At first, all they could find was death. The first corridor they walked down was nothing more than a burned-out shell. The troopers had to pick their way through the remains of an entire nohan damage-control party who had fried inside their armor. Farther on they came across three dead sluicers, huddled together in positions of mutual protection. They must have been caught out by the jump and succumbed to the heart-stopping horror of the hallucinations. In the final moments of terror they had clawed their lightweight radiation suits to shreds.

"Looks like we got lucky, holing up in that dropcraft."

Rance didn't bother to point out that their survival might have had more to do with his own quick thinking than with luck. "Let's keep on going."

Right from the start, it was obvious that the ship had taken a terrible pounding. Although there was still air and gravity throughout the ship, the lights had gone in a number of sections. Small fires burned all over, and there were major conflagrations in some of the larger compartments. Flares of energy arced across breaks in cables and the gaps in ruptured ducts. The decks were littered with debris, and repeatedly the squad had to climb over tangled barriers of wreckage. Their first encounter with life was less than encouraging. The two e-vac crewmen were wandering aimlessly. No one was home behind their blank eyes. So when the strange voice came over the communicators, it brought both shock and a release of fear. There was at least some kind of authority. For all their rebellious anger, the troopers still craved someone to tell them what to do.

"All uninjured personnel who are not engaged in repair or fire-fighting should proceed immediately to section eighty-two."

"What the hell is that?"

Although the voice had been speaking in their language, it was definitely not human.

"Section eighty-two is median country."

Rance halted and faced the men. "I think I know what that was."

"You don't look too happy about it."

"Anybody know what the interpreters are?"

"Some kind of alien, right?"

"We never see them. I heard they were ugly suckers, kind of blue globs with tentacles."

"Is it true they can talk everyone's language?"

"They're supposed to be part instinctive linguists and part telepaths. Their function is interspecies communication. If one of them is issuing orders, there can't be too many of us left alive on this hulk."

Section 82 was just inside the ship's hull. Its center was a transparent fire-control dome. Although most of the equipment was burned out and the dome was badly scarred, it was still intact and airtight. When Rance's squad arrived, there was already quite a big gathering in the large circular area. It was a gathering that only a few days earlier they would not have envisioned even in their wildest dreams. Almost every species on the ship was represented, including a number of aliens that the men had never seen before. The atmosphere was set for humans, and three of the alien species present were contained in their sealed environmental enclosures. The trooper who had described the interpreters as blue globs with tentacles had been very close to the truth. There were three of them in their tank, floating in a soup of methane and ammonia. One side of their mobile tank was covered in a complex of communication equipment. The lone lantere was still in its battle armor, as were the pair of wormlike dauquoi. Another tank contained a dim, constantly changing shape.

Hark whispered to Dyrkin. "You know what that is?"

"It's a navigator, boy. I doubt even the medians saw a navigator before. Nobody ever sees the navigators. Nobody. They live in the heart of the ship in their own sealed environment."

"What exactly do they do?"

"What their name says. They navigate. Don't ask me to explain it in detail. They navigate the cluster through jumpspace. They know instinctively where we are, and they sculpt the jumps accordingly."

"Weird."

"You said it."

Including Rance's troopers, there were some thirty humans in the room. Most were rank and file, other troopers, spacecrew, riggers, sluicers, a motley bunch who had managed simply to survive both the attack and the jump. The medians stood apart from the others of their kind. Rance noted that there wasn't a single officer present.

The interpreter's voice came again.

"We are in a unique position. The Therem on this ship are all dead." The alien's voice echoed strangely; somehow it was speaking in a number of languages at once. "We have also lost the other ships in the cluster."

Everything with eyes looked up through the dome. It was true—they were alone in space. Beyond the dome, there were no other ships, just the stars. The closest object was a glowing cloud of gas that hung in space like a furled silver flag. The emptiness seemed very close.

"What of the Yal?"

"It's unlikely that they are able to track or follow us. They probably believe that this ship was destroyed along with the others."

One of the medians had a question.

"How badly is the ship damaged?"

"A number of levels are out of commission. We have

no weapons capacity, but the ship has spatial mobility, and it's capable of short jumps."

"Do we know where we are?"

A dim green light glowed in the navigator's tank. The interpreter's equipment translated.

"We know where we are. We are away from the normal avenues of combat. Do you require the coordinates?"

The median shook his head. "It would appear that our duty is clear. We should proceed, in short stages, to the nearest Alliance base and await orders."

The lantere made a noise that was a cross between a grunt and a bellow.

"That might be open to a certain amount of discussion," came the translation.

The median's voice was cold and particular. "Surely any such discussion might be construed as treason when our duty is so obvious."

This time the interpreter spoke for itself. "There are those of us who don't see it as quite so obvious. Some might say that fate has freed us from the Therem and our duty might, in fact, be to pursue that fate."

"We still belong to the Therem Alliance," the median argued.

There was a rumble from the dauquoi. "You mean we still belong to the Therem."

"We still belong to the war."

The navigator blinked and bubbled. "Ah, yes, the war. It was never a war of our choosing."

"There is no escaping the war."

"Do the other humans share their median's devotion to our master's war?" the interpreter asked.

Rance looked around, wondering who was being addressed. Then he realized that everyone had turned in his direction.

"I . . . don't think we're crazy about going back to the war. Is there any alternative?"

The median cut him off. "There is no alternative."

"Let the humans speak for themselves."

The median took a step forward. His tone was now coolly threatening. "My men don't need to speak. They do what they're told."

Rance started receiving a telepathic image. It showed him and his men burning down the medians. He realized that the men were seeing it, too. They were looking to him for direction. The median must have also received the image. He started to draw a sidearm.

"You men will stay exactly where you are!"

Rance fired without thinking. The other men did the same. The three medians were cut down by a withering hail of MEW fire. The troopers kept on firing until the medians' bodies were nothing more than shapeless blackened stumps. The interpreter was making a high-pitched keening. Rance slowly lowered his weapon.

"What now?"

The interpreter got its voice back under control. "You must pardon me. I find it very distressing to be in close proximity to death."

"We've just committed grand mutiny. What are we supposed to do now?"

"You have killed all your remaining superiors. What you do now is your decision."

"There are no more medians and no officers?"

"The human officers' level was destroyed in one of the first explosions. No one survived. The other medians died later."

"What do you intend to do?"

"We have a plan that we will outline."

The aliens' plan was a relatively simple one. They would take the *Anah 5* and get as far away from both the Yal and the Therem as possible. Their offer to the troopers and the other humans still on board was a free ride to the planet of their choice. The best choice, as the aliens saw it, was a planet in a system three jumps away. It had recently been terraformed by a party from the *Anah* cluster.

"The existence of the planet would only have been recorded in the cluster's brain net. Now that has been destroyed; only we know that it's there. It's a bleak, bare place where it rains a lot of the time, but over the years, conditions will improve. The important thing is that the odds against being discovered are astronomical."

Rance shook his head. "I don't know if the surviving men can stand up to three jumps in quick succession."

"Di-trexane."

"What?"

"Di-trexane. It was issued to the medians and officers to ease them through the jump. It wasn't issued to you."

The anger among the men was like a physical presence.

"I fucking knew they had something."

There was real disappointment that nobody was left to kill. The jumps had been bad enough when they'd seemed unavoidable. Not it was like some hideous conspiracy of pain.

"But why?"

"The Therem move according to strange logic."

"Don't they just."

There was one other major flaw in the aliens' plan. It was Renchett who voiced it.

"We don't have no women."

"I beg your pardon?"

"Women. We don't have none. It going to be a pretty sad little colony with just a bunch of old soldiers getting older."

"I'm sorry, I don't understand you."

"Seems simple to me."

Rance stepped in. "Without females, our species cannot reproduce."

"We didn't know that."

Renchett was getting angry. "Everybody knows that."

"We are all specialists. None of us have a grounding in comparative biology."

"That's as may be. The question still remains. What are we going to do about it?"

The interpreter moved an unhappy tentacle. "There seems to be nothing we can do about it."

Renchett bristled. "There damn well is."

"There is?"

"We could head back to the last recstar and liberate the women there."

There was a murmur of agreement from the humans. Then the lantere boomed.

"That's impossible. Even if this ship had operational weapons and shields, it couldn't take on an asteroid base."

The other aliens signified agreement.

"We can't go back into combat space."

"And we ain't sitting around on some mudball waiting to be the last one to die."

Rance held up a hand. "Wait a minute. There could be a way to do this. How many fighting men could the ship muster if it really came to it?"

"Perhaps two hundred if we armed the technical personnel."

"We could take a recstar with two hundred motivated troops."

Renchett grinned. "And we'd sure as hell be motivated."

The navigator emitted bubbles.

"It's impossible."

"No, it's not. Listen, we could approach the recstar pretending to be exactly what we are, the lone crippled survivor of a destroyed cluster. They must know by now that the *Anah* was wiped out in the JD4 system, and they won't suspect anything. We limp in, and we dock. While we're docking, the ground troops drop to the surface of the asteroid. We hit 'em hard before they know what's happening. The women will join with us. We'll have the ship ready-powered so we can jump immediately everyone's back on board."

The interpreter conjured an image of men silently floating down across the asteroid's rocky terrain. "It has a certain plausibility."

The dauquoi didn't agree. "The rest of us can't risk our new freedom for the comfort of one species." The lantere rumbled agreement.

Rance looked meaningfully at his weapon. "As a representative of that species, I can assure you all that we take our comfort very seriously."

Topman Benset moved up beside Rance. "It's more than comfort. It's the continuing freedom of our species. We're prepared to fight for that."

There was a sudden tension in the dome. The interpreter started pumping out calming abstracts, but they had little effect on the increasingly belligerent lantere.

"Are you threatening us?"

"We're trying not to, but if we don't do this our way, I think you're going to have problems with our future cooperation. We do have the firepower."

Weapons were being hefted to emphasize the point. The interpreter seemed to accept the situation.

"I think we have to go along with the humans' proposal."

The lantere was still being stubborn.

"If we were to attack the asteroid base, I could find myself fighting against my own kind."

Rance nodded grimly at the charred bodies of the medians.

"That can sometimes be the price of your freedom."

There was a long silence. Finally the lantere gave in.

"Very well, I will agree to this foolhardy expedition, but I still have grave doubts."

Renchett whooped and spun his weapon. "Let's get ourselves some girls!"

Rance looked at him. He wasn't smiling.

"This may not be that easy."

# SIXTEEN

"THE suits don't work," Dyrkin told Rance.

"What do you mean the suits don't work?"

"Try one. They go on the way they always did, but once they're on, there's no flexibility. You can't move your arms and legs. Also, they're secreting something that's got everyone close to throwing up."

"What the hell is going on? We're only hours out from the recstar. There's never been a problem with the suits before. Why now?"

Rance followed Dyrkin to the messdeck. The ship had completed its third and final jump, and preparations were under way for the attack. A problem with the suits was little short of a disaster. Rance immediately stripped off his dress tans.

"Somebody throw me a suit."

Hark tossed across one of the shapeless black blobs.

"It's like they know what we're doing and they're refusing to go along with it. It's like they won't go against the Therem."

"That's ridiculous superstition. The suits don't have the brains for anything like that."

Rance placed the suit on the deck and stood on it. The

268

suit began to crawl up his leg, but it moved more slowly than usual. The slowness was easy to interpret as reluctance. When the suit covered his body, he experimentally flexed his arms. The suit resisted. The same happened when he tried to bend his legs.

"See what we mean?"

"We're not going to be able to use them."

"What are we going to do? We can't go into combat without suits."

"We could use radiation armor."

"It's goddamn bulky. It's going to really cut down on our mobility."

"What the hell else can we do?"

"Nothing. We'll have to go with the radiation suits. Dyrkin, scout around and see how many you can come up with."

"What are we going to do with the suits?"

Rance shook his head. "I don't know. I'm going to talk to the aliens and see if they've got a line on any of this."

The meeting with the aliens was brief. They had nothing to contribute as to why the suits should be behaving the way they were. Strangely, they seemed more inclined than Rance to accept the men's idea that the creatures were actually refusing to act against the interests of the Therem.

"Even though it seems at the time to defy logic, an intuitive feeling may be a pointer to the truth."

"Sure."

"We don't feel that these things should be allowed to remain loose in the ship. The current loss of function may be only the start of an entire destructive cycle. We have no idea what might be built into their genetic code. We urge you to destroy them."

"The suits are not that easily destroyed," Rance reminded them.

"So simply jettison them into space."

"You want us to do that?"

"It would seem the obvious solution."

"The men aren't going to like this. They've been a long way with those suits. Remember that we and the suits are symbiotic."

"The men would probably like it even less if someone else disposed of the suits."

"You've got a point there."

The men didn't like it. The announcement was received by a hard silence. No one cursed and no one complained, but also no one moved. Nobody wanted to be the first. Finally Dyrkin broke the deadlock.

"He's right. They're going to have to go. They ain't working with us no more."

"Maybe it's just a delayed-action side effect of the jumps. Maybe they'll come back to normal."

"Damn it, you know that ain't true. They've left us, and we've got to dump them. They could turn on us."

Rance quickly took control before the mood could alter. "Load them on a pallet and let's get it over with. Dyrkin, pick a squad to take care of this."

To his complete surprise, Dyrkin turned on him with something close to a snarl.

"No way, Rance. Each man does his own. As each man gets his radiation armor, he goes to the lock and blows out the old suit."

Rance nodded. "As you want it."

It became a solemn procession. The radiation armor was brought down to the messdecks. It had been hastily sprayed black so those wearing it wouldn't present too obvious a target. Each man in turn received his issue, fitted the suit, and checked the servos. Then he picked up the black blob of dormant suit and started the long walk to the nearest lock. Each would pause for a mo-

ment as his suit floated into the void, and then he'd turn
and make the walk back.

Communications started coming in from the asteroid.
The survival of one of the *Anah* cluster seemed to be
causing some degree of excitement. There were constant
demands for information. The ship sent a broken, ragged
signal of modulated static, as if the communication
equipment were much more badly damaged than it really
was. A number of shuttle craft came out to meet the
*Anah 5*, but they seemed content to remain at a distance,
merely inspecting the disabled newcomer. The asteroid
base appeared to be accepting the slowly limping ship on
face value. The men moved into the lower drop bay from
where they were going to launch their attack. They were
very quiet. Rance had worried that the discarding of the
suits would have had a dampening effect on the men's
spirits, but it seemed to have had quite the opposite result. They were quiet but deadly. They were fighting for
themselves, and they weren't going to let anything stop
them.

The asteroid was starting to broadcast warnings. They
wanted the *Anah 5* to stand off in deep space. Shuttles
would be sent to take off the crew. This was understand-
able. Those on the asteroid had no idea of the levels of
damage. For all they knew, the ship might be five minutes away from blowing itself to atoms. The *Anah 5* ignored the warnings and kept on coming. It went right on
broadcasting the unintelligible signal. The messages from
the recstar began to sound more than a little spooked.
The two bodies were now in visual contact. On the asteroid, they had to be entertaining the idea that the *Anah
5* wasn't capable of stopping and was going to run right
into them. The warnings started to be a good deal more
threatening. There was a first tentative mention of force,
although it was actually too late for that. The ship and
the asteroid were now so close that neither could damage

the other without doing damage to itself. The asteroid population must have been wondering if anybody was left alive on the cluster ship or if it was just a drifting hulk sending an automatic signal. The interpreter seemed to derive a lot of entertainment from imagining the state of mind of what was now being thought of as the enemy. It seemed to take a positive delight in directing the overall operation.

A more serious warning came in.

"Reverse spatial motion or we will be forced to deflect you with our heavy weapons. Please acknowledge."

This was the moment to change signal. A prepared message was sent. The deliberately desperate voice of a lantere cut through the storm of jagged static. The fact that it was a lantere sending should have alerted the base to the fact that things were very wrong on the cluster ship. The big crustaceans were natural engineers, but they never operated ship-to-ship communication.

"We are reducing spatial motion as best we can. We are coming round onto your darkside. It will be a close dock."

The static took over again, but the *Anah 5* did begin to slow as the two bodies came closer and closer. It still looked as if they were going to touch, but then, at the very last moment, the cluster ship started to curve around the asteroid.

"Ground troops stand by."

In the drop bay, the fighting men sealed their armor, concentrating fixedly on the small details rather than speculating about what was to come. The lights went out, and the bay's atmosphere was allowed to whistle into space. The eerie, drawn-out noise scraped on their already stretched nerves. The *Anah 5* entered the asteroid's shadow. The bay doors open. Below them was the dark expanse of rock with its clusters of steadily shining lights.

"Let's hit it! By the numbers."

The first troopers launched themselves into the void. They jumped in groups of five, five men clinging to a soft, lozenge-shaped floater. The nulgrav floater compensated for the opposing gravity fields of the ship and the asteroid and sank lightly and silently toward the recstar's surface. The troopers' one advantage was that the asteroid had no appreciable ground defenses. In normal combat, such a heavily armed installation would have been reduced to red-hot slag before ground forces could hope to set foot on it. The Therem had never planned for piracy. The men of the *Anah 5* were able to float down shielded from all sensors by the bulk of the ship. As long as they observed helmet silence, their presence would not be detected until they actually entered the base.

Rance was in the fourth party to drop. Renchett, Dyrkin, and Hark were hanging onto the same floater. Rance was coming to rely on these veterans, and he wanted them beside him on what might conceivably be their last mission. The first three groups touched down without mishap. In the final moments, the ground seemed suddenly to rush up at them. Rance told himself that it was only an illusion and braced himself. They touched with only the slightest of shocks. He detached his armor from the webbing on the floater and looked around. Men were drifting down all around him. Above them, the *Anah 5* filled the sky. Using only hand signals, he started moving the men who were already down out of the immediate landing area. One group's floater, when it was only a few meters off the ground, did a sudden flip and came down on its edge. There were muffled curses in everyone's communicator. It was a breach, but Rance hoped that nobody on the asteroid would notice the brief, random noise.

The *Anah 5*'s damaged subbrain had yielded only a partial plan of the recstar. Rance displayed their immediate surroundings on his visor. If they'd come down in the right place, there should be a main exhaust vent over on their right. He peered into the darkness. It was only after a minute or so that he spotted the containing wall. It was time to break helmet silence.

"Bearing 351 on dead reckoning. That's our back door; let's go!"

The men moved forward, pulling the weightless floaters behind them. They were forced to traverse giant conduits and other enormous pieces of equipment. Everything on the outside of the asteroid was so huge that the men started to feel like microscopic parasites crawling across the outside of something that they hardly even understood. The containing wall around the vent was a little more human in scale. It was smooth, circular, and maybe fifty meters high. As they approached it, Rance issued another order.

"Grappels forward."

There were three puffs of smoke as grappling hooks were fired up and over the wall. The trailing lines would be used to haul men and floaters up and over the wall. At the top they'd strap on to the floaters again and descend slowly down the vent. Everything went well until they started dropping down the wide shaft. A man lost his hold on his floater and tumbled headlong into the vent. Even in the asteroid's low natural gravity, he was certain to be killed by the fall. As he fell, he screamed. The dragged-out howl echoed blood-chillingly in everyone's helmet. If anyone on the asteroid had spotted them and was monitoring, he'd be scanning the whole area by now.

The schematic didn't show how deep the tunnel went. Rance knew from the previous visit that the human environment was pretty deep inside this particular installation. On the other hand, if he went too low, he'd risk the chance of his whole force being sucked to their deaths at the core. At regular intervals, the vent intersected with smaller lateral tunnels. Rance let five of these go by, and then he decided that they'd gone low enough.

"Steer your floaters into the next tunnel and set down."

The pitch-dark tunnel ran on for what seemed like forever. It had to be some kind of emergency runoff from the power system. There wasn't enough heat in the bone-cold rock to register on their redscopes, and they had to rely on their helmet lights. Not that there was too much to see. The walls were smooth and unbroken rock, and the troopers had walked for some minutes before they came to an inspection port. Rance motioned for the main force to hold back. He waved to Hark to check it out. Hark examined the door and indicated that it was locked from the inside.

"Burn through it, but be careful. There's probably atmosphere on the other side."

Weapons flared in the dark, throwing the men around the door into stark relief. After a few seconds, the door blew back in a rush of pressure.

"They know about us now, for sure. We've got to move fast from now on."

Rance put five troopers through the lock. Escaping air shrieked past them. When they drew no fire, he sent another five through, then he went through himself, followed by Dyrkin, Renchett, and Hark. The ten men had fanned out into a semicircle around the blown port. The lights were on in a perfectly ordinary, if deserted, corridor. The only thing that wasn't strictly normal was the flashing of pressure-drop alarms. The section of corridor had undoubtedly sealed itself, and if nothing else, a repair crew would be on its way.

"Benset, get the rest of the men through into this section." Rance looked at the longtimers. "You three come with me. We've got to find an elevator."

They moved up the corridor at a run. As Rance had

expected, they quickly came to a closed emergency door.

Hark grinned. "You want me to get it?"

Rance nodded.

Hark took down the inspection cover. "How come I suddenly became the door expert?"

"You've got the touch."

There was another rush of escaping pressure as Hark bypassed the automatic safety control. The doors opened on a surprised dauquoi repair crew that took one look at the armed and armored men, turned tail, and wriggled away.

Renchett raised his MEW, but Rance stopped him.

"Let them go."

"There goes the element of surprise."

"They still don't know what we're doing here."

The elevators were three sections on. Rance sent Dyrkin back to bring up the rest of the men while the others waited tensely beside the bank of elevators.

"We can't have too much longer. Somebody's going to be along to investigate any minute."

Men started streaming down the corridor. Rance used the first to arrive as a defensive circle around the elevator banks. Then he left Benset in charge of loading the rest of the men onto elevators and rode down on the first one. No word of the attack had come down to the women's level. As the doors opened, the troopers confronted a small group of women routinely waiting for the elevators. With no major ships docked at the asteroid, it was a quiet period in the recreation area. The women, who were plainly and functionally dressed, stared at the men in amazement.

"What are you supposed to be?"

In all his planning, it hadn't occurred to Rance that he'd actually have to explain himself to the women.

"We've come to take you out of here."

"You're out of your mind. You're only going to get yourselves killed."

"Where did you come from?"

"We need to talk to someone in charge."

"The shores will be here soon enough."

Hark quickly stepped in. "We need to see a Venerable Madame."

Rance glanced at him. "You know about this stuff?"

Hark nodded. The women looked at each other uncertainly. A small crowd had started to gather.

"This is going to end in a lot of trouble," one of the women said.

"This could end with us getting free of the Therem," Hark said.

A second elevator full of men arrived, and then a third. The women's attitude began to change. A plump young woman with short-cropped blond hair stepped up to Hark.

"I'll take you to Conchela."

"Conchela is a Venerable Madame?"

"You know Conchela?"

"I did once."

Hark felt a little sick. He had forgotten about the time distortion. Conchela would be an old woman by now. He wasn't sure how he felt about seeing her. Rance was starting to look anxious. Men were pouring out of the elevators, and they had nowhere to go.

"Can we speed this up?" Rance said.

He and Hark took a squad of men and followed the blond girl. The rest of the troopers took up a position by the elevators. The advance walked between the avenues of closed and empty booths. The quiet, deserted area had a strange effect on the men. They looked around nervously, almost as if they were trespassing. Conchela's home was a good deal larger than the one to which she had taken Hark. Presumably a Venerable Madame had certain privileges. She still crafted jewelery, however. As Hark and Rance came through the entrance, Conchela had her back to them. She was wearing a simple kaftan. She turned and stepped back in shock.

"Have you come to arrest me?"

Hark quickly removed his helmet. "It's me. Harkaan." She sadly shook her head. "Don't you men ever age."

·She wasn't exactly old, maybe in her mid-fifties and well preserved. Her hair was a natural gray, and there was a strength about her face and bearing that spoke of intelligence and authority. Maybe, by becoming a leader of women, Hark thought, she was fulfilling a destiny that had started when she had served in the Lodge of the Spirits.

When Rance had explained the situation, Conchela wasted no time with unnecessary questions or expressions of disbelief.

"So you've come to take us out of here. We've dreamed of this moment all our lives, but when it finally comes...what can I say? It's frightening. It's a huge step into the unknown."

"At least it'll be our unknown."

"Do you think you can really pull this off?"

"I think we have a chance."

"I'll mobilize the women. How do you plan to get off this rock?"

"That's the tricky part. We have to fight our way into the shuttle dock and hold it long enough to get us all off. We also have to neutralize the main fire-control center so they can't shoot us down on the way out."

"You'll be taking on the lanteres."

"I have two hundred men, all armed and as mean as hell. Do you women have any weapons?"

"A few."

"There were explosives the last time I was here."

"That was a long time ago. They clamped down on that, but I expect there's some about. Where do you want the women to assemble?"

"In front of the elevator banks. As soon as you can. Tell them to keep the stuff they bring with them to an absolute minimum. No more than they can easily carry."

As Rance and Hark left Conchela to start marshaling the women, alarms started to shrill all over the environment.

"Seems like they're on to us."

"It took them long enough."

After a full minute of clamor, the alarms were replaced by a full-power authority voice.

"This is addressed to the unauthorized men by the elevators. You will lay down your weapons and prepare to identify yourselves."

Rance, Hark, and the men with them broke into a run. The announcement was repeated once more. There was the sound of shore patrol sirens on the other side of the area. Rance reached the elevators just in front of the shore patrol.

"Hold your fire! Nobody fire unless you have to."

The shore patrol came out of the central avenue. There were six of them in servo suits and maybe a dozen more on foot. When they saw the size of the force from the *Anah 5*, they stopped in their tracks. Clearly no one had told them what they were up against. Rance gave thanks for the confusion. The leader of the squad dismounted from her servo and walked uncertainly toward the men.

"What the hell is going on here?"

"We're liberating you."

The squad leader halted. "Liberating?"

Rance talked fast. At first the squad leader refused to believe him, but in the end, the obvious evidence of the large force of men was just too overwhelming.

"So, are you with us, or do we all have to start shooting each other?"

The squad leader looked totally confused. "I don't know. I've got to talk to my people."

"No communicators."

"I just want to talk to the people with me."

She walked back to her squad, and they went into a huddle. Rance shook his head.

"I wish they'd hurry it up. Time is not on our side."

At that moment, Conchela emerged from a side corridor with a crowd of women behind her. Quickly she detached herself and hurried over to the shore patrol. There was further discussion, then she and the squad leader came back to Rance together.

"It looks good," Conchela said.

"We'll throw in with you. It may be the only chance that we ever get. I hope you can pull this off, because if you can't, we're all dead."

"We can try," Rance said.

"Well, you better make it fast. We were ordered to investigate a disturbance, but we had no details. Up on the surface they don't know what's happening. A couple of dauquoi called in a seven-twenty, but the lanteres didn't believe them. If we don't report pretty soon, the lanteres will be down to see for themselves."

"Can you stall them?"

"Not for long."

Women began to come out from all over the environment. They came with bags and bundles. Most had followed Rance's instructions, but some were hopelessly loaded down with possessions. Some were even brandishing homemade weapons. Their attitude was one of grim determination, although not without fear. More of the shore patrol came across and joined the breakout. There were even some men from the recstar's permanent complement. The crowd by the elevators grew until it threatened to become a real problem. There were close to three hundred women and further fifty men.

"Is this all of them?" Rance asked.

"All that want to come. The others are either too brainwashed or too frightened. They think we're all going to be killed."

Rance could almost sympathize with them. It was only now that he realized the enormous logistic problem that he'd set himself. Fortunately, Conchela had her own chain of command through the covens that helped to control the situation.

"We should start moving up." Rance looked for the squad leader, who seemed to have assumed the leadership of those members of the shore patrol who had come over to the mutineers' side. "How are we doing with the lanteres?"

"We're faking a communications screwup, but they're getting impatient."

"If they came down here, would they use these elevators."

"With their bulk, they'd be more likely to use the emergency chutes on the other side of the environment."

"Then we'll position a rear guard there."

"My women and a detachment of your men could hold them there for a while. They can only come out of the chutes two at a time. We could bottle them up there."

"What's the fastest way to the shuttle dock?"

"With human atmosphere all the way?"

Rance looked at the crowd of women. None of them had suits. "It'll have to be."

"Okay, you take these elevators to level 1. That's directly under the surface. At the elevator head you take the corridor to the right for two sections. After that, you use the lat tunnel to bypass the lantere atmosphere. Most of level 1 is lantere."

"So we'd have to secure two sections of corridor and the passage."

"As well as the dock itself."

"Damn."

"None of it is that well guarded. There's never been an attack from inside. One thing, though, we ought to get as many breathing masks as we can. It's possible for the lanteres to breach the tunnel. That soup they live in could kill the women as effectively as blaster fire."

"Are there masks?"

"Theoretically there should be a mask for every woman in the emergency dispensers. How good they are is another matter. They haven't been used in years."

Rance shouted to Conchela. "Have your people break out all the breathing masks they can find. We may need them."

He turned back to the squad leader.

"One more thing. I need a technician to rig the elevators so they can only be controlled from here."

The squad leader beckoned to one of her women. "Hey, Jacka, get up here. Move it."

With the elevators gimmicked, the great move to the surface began. The armored men went first. The others waited until the route to the shuttles was secured. As he rode up on the first elevator, Rance gave his last-minute instructions.

"While we're in here, were bottled up. If we can't break out immediately, we're dead. There may well be lanteres waiting for us at the top. I want a firing line right inside the door. Directly the doors open, start blasting and move out. The lanteres may be big, but they're slow. That's our main advantage."

The men arranged themselves accordingly. The elevator seemed to be rising painfully slowly. It eased to a halt. The front line tensed. The doors started to roll back. The MEWs opened up. There were lanteres.

Everyone pressed forward. Hark, who was positioned right behind Rance, found himself yet again caught up in the confusion and isolation of combat. No matter how many times he went through it, he never lost the jagged sense of fear and breathless excitement. He was in among the huge crustaceans, pumping his weapon at anything that presented itself. One of them loomed over him, bringing around a posicannon. He ripped the creature with a sustained blast. Its armor smoked as it toppled backward. The deck plates were becoming slick with colorless crustacean blood. There was a constant alien screaming in his communicator.

They were in the right-hand corridor, and for the moment, there was no more opposition. The half dozen lanteres that had been guarding the elevator head had been overcome with no human losses. More men were coming from the elevator cages. Rance moved them forward, leaving detachments at each crucial point along the way. Hark noticed that among the men from the *Anah 5* there were also shore patrol and even civilian women wearing facemasks and carrying improvised weapons. Two were lugging one of the heavy posicannons that had been dropped by the dead lanteres.

Hark, along with Renchett and Dyrkin, was in the advance party. They reached the first corridor intersection without incident. There was the sound of firing from behind them. Something was happening back at the elevators. Dyrkin waved the party to a halt.

"If we get too far ahead, we'll be cut off." He spoke into his communicator. "Rance, can you hear me?"

"I hear you."

"What's happening back there?"

"More lanteres, but we're holding the bastards. I'm going to start bringing up the women."

"We're at the first intersection, but we need more men to hold it before we can go on."

"They're on their way."

At that moment, a number of human figures appeared in one of the side corridors. They wore the tabards of field police and carried MEWs.

"Hurry it up, Rance. We got company."

A headhunter voice was in their helmets on the general frequency. "Drop your weapons or we open fire!"

The men of the *Anah 5* didn't need an order. Their response was instant and deadly. The burned down the field police with something close to relish. The e-vac fields on JD4, and the scars that went with them, were still fresh in their memories. Troopers were coming up from behind to reinforce the corridor. The two women with the posicannon were among them. They seemed to be determined to use the thing as makeshift artillery.

"Let's move up."

Again they made the intersection without incident, and once again they had to wait as more troops came up to hold the position. Now there was just the bypass tunnel in front of them. That, too, seemed at first to be unguarded. It was halfway along that all hell broke loose. The lights suddenly went out, and the bolts of red fire were flashing at them and ricocheting off the walls of the tunnel. There were screams and curses.

"Get your redscopes on!"

A heavyweight energy weapon had been set up at the far end of the tunnel behind an improvised barricade. Finally someone was ready for them. Leaving four dead, the advance party quickly retreated to a point where a curve in the tunnel would give them cover.

"What the hell do we do?"

"We can't rush that thing."

Rance was on the communicator. "I'm moving the women up into the corridor."

"You can't do that! We're pinned down in the tunnel by a heavyweight."

"Can you do anything about it?"

"Not a damn thing. We'd have to rush down a straight tunnel. We'd be cut down before we got halfway."

Rance sounded desperate. "I've got to start moving these people up into the corridors. We're being pressed too hard here at the elevators. We're stretched too thin."

"You got any ideas?"

"What's manning the EW?"

"Hold on . . . Renchett, take a look at what's firing that thing."

"Stick your own goddamn head out."

"Don't screw around, man!"

"Okay."

Renchett craned forward. Fire burst above his head, and he jerked back.

"Dauquoi."

"At least they won't be rushing us in a hurry. They squirm too slow."

"So what's the story, Rance?"

"Wait a minute, we might have something back here."

More fire hit the wall. Molten rock spattered their armor.

"You better make it fast."

"I've got six shores here with their servo suits. They figure they could rush this gun nest. They might pull it off. They've got the speed and they've got the armor. They'll be coming at a power-assist run, so don't get in their way."

"We'll be here."

There was a lull in the firing. The dauquoi seemed willing to wait out the humans. After a couple of minutes, the men in the tunnel heard the first metallic crash of power-stepping coming down the tunnel behind them. The servos had their lights flashing and panning from side to side to confuse the dauquoi. They were coming fast, faster, in fact, than most of the men thought a servo suit was capable. Two extra shore patrol clung to the back of each one, firing under its huge arms. The troopers flattened against the wall as the machines thundered past.

"Get in behind them."

The servos' armor seemed to be withstanding all of the dauquoi fire. Then a cascade of sparks fountained from the leg of the lead machine. It reeled like a drunken man as the operator lost control, staggered a few paces, then fell headlong. The others didn't hesitate, however. They kept on going. A second servo was hit. Smoke streamed from the upper half of its torso. It lurched off course and smashed into the tunnel wall. The remaining three steered around it. They were in among the dauquoi, pumping fire and even stomping down on them with crushing steel feet. Purple slime sprayed the tunnel wall and dripped from the ceiling as the wormlike aliens literally burst apart.

"Rance, we're into the shuttle dock. You can move everyone up."

The troopers practically had to wade through the debris of the dauquoi. The purple slime seemed to be everywhere. Renchett looked genuinely amazed. He scooped up some of it with his fingertips and held it up to his visor. For one horrible moment, it looked as if he were going to taste the stuff.

"Never thought they looked like that on the inside."

"Shut the hell up, Renchett, you're making me sick."

"Somebody bring along that EW. We may need it."

They were in a brightly lit, transparent gallery that ran along the rear of the large shuttle dock, overlooking the individual reaction pads. There were five of the hemispherical craft parked in the dock, and umbilical walkways ran out to their pressure locks. Each one could lift 150 human passengers. There didn't seem to be any further guards of any species.

The surviving shore patrol dismounted from their servos. The advance party walked slowly down the gallery with the same dazed look that always followed combat. Both the men and the women were gazing up through the curved canopy that covered the gallery. The stars were visible where the dock was open to space; it was the first time most of the women had seen the stars since they had been taken from their own worlds. Then the *Anah 5* came around on its orbit and blotted out everything else.

One of the shore patrol looked at Hark. "Is that your ship?"

"That's her."

"Then it looks like we really made it."

"When the pilots get up here."

Dyrkin broke the spell. "Some of you secure that far entrance. Take the EW. I don't want anything coming through there."

"We still have to knock out the main fire control. It's just above here."

Renchett scowled at Hark. "And guess who'll do the knocking."

"We'll wait until Rance gets up here and see what he wants."

Rance wasn't long in coming. There was the sound of firing and the sight of flashing in the dark of the tunnel. Women started to pour into the gallery. Dyrkin remained in control. He started to direct the women down the umbilicals.

"Keep on going! Down into the ships. You'll be safer there."

The troopers were now backing out of the tunnel, firing as they retreated. A large force of lanteres was pressing them hard.

"You men! Get back there and help them out! We've

got to keep those suckers back...Rance? Where are you?"

"Over here!"

Dyrkin spotted the topman backing out of the middle of the fighting. There were four men with him in blue flight suits and helmets.

"Are those the pilots?"

"That's them," Rance said. "I've been watching over them like a mother."

"Better get them down into the ships. It'll take time to get those shuttles powered up."

"They're on their way."

Firing started at the far end of the gallery. The EW opened up. A second force of lanteres was attacking from that direction. Rance looked quickly around. The situation could actually have been a lot worse. For the moment, the humans were holding both entrances. In the tunnel, the lanteres were pinned down in the same way that Dyrkin and his men had been just minutes earlier. At the other entrance, they had yet to mass in sufficient force to be able to overrun the EW. Rance, having taken stock of the situation, moved up next to Dyrkin.

"I think we got them stopped. We should start pulling back into the umbilicals."

"What about fire control?"

"Can you take some men and handle it?"

"You're getting predictable."

Abruptly the firing ceased.

"Wha—"

The lanteres had stopped firing, and at the same time, men were also lowering their weapons. They were backing away from the mouth of the tunnel.

"What the hell is going on?"

A light appeared in the tunnel, white and brilliant, and murmuring among the humans. Hark was one of the last to feel it, and Renchett the first to realize what it was.

"A Therem. A goddamn Therem. Right here."

Hark's MEW was very heavy in his hands. He wanted to put it down. His legs felt weak, and a warm languor was spreading all through his body. He knew that he should be angry, that he should do something, but he couldn't force his mind to focus. He was staring through his visor at the weapon in his gloved hands. Even reality was wavering. What the hell was this thing that he was holding? He wanted to lie down and sleep. All around him, men and women stood and stared as if they were in a trance. Even the attacking aliens were rooted to the spot.

"Mindlock."

A tiny surge of anger managed to break free, but it was almost immediately smothered. He searched for another, but the influence of the Therem was like a warm smothering blanket. Resentment still smoldered, but he couldn't reach it and bring it to violent life. The whole escape was coming to pieces, and there's wasn't a damn thing he could do about it.

They came out of the tunnel. Two of the familiar red spheres flanked a third, larger one of a kind that Hark had never seen before. This was the source of the white light. It was hard to even guess at the material from which it was constructed. The light didn't seem to come from inside the sphere but to halo around it like an aura. The surface of the sphere was even more of a puzzle. It constantly changed. At one moment it was a polished, reflective mirror, and the next it would be pale opaline, with faint rainbows drifting across its surface. The only thing about which there was no doubt at all was that this sphere contained one of the beings that had been the Masters of humanity for countless generations. There was a Therem inside the sphere. Perhaps this was the ultimate irony. This human rebellion was finally being subdued by an actual Therem, but the poor forsaken humans weren't being allowed to so much as see it before they died.

"Nooooo!"

The scream rang through the gallery.

"Nooooo!"

As if out of nowhere, red fire was pouring at the underside of the sphere. Hark was only dimly aware that the fire was coming from his own weapon. The front of his mind simply couldn't accept it, but some intensely human and profoundly deep part of his unconcious had broken the mindlock, raised his arms, and set his fingers on the triggers. The sphere seemed to be caught in the fire, unable to move. It simply hung in the air, vibrating with increasing violence. The smothering blanket was slowly lifting. Hark found that he could use his voice again.

"Help me! I'm holding it, but I can't destroy it. Everybody fire at the thing."

The weapons were coming up, but the men were still moving sluggishly. The Therem was trying to reestablish control but not quite making it. Sporadic fire was now being directed at the sphere, which was glowing brighter.

"It's a shield. The bastard's got its own miniature shield. Keep firing and it'll burn out."

Rance's voice joined Hark's. "Watch the lanteres, though. They may come alive again."

Fire was hitting the sphere from every side. The halo turned a blinding white, although it radiated no heat despite the energy that it was absorbing. It seemed to be trying to rise in the air, but it managed only about a half meter before it fell back to its original position.

"Keep going. I think we got it!"

Something was happening to the shape inside the halo. It appeared to be collapsing on itself. The outer skin wrinkled and sagged. Suddenly Hark had a vision of the sphere's occupant. It was preparing to die, and it was letting him see. Few creatures had ever killed a Therem, and he was being allowed to witness what he'd done. The shock almost paralyzed him. It was such a tiny thing, a thing of air and filaments. Its only strength was in its mind and its millions of years of culture. The Therem was a little spherical puffball held in stasis at the very center of the sphere that was its armor. It was so small that a man could enfold it in the palm of his hand. Humanity had been enslaved by something that even a child could crush in its fist. There was a terrible absurdity here. The sphere started to melt. Large molten drops formed on the underside.

"Get out from under that stuff! Don't let it touch you."

A drop about the size of a man's head detached from the sphere and fell to the deck. Where it touched, the deck plate bubbled and smoked.

"It's finished!"

The halo vanished as if it had never been. The two red spheres vanished with it. The Therem was gone. Hark knew that he had killed a God. The white sphere, which was now just a blob of gray molten material, burst on the deck in a spray of acrid smoke and acid foam. The lanteres were starting to crawl ponderously forward. They didn't seem to have recovered sufficiently from the Therem mindlock to start shooting.

"Finish those things and let's get out of here."

The people with weapons tore into the lanteres while the others hurried down the umbilicals. Rance turned to the three longtimers.

"Let's go put their guns out of action. We need to go up a level."

Renchett shook his head. "What did I tell you guys?"

Rance grinned. "What did you expect?"

They rode up in a small elevator to the rear of the gallery.

"Don't take any chances. The Therem effect may not have reached up here."

"What are you telling us? This is another suicide mission?"

"What's it ever been?"

# SEVENTEEN

THE *Anah 5* had entered orbit. The planet hung above them, a huge blue-green orb almost totally swathed in cloud. There were twenty or so humans standing under the observation dome. They stared in silence at their new home. In half a standard, the shuttles and the converted e-vacs would drop from the big ship, carrying the people and the equipment down to what would become the first human colony. The aliens would then take the *Anah 5* on to whatever strange destiny they had planned for it. When the small ships made planetfall, a whole new struggle would start. The planet would prove a stubborn, inhospitable host. Its terraforming was in an early stage; there was only a basic grounding of flora and fauna. The early days were going to be rugged, and the colonists' only consolation was that it couldn't be too much worse than what had gone before. The anticipation of the hard times to come made it all the more of a luxury to simply stand and stare.

"I wish we could see more of the surface," Hark commented.

"I'd like to think of it as a mystery for a while longer.

I'm sure we're going to be all too bloody familiar with it before very long," Dyrkin said.

Drykin, Renchett, and Hark stood by themselves. Since the destruction of the asteroid's fire control and their spectacular dash to board the last shuttle, the three of them had become something of a legend among the human escapees, and although they wouldn't admit it, they felt a little awkward around people. There was even talk that they might be the fulfillment of Mystic Heda's prophecy. Renchett had taken to growling whenever the subject came up.

"No asshole ever prophesied me."

Rance and Conchela walked over to join them. These five, plus some six or seven others who had distinguished themselves during the liberation, had been informally appointed as a basic steering committee until they were down on the planet and a more structured government could be devised. Rance and Conchela seemed to be spending a good deal of time in each other's company. Hark, on the other hand, still felt a little awkward around Conchela. He hated the way in which their ages had been distorted, and he stiffened a little when she spoke to him.

"You really think we're going to make it on our own after a lifetime of indoctrination and brainwashing?"

Hark frowned but didn't look away from the planet. "I can hardly believe that we're free of them. I keep catching myself wondering if all this is just some diabolical Therem plot."

Rance's voice was very quiet. "We're free of them."

"Hell, boy, you killed a Therem." By unconscious habit, Renchett had pulled out his knife and was feeling the edge with his thumb. "Sure, we're going to make it."

Rance raised an eyebrow. "And what are you going to do with that knife? There won't be no ears to collect down there except ours."

"You never know what will come along."

Conchela turned away from the skyscape. "Oh, hell, I pray nothing will come along. You believe that the rec-star really was destroyed when we jumped?"

Rance nodded. "The aliens think that it was vaporized by the backwash."

Renchett grinned. "And the Therem will assume it was the Yal."

Conchela shook her head. "I can't help thinking of all those women we left behind."

Renchett stiffened and put away his knife. "It was their choice. They thought they'd be safer as slaves."

There were sirens calling somewhere in the depths of the ship. There was a strange sadness about them.

Rance turned to go. "I guess we'd better go and start things rolling."

# ABOUT THE AUTHOR

Mick Farren was born in Cheltenham, England, on September 3, 1944, was educated at St. Martin's School of Art, and hasn't held a steady job since the mid-sixties. Instead he has divided his time between science fiction, popular music, and media criticism. During the late sixties and early seventies he was the lead singer with the notorious Deviants, who have frequently been cited as one of the major precursors of punk rock. He has published a number of novels both in Britain and the USA, as well as nonfiction works on rock music and pop culture. In addition, he has published comic books and also worked on TV and movie scripts. In 1980, lured by the city's essential craziness, he moved from London to New York and currently lives in lower Manhattan where he continues to write fiction, contribute to a wide range of magazines, and participate in various musical projects.